Top scores for
FINAL SCORE!

"A larcenous chess puzzle with each move foolproof and even more telling."

—*Publishers Weekly*

". . . a feisty superheist . . . funny, street-smart and combustible—full of scuzzy characters and sophisticated tools."

—*Kirkus Reviews*

"Strong, hard, streetwise."

—*Bruce Jay Friedman*

"A fascinating story."

—*William Burroughs*

"FINAL SCORE is about ordinary citizens—coke runners, pimps, homicidal religious maniacs, mother and daughter prostitution teams, loan sharks, wheel girls, Pete men . . . so run along and get streetwise."

—*The New York Times Book Review*

FINAL SCORE

Emmett Grogan

BALLANTINE BOOKS • NEW YORK

Lyrics for the song "Qualified" written by Mac Rebenneck and
Jesse Hill, published by Ten East Music.

Library of Congress Catalog Card Number: 76-3979

ISBN 0-345-25907-6

This edition published by arrangement with
Holt, Rinehart and Winston

Manufactured in the United States of America

First Ballantine Books Edition: November 1977

For MAX
and
As Always
LOUISE

"Dat's Mistuh Grogan . . . (a trifle apologetically). He's been drinkin' a little so don't pay no attention to anyt'ing he says. . . . He didn't mean nuttin' by it—(with ponderous assurance) Nah-h! . . . He's one of duh nicest guys yuh ever saw when he's not drinkin' . . . he's only kiddin' anyway. . . . He don't mean nuttin' by it . . . but JE-SUS!"

—Thomas Wolfe, *From Death to Morning*

1

LEO WARREN stood looking at the traffic out of his eyecorners. He stood still with his jaw set, his teeth clenched, and his left hand bleached from holding on to a shopping bag too tight. The sweat streamed from beneath the brim of an old felt hat. Trickling down his face and neck, it ran under his soaked open collar to form pools of perspiration from every pore of his six-foot, two-hundred-pound, fifty-seven-year-old body.

Each time a car entered the periphery of his vision Leo would get ready by pressing the fingers of his right hand sternly together, tense his feet inside the puddles of his shoes, and stiffen every muscle taut.

He had planted himself by the side of the road for nearly an hour and he didn't know how much longer he could take. The washed-out, brown gabardine suit he wore was short in the sleeves, exposing his skin, sending a chill screaming up his arms.

He was drenched with sweat by the time what he'd been waiting for pulled slowly over to the soft shoulder of the road. He didn't move. Only his eyes moved. The rest of him was stiff.

Her face smiled at him from behind the windshield. He just looked at her with whatever kind of eyes he had by then. When she realized his deadpan wasn't going to crack, she switched off the engine and bounced her slender, sassy body from the car, walking with the confidence of a woman who'd made her living on the streets for most of her thirty-four years.

She talked as she approached. "Leo, I'm sorry I'm late. But I had a . . ." Leo Warren's right arm snapped loose from his hip. His open hand caught her left cheek, slapping it solidly to the other side. "That's for

1

everything I don't wanna hear," he said, as she weathered the blow and cautiously turned back toward him with eyes wet with insult. He caressed the nape of her neck, edging her close, saying, "This is for everything I do wanna hear," and kissed her.

Walking over to the Olds Toronado, the difference between them was all a matter of appearance. Her gait was springy and her face tanned. His feet shuffled and his skin had the pallor of an albino's ass. He'd just been released from Folsom Prison, where he'd done every minute of a five-year bit. The woman was Joanie Brown, a hustler who kept herself busier than any hooker with two beds full.

Leo dropped the shopping bag semifilled with shaving gear and the rest of his belongings into the rear. Then he slid his weary self into the Naugahyde front seat, collapsing with the fatigue of having been abruptly awakened from the slow time of a half-decade's hibernation.

The Camels he pulled from the shirt pocket were sopping wet. Joanie leaned forward, flipping open the glove compartment, producing a full carton. While Leo lit up a fresh cigarette with the car's lighter, she turned the ignition and watched her old man close his eyes. She took the lighter from his hand and, replacing it in its socket, said, "Where we going, honey?"

"We're going slow."

2

IT WAS a rare-weather day for Brooklyn. An especially insistent sun softened February's winter edge, and kids ran around the streets yelling as they played those games usually reserved for warmer months.

Shading his bright eyes from the sunshine, Poley

Grymes walked so fast along Flatbush Avenue, he was winded by the time he climbed up on a stool at the bar of the Sure Enuf Saloon. He wagged his finger for the usual and Joe Cobez tended him a rye with a short beer back.

"Who shot him, Cobez?"

"Somebody with a gun."

"Hey, this ain't no joke."

"Neither is somebody with a gun."

"But who'd wanna kill Ulric?"

"Whadda I know, Poley? The old man just caught a tough break."

"A tough break!"

"Yeah, the world's full of 'em."

"A nice old guy didn't have a dime and never hurt nobody, gets shot in the back while he's floppin' in a doorway on Seventh Avenue, and you call it a tough break!"

"What'd you call it?"

"I'd call it murder."

"Well, what's murder if it ain't a tough break? You wanna 'nother round, Poley?"

"Jesus!"

"Well?"

"Yeah. Yeah."

Poley Grymes was medium height and 180 pounds. Some of it was fat, but not all of it. He'd been intentionally unemployed through most of his middle years; however, his face still had the pinch of character that salt water gives to men who spend their youth at sea. He sat at the bar, burning Pall Malls and dumping whiskey into his mouth, keeping it there until he had to swallow in order to breathe.

A skinny black woman with an injured nose in the middle of a bony, pockmarked face walked across the beaten linoleum of the barroom. Her hand was wrapped around a glass of gin.

"You know, Poley, it's funny," she said.

"Whadda you talking about, Etta?"

"I means Ulric gettin' done the way he did."

"What's funny about it?"

"Well, last week Bertha May was found inna alley offa St. Marks Place. . . ."

"Bertha May?"

"Yep. You know. Big quiet woman come up from Barbados. Always carrin' them shoppin' bags around 'n drinkin' rum. . . ."

"Yeah, I remember. So, she was found in an alley. So what?"

"So, she was dead."

"I sorta figured that out for myself."

"Shot dead!"

"What?"

"Shot dead right through the back of her head, Poley."

"Like Ulric?"

"Like I said, it's funny. Ain't it?"

"Hey, Cobez! They shot Bertha May, too!"

"Who's they?"

3

THE SUN dimmed and the place was nearly dark. The surprisingly warm day was quickly becoming an ordinary cold evening. But he crouched there anyway, reading one more time what he'd read so many times before.

William Marcus O'Brien
Devoted Father
B. April 1, 1929—D. January 1, 1970
DEUS VIAM INVENIERAT
NAM OMNE QUOD NASCITUR

As always, the Latin inscription swelled him with feeling. His father had lived and died behind that home-cooked creed. "God has found a way for everything that is born." The son carried the phrase inside his belly, while slowly walking through Green-Wood Cemetery toward the small, austere apartment in which there'd never been a woman and where his father had left him to go it alone.

It'd been five years since the late Mr. O'Brien died on the job. He was working as a gaffer for the Ringling Bros., Barnum and Bailey Circus in Madison Square Garden, tightening the high wire, when he suddenly fell smack-dab in the middle of an animal cage, freaking all hell out of the dozing lions who naturally ripped him apart for his invasion of their slumber. A few inches, more or less, and he'd have dropped to the sawdust, only breaking an arm or leg. His son never wondered about that, or about anything else. He'd been raised not to.

Billy Jamaic O'Brien was his full name, but no one ever bothered with the O'Brien. Everyone simply knew him as Billy Jamaic, a name his father gave him out of respect for the Jamaica bayberry whose oil was used to make his favorite rum and whose scented leaves his son had mixed with the usual incense whenever he'd been the censer bearer during his hallowed career as an altar boy. This career, which had assured vocation to priesthood, ended unexpectedly after Billy assisted at the funeral service and burial of his father. He also dropped out of the senior class at his academy immediately afterward, in order to retreat into the solitude of himself and the teachings of the renowned Bishop of Hippo, Saint Augustine.

William Marcus O'Brien had spent most of his life misinterpreting the words of the saint whom he considered to be his patron. Therefore it was logical for his son to conclude that his duty was the righteous continuation of his lamented father's work. And so, where Saint Augustine had developed the doctrines of Absolute Predestination and the immediate efficacy of grace or mercy; and where Mr. O'Brien had totally believed in the power of prayer to produce supernatural effects, even though he hadn't remembered to say one as he fell; Billy Jamaic stretched the theories to imply that, as an earthly servant of God, he could and should intervene in the lives of the wretched by putting them out of their misery. Thus, feeling guided by the providential hand of the Divine, Billy Jamaic became a rather competent mercy slayer. He performed his helpful deeds gratuitously, of course, and considering them no more than mere pats on the back from the Divinity, he called his chosen work "Godspeed."

These small pats on the back, which indeed speeded the "miserable" to God, were delivered from the barrel of a snub-nosed .32 caliber automatic Billy Jamaic carried in his pocket along with a bottle of holy oil. After one of his bullets introduced an unfortunate to his Maker, Billy tried his best to see that the meeting would be cordial. He did this through the application of the holy oil to the organs of sense and a recital of prayer over the newly departed. The act of anointing, as a symbol of consecration, needed no given name, for it had forever been known as Extreme Unction. And the summoned Billy Jamaic took special pains to always administer this sacrament with ritual care whenever he bade somebody Godspeed.

4

THE BEST part of that first day for Leo Warren came the next morning, when he woke up and found out he wasn't in jail. It was just after dawn. The sleeping pill he'd taken the previous night had drowned all noise, but it hadn't quenched the sound of the buzzer they ring in Folsom to get the cons up and out of their bunks. That was a memory which had to be forgotten.

Even though the sleeper had only done half its job, Leo was still groggy. He slid from beneath the sheet and carefully lifted himself off the king-sized bed without disturbing or looking at Joanie. He was too busy looking for a match. There was none. He ordered some from room service, along with a large pot of coffee. He waited under a cold shower for it to arrive. When he heard the knock on the door, he didn't bother drying himself. He just wrapped a towel around his waist, draped another around his shoulders, and let his breakfast in. Although he was singularly right-handed, he initialed the check with his left. Then he sat comfortably on the sofa, enjoying the fine coffee, fresh cigarettes, and the expansiveness of the Fairmont suite.

Whenever he was in San Francisco, Leo would always try to either register at that hotel or sublet an apartment in the same rather exclusive Nob Hill area. He learned when he was very young that the surest way to avoid any heat was to eat, drink, and stay only in the best places of any town. Mainly because coppers seldom, if ever, go to the best places. They can't afford to, for many more reasons than money. So the best places to go really are the best places to go. Especially when your profession is stealing.

Joanie rolled onto her back, her right arm dangling over the side of the bed with its palm up, almost touching the floor. She was open-mouthed unconscious. That's what barbiturates like three-grain Tuinals are for. They keep you from the possibility of dream.

The position of her arm grabbed Leo's eyes. He leaned his look forward to see whether the tracks lining her veins were the same old ones, or new. A few of the scars had the bluish pink of new but not the bright red of fresh needle marks. He calmly figured she'd been on a couple or more runs since he'd been away, but had cleaned up her junk habit before he was cut loose from the penitentiary. Or maybe she was just coasting on methadone, and joy-popping now and again?

He didn't let it bother him. He would find out what was what. Later.

Instead, he wandered his gaze up to her blond, wavy hair and down over her firm breasts, defined rib cage, and thinnest of waists. For a moment, but only for a moment, Leo allowed himself to remember that night during the late fifties in Detroit when he'd first met Joanie Brown in what was the biggest night-club in the world, Uncle Tom's Plantation. She was just a kid then, but already a hustler. He'd bought a few rounds of drinks, then shacked up with her for nearly a week. During that time, she discovered who Leo Warren really was and what he did and what a rep he'd made doing it. Ever since, Joanie was always by his side whenever he wanted it that way. She never asked him any questions and he never had to tell her any lies. Unlike square-john broads who were always trouble, she was a natural. A pleasure born of pain.

The alarm sounded; the past was a long time gone. Leo shut it off. It was eight o'clock and he had business to take care of.

He emptied the trouser pockets of some odds and ends, as well as the fifty dollars the State had given him upon his release, and tossed the cheap gabardine in a trash basket. He then unzipped a plastic clothes bag, pulling out an inconspicuous sports jacket–slacks combination which smelled a bit from having been stored in mothballs. He didn't bother trying them on; just left them on the hanger while he shaved. He knew they would fit. Leo hadn't gained or lost a pound since the day a tailor wardrobed him six years before. For a man his age and size, he looked much younger and was more than in shape. He was smart.

"Am downstairs in lobby phone booth trying to root Sage," read the note he left for Joanie where he'd always left her notes: at the bottom of an unopened pack of his cigarettes on the floor near the bed.

5

THE FACE didn't have the withered characterless-
ness he usually found on park benches. But given a
few more years, it certainly could have. So Billy
Jamaic thought it best to nip the obviously doomed
life in the bud before it had to suffer the torments of
utter desolation. He moved closer with his hand tightening on the gun in his overcoat pocket. And every
cell in Terry Sage's slim, nicely ridged, snaky body
became aware of the presence of someone walking
too softly not to be dangerous. He kept his eyes
shut and his head down, as if he were still nodding on
the opium chinois that'd made Prospect Park seem
paradise earlier, when the morning was still the previous night.

As Jamaic neared behind the bench, Terry sprang
to his feet and spun around. This surprised the little
runt, but it didn't exactly take his breath away. It
only forced him to raise his gun, until it was aimed
at the center of Terry Sage's face.

"Will you please turn your back to me again."

The order wasn't questioned, but very slowly
obeyed in silence. Words are only a good argument
against bullets in the movies. He almost charged the
gun. The bench blocked him. As soon as he heard
"Godspeed," Terry thought, You betcha ass!, ducked
low, and jumped on out of there. He felt something
sting his ear right before the sound of the report
reached him. With the fury of anger trying to outrun
fear, Terry raced through the park.

There was another shot as Terry flew across the
wide-open deserted space of Grand Army Plaza, bit-
terly wondering where everybody was. He didn't

bother puzzling over the guy who was chasing him, or why he was shooting. He didn't want to boggle his mind. He needed to keep it on one track: losing the son of a bitch and staying alive.

Once in the streets, Terry began breaking his field, running between and on either side of parked cars. Another shot assured him he was still doing it all for a good reason.

A fourth bullet blew out a windshield as he tore around the corner onto a vacant Flatbush Avenue. He sailed by a newsstand then he leaped down the stairs of a subway entrance, whipped past the token booth through the station, and bounded up the steps of the exit on the far side of the avenue. He kept sprinting all the way to the Sure Enuf Saloon.

Billy Jamaic quit the chase at Union Street, where he turned and walked down to Sixth Avenue and Saint Augustine's Church. There he attended mass and prayed to be granted wisdom, before his merciful role toward the Brooklyn diocese's miserable was revealed.

While God was being asked for his deliverance, Terry Sage was sitting on a bowl in a stall of the Sure Enuf Saloon's men's room, calming his overexerted respiration and cooling his hypered nerves. He was also thinking a lot about who the fuck that guy was. He knew he wasn't a contracted killer because Terry would've been dead thirty minutes ago. And neither was he someone Terry had wronged. He would've mentioned a name. Those kind always mention a name. No, he was sure the guy was some kind of nutter. An insane freak who'd played with murder enough to get to like it in an uncontrollable sort of way. That made it unnecessary for Terry to dwell on the question, Why me? He'd been picked as a target simply because he'd been sitting on the range. But, where there really had been no reason, there certainly was a damn good one now. He'd seen the crazy punk's maddened face. A face he wasn't ever likely to forget and whose identity he might discover at any moment.

Like I didn't have enough problems! Now I got to keep watch this motherfucker don't see me before I see him. But . . . maybe he's not from around here. Sure! Who the hell'd go around trying to shoot strangers in their own neighborhood, anyway? No. No one shits in his own backyard. No one . . . no one, except stark raving lunatics. Fuck me!

He never considered notifying the police. Terry Sage only called a cop once in his life. That was in Los Angeles, back in the summer of '69. He called him a prick.

Leaving the bathroom, Terry checked in the mirror and saw something for which he was mildly grateful. His ear had only been nicked on the lobe. He sardonically thought that was terrific!

The saloon was already Saturday-morning busy with the low-money crowd standing at the bar, and the usual high rollers in their respective booths, drinking coffee laced with whiskey and conducting their various businesses which they considered legitimate. Others might claim it was criminal conspiracy. These businessmen, however, were unconcerned by those others because the jukebox made it practically impossible for anyone to be arrested for a conversation. Much less go to jail.

The music at the Sure Enuf was soft, Louisianan loud. All the singles and LPs were recorded by musicians who'd learned their craft down the bayous, along streets with names like Magnolia, and in the back rooms of New Orleans. Every main name who ever contributed to or vitally continued that specially funky sound was on the charts of the juke, which had a speaker box in every booth.

Joe Cobez wanted it that way. He didn't give a good goddamn what his place looked like, as long as it smelled like gumbo and sounded like home. The home he was forced to flee for having made the serious mistake of cuckolding a man whose trade was the impairment of health and who sought Cobez dead for his having bo-diddlied him. Joe had left his beloved city of New Orleans and, after hearing that the man's wife was found beaten to death, had also left the state. The move north had changed him into a quiet sort of dude, saving all the words he could.

"Terry."

"What?"

"DayDream phoned."

"Well?"

"She got a message."

"Thanks."

"Rien."

Poley Grymes was just coming in as Terry Sage was going out. He stood at the door with a grin on his face. Terry Sage wiped it off.

"What the fuck you expect me to say, 'hello'?"

6

SHE WAS DayDream because she acted with the distracted air of a woman searching for something she couldn't have defined. A deeply sensual, completely natural, unaffected, leggy beauty of twenty-three with the placidity of a child. A somnambulist, so unemotional of voice and face she was capable of reducing murder to an act as irrelevant as crossing the street. A prowling feline who was sure about the proper uses for practically everything, especially the automobile. She could make a polo pony out of almost any car worth her trouble to drive. She drove as well, or better, than many a good wheelman. Which was her occupation.

There was no question of love between DayDream and Sage. They didn't talk to each other that way. They just lived together, sharing one another's bodies. Seldom their thoughts. For Terry was a brooding, rebellious, sensitive presence who maintained his respect by never tolerating discussion.

He was thirty years old and he'd kept at a distance for every one of them. But he treated his woman like he treated himself and everything was all right.

One large corner of their spacious loft apartment was enormously pillow-comfortable. The rest was bare wooden floor between plaster white walls. There were no posters, paintings, or other artistic hangings, unless huge, finely detailed street maps and heightened photographs of specific buildings were works of art. They sure looked good to Terry. And every time he returned, he'd eeny-meeny-miny-moe them. Just as he did now, closing the door behind him.

"She give you the clap, handsome?"

"Quit the baby talk."

"Rubba dub dub . . ."

"Who flew the kite?"

"California."

"California who?"

"Called himself Pete Man."

"What'd he say?"

"A telephone number."

Terry looked thoughtful for a moment, then went into the kitchenette without saying or showing what he'd thought about.

Pete Man wasn't anybody's name. It was slang for safe-cracker. A professional who just leaves word because it's the other guy's prerogative to respond. Leo Warren was out and the caper was on. It was only up to Terry whether or not he himself was in.

A decision not quick to make. Too much had gone over the bridge. His life was a series of contradictions. He'd been this and that so many times, he'd almost gone blind looking for the bright side.

There was one definite consistency about him though: ever since he could walk, he'd been a thief.

So Sage forgot about making coffee and lay back on the sofa, as DayDream left him alone to figure out whether he should perform one more time before resigning from the race.

7

THE MIRROR reflected a floozy deadpan and a some-what kooky image of a woman who had seen too much, lived too hard. The circles under her eyes and the un-definable sadness of her face, however, did not remind Joanie Brown of any generous visions of youth. They were the teasing traces of an eroticism that made her feel more desirable, better than ever.

Sitting at the dressing table and watching herself smoke a cigarette, she thought it was a drag that she wasn't in the movies.

She heard the door open and listened as it was un-deftly latched. The fumbling meant something was wrong. Her eyes passed over the looking glass, and giv-ing her double a satisfied wink, Joanie sailed into the suite.

Leo was slumped on the sofa, flushed with exhaus-tion. He was breathing heavily, almost panting.

Joanie felt what was the matter, but asked anyway.

"Nothing!" Leo snapped.

"Nothing's just another word for nothing left to lose."

"What that fuck's that supposed to mean?"

"Freedom."

"Bullshit!"

"Still, it's a catchy phrase."

"It's dumb."

Joanie paused briefly to light a fresh cigarette before she popped the question, opening the way for Leo to blow out what he was trying to smother, as a child holds his breath.

"How was it outside this morning, honey?" she said.

"Rough! Everything's so fucking much faster, you'd

think there was some other kinda race going on. All
that mad rushing around ain't normal. It's a sick condition, scared. All of them. Worried, hurried. Wham!
Bam! They need a fucking doctor.

"I've been cut loose after doing flat time before, but
never like this. I'm telling you, the citizens have gone
fucking crazy. At least a dozen of them bumped right
into me when we were all walking in the same fucking
direction. I mean collided into me from behind. Each
time it happened, I couldn't believe it. Then it'd happen
again. No 'excuse me,' no 'sorry,' no nothing.

"With all these cocksuckers hauling ass, I felt like a
madman looking for a fight. So I figured I better cool
it, when up comes this freak and, without a fucking
word, hands me a business card and walks away.

"I decided enough's enough and started back here to
the hotel. I was waiting for a light to change when I
read the freak's card. 'You can have your cake and eat
it too,' it says. 'Just call anytime 415-552-2155.'
There's a phone booth on the corner, and the crowd's
pushing and shoving, so I ducked inside for a breather
and to see what kind of scam the freak had going for
him. I dialed the number on the card, and guess who
the fuck answered? A goddamn Fed! It's the fucking
FBI office downtown."

Joanie went into full laughter, asking, "What'd you
say to 'em?"

Leo was indignant. "Say? I hung up. That's what I
said. And it's not so goddamn funny either 'cause by
the time I got back to the lobby downstairs I was paranoid. And to cap it all, an outta town ding clamped
his fucking hands on my shoulder. I thought it was a
roust. I froze. Then the clown asked me if I could direct him to the Wax Museum. The goddamn Wax
Museum! The asshole'll never know how close he
came to a mortuary, forget museum. The elevator kid
saved the son of a bitch, shouting 'Going up!' right in
my fucking ear."

The smile heightening Joanie's lips was no longer
wide with amusement but softly drawn in sympathy.
She fully understood what Leo Warren was going
through. And so she mellowed the anxiety between his

words with compassionate hands, firmly soothing the
tense muscles that columned his spine. His body
wasn't swift to relax, but once it began, her fingers reacted nimbly, coaxing off his clothes and maneuvering
him down on the sofa. When he was silent, she put her
mouth to work, gracefully lacing her tongue, gently
licking his wounds.

She shared his hurt. Not the occupational scars that
were simply the results of hazards spanning the four
decades of his career, but this harrowed pain which
had him going hard with a staggered mind. The uneasy
trouble of his waking up from a 43,862-hour maximum
security nightmare and walking out of the 10½ by
4½ solitude of a cell straight into the massive loneliness of society.

As she eased his pangs with continuous touch, she
thought about how it was her fault that Leo was now
in the throes of undoing what Folsom had done to him.
The toughest penitentiary on the West Coast, where
he'd never have been sent down if it had not been for
her.

It happened in '68. Leo had been living on the dodge
for over three years with wanted sheets out in a dozen
states, his photograph decorating every post office wall
in America. All this attention was due to his being
the prime suspect in a burglary involving a quarter of
a million dollars, most of which was undeclared funds.
In fact, he was the only suspect, according to fifty
eyewitnesses who were shooting a sunrise ballet for
Public Television that Sunday morning, when Leo's
exit from the building housing a shady restaurant was
inadvertently videotaped on an otherwise deserted Wall
Street. After the tape was privately screened for a
Grand Jury, an indictment was handed down and appropriate warrants issued for his arrest. By then he
was a high-power fugitive, since the videotaped publicity inspired the NYPD to file on him for a series of
unsolved cases he'd nothing to do with.

During the years of his cruising around the country,
Leo would caper and regularly send money through
Joanie to his attorney, who'd stash it waiting for the
heat to lower, making a timely payoff possible. The

restaurant owner and his associates were repaid immediately after Leo had been identified, which was why he was still alive the day he had his rendezvous with Joanie in Los Angeles. He'd accumulated enough cash from his scores by then to fix whatever had to be arranged through his attorney, with whom he also intended to surrender to the authorities.

Joanie had rented a furnished house in the Hollywood hills a week before Leo arrived to find her crumpled on a vomit-stained bed, dying from a savage cold-turkey withdrawal. She'd been lying there for days with the loneliest companion in the world—pain. Every cell in her body was violently suing for the abrupt nonsupport of a $200-a-day heroin habit religiously maintained for years in a half-dozen different towns.

Los Angeles wasn't one of them. She didn't even know anyone there. She only knew telephone numbers and all of them were disconnected. By the time she'd bothered to discover that brutal fact, she was already sick. But not as sick as she became when she discovered there was also a panic on in the streets and nothing was for sale at any price. That's when she lay down without ever thinking it might be to die.

Leo didn't call an ambulance, because a hospital would just strap her into another bed. He also couldn't phone any characters to get the name of a doctor who'd write a scrip. He was afraid he'd be traded in to fade a beef one of them might have with the LAPD, who were notorious. That's why he seldom worked that city, using it only as a drop.

There was no easy way. He needed Joanie to deliver the remaining down payment on his future. To do that, she had to be put on her feet. Which was what he intended to do when he broke into the pharmacy on Santa Monica Boulevard.

The narcotics cabinet was a tin box, and he opened it like a can of beer. He quickly found what he was after, scooping a hundred-odd morphine tablets and twice as many Dolophines into a discarded vitamin bottle. As soon as he resealed everything and was shutting the cabinet door, he saw the red lights silently flashing on the slowly approaching squad cars.

He dropped to the floor and rapidly wormed his way between the series of shelves that stranded the center of the store. After carefully hiding the brown bottle of evidence behind an oversupply of Kaopectate, he crawled along the aisle bordering the shelves to a different row, where he completely undressed.

Leo was wise to what the LA police do when they come upon a crime in progress. They shoot to kill. His only chance was his nakedness. It's relatively easy for officials to explain away the death of an unarmed man as justifiable homicide. But they'd be hard put to find an excuse for the shotgunning of a nude male. Unless the cops swore they mistook his penis for a pistol.

He waited until a brace of spotlights brightened up the entrance and the officer in charge got on a loud-speaker to tell him the obvious and what to do about it "with your hands on top of your head!" It didn't surprise Leo that the officer knew he was speaking to only one person inside. A citizen must have spotted him making his entry, while he bypassed the perimeter alarm. As he slowly rose and carefully appeared in the bath of light, Leo blanked his mind to all thought of life and death, relying solely on his instincts to carry him out onto the sidewalk.

It worked. The police were clearly expecting a flaky dope fiend and not an unclad middle-aged man with a stomach as flat as a brick. The uniformed cops were more than a bit startled as they cuffed Leo and hustled him into the back of a squadrol.

The next morning, Leo's attorney flew into Los Angeles, visited County Jail and that afternoon was in the same pharmacy buying Kaopectate and retrieving the bottle of medicine that had been left behind for Joanie. He gave her the pills that saved her life in exchange for the last installment his client had stored at the house in the Hollywood hills. It took every cent Leo had labored to steal and stash with his lawyer over those years to cancel his outstanding warrants in New York City and ease the way for an LA prosecutor and a Superior Court judge to agree that he should not be sentenced indeterminately or for life as a habitual criminal, but simply to three five-year terms to be served concurrently at Folsom Prison.

Now the steady massage of Joanie's hands and lips had Leo deeply asleep, snoring approval. She covered him with a blanket from the bedroom. Then sat in a nearby chair, satisfied to regard the only other being she'd ever cared for besides herself.

They were both in love, without either having ever thought so.

8

POLEY GRYMES was talking at the Sure Enuf Saloon, his belly rubbing against the wood of the bar, swaying with his words.

"Ulric was always doing something funny. Once I found him crawling on all fours right up the middle of Flatbush Avenue. I asked him what he was up to, and you know what he said, Myrtle?"

A gaunt woman with a tried and sallow face moved a dry encrusted mouth to answer, "No."

"He said he was breaking in a new pair of gloves! That old man and those gloves of his. He was something."

"What gloves?"

"Ulric's. He always wore gloves. Winter and summer. Never seen him without gloves on in all the years I knew him. Never even would take them off for a second. You know, one time I hit the number and, after Stalebread over there paid me, I told Ulric I'd give him a twenty if he'd just take off his gloves for a single minute. Twenty bucks! Just for a stinking minute. He looked at me as if I was crazy or something. Then said I'd insulted him and walked right outta here. Nope. No way he'd ever take those gloves off his hands. Why, another time . . ."

"There were no gloves."

"Huh?"

"Yesterday. There were no gloves yesterday."

"Whatta you talking about, yesterday?"

"Ulric. I was there when they found him dead yesterday morning."

"Yeah?"

"And there were no gloves."

"You mean they weren't on his hands?"

"I mean they weren't anywheres. They were gone."

"Cobez! Listen. What happened to Ulric's gloves?"

"Don't ask me no riddles, Poley."

"But his gloves. Ulric's gloves. Myrtle here says they were gone."

"So's Ulric. And he don't need 'em."

9

"I'VE GOT you now and you'll never get out of my sight, much less get away," were the last words Humphrey Bogart said to the woman before she leaped out of the apartment window, taking the proof of his innocence down with her. Agnes Moorehead, just before she jumped, delivered that greatest proverbial last laugh ever filmed. The stunned look on Bogart's face was the reward for her suicide in the movie *Dark Passage,* which Terry Sage was watching on the "Late Show." He particularly enjoyed it for the way the camera favored San Francisco, the city that had been on his mind all day.

Ever since he got the word early that morning, he'd been thinking over all the angles. Reexamining the various stages of the venture that began as an outlandish idea in 1969 and developed over the years since into a well-devised scheme. Until now, it was simply a tall order with someone waiting for it to be filled.

The plans were exact and as solid as the people who were to carry them out. This was what had Terry bothered. For hours he'd undergone a self-examination, asking questions he'd already answered, to the point where he felt he was jerking himself off. Was he this? Was he that? Of course. He was in terrific shape and ready to go. There was nothing blurred about him. Nothing indecisive at all. But what about Leo?

He tuned out the television and went to the refrigerator, dropping ice from the tray into a glass and pouring malt whiskey over the cubes. He lit a Chesterfield and sat on the floor with his back against the wall, staring at the far side of the loft.

Is Leo Warren ready? Still together enough to do what has to be done? Terry was embarrassed by those thoughts. How could he lack confidence in a man whose reputation stretched back to his teens? Doubt a man who became a legend, buying his way out of Alcatraz, his twenty-year sentence commuted by a powerful politician who understood the value of a tax-free cash contribution to a financially troubled campaign. Not pin his trust on the savvy of a professional whose career was seldom interrupted. Hesitate in betting on a sure card of a man who had earned every rung to rank at the top of a ladder erected on the shells of a thousand cracked safes.

No way! was the opinion that scattered the discussion in his brain, as Terry Sage went to call Leo from a pay phone across the street.

The answer to what the past five years in Folsom might possibly have changed in the man he'd met at the LA County Jail in 1969 would be known within the week. And the answer would be: nothing.

BUNDLED IN her dark, dirty, patched coat, Myrtle
Wilson shuffled along Flatbush Avenue, the gray quiet
of the damp, cold night broken by the plodding of
her oversized galoshes. Her red-lined eyes jerked narrow for a moment in a feeble attempt to focus on
Terry Sage dialing a number inside a nearby booth.
She shambled past him and on toward a street behind
the Long Island Railroad terminal where she planned
to flop in the usual abandoned tenement.

Her plans changed when she crossed Atlantic Avenue and moved into the shadows of South Elliott Place.
She thought she heard something. If she did, it was
only Billy Jamaic softly wishing "Godspeed" an instant
before he squeezed the trigger. The bullet punched a
neat little hole in the base of her skull where her hair
was tucked beneath a woolly hat and pitched her body
forward onto the sidewalk in a lifeless heap. It didn't
hurt Myrtle Wilson a bit to die.

The swift accuracy of it all pleased Billy Jamaic as
he knelt beside the corpse to complete his task. He
slipped the automatic into his overcoat and removed
the cruet of holy oil from another pocket. He quickly
performed the Last Rites, carefully anointing the
newly departed. Not being ecumenical by nature, he
preferred the traditional Latin prayer rather than the
modern English version. He chanted the words rapidly.

When he finished, he stood and stepped back into
the shadows to approvingly regard the peace he had
made. Satisfied, Billy Jamaic bid the soul of Myrtle
Wilson a final valediction. "Te Deum" was all he said
before he withdrew, feeling palpably somber.

11

JOANIE BROWN sat and smoked all the twenty
minutes Leo was gone. When he returned from the
lobby, his face was composed and his eyes were bright
with thinking. He phoned room service, ordering a
late champagne and wine supper for the both of them.
Then he kicked off his shoes and dropped comfortably into an easy chair, resting his feet on the coffee
table. He was smiling.

Putting the cigarette in a corner of her mouth,
Joanie wanted to know about the smile.

"Well?"

"Well what?" Leo said.

"What'd he say?"

"He said, 'sure.' "

"When are we going?"

"In a couple days."

"We gonna drive there?"

"No. You are. I'm taking trains."

"Why can't we go together? The car can be shipped
by train. . . ."

"The car's only got three hundred some miles on it.
You're gonna break it in."

"But nearly every damn road in the country has a
fifty-five-mile speed limit now. Might take me a fucking year to reach the East Coast."

"It'll take you less than two weeks. That includes
the stopover in Denver."

"What stopover in Denver."

"At the Brown Palace Hotel. There'll be a guy waiting in a suite for you. He's the mechanic's gonna
outfit the car with the extras."

"What extras?"

23

"Special shocks, springs, supercharger. Whadda you care what extras? You give the man the car, he gives you the suite. And you lay up there until he brings it back. Stay off the streets."

"How long will it take him?"

"Depends on what time you arrive. But I'd say two days on the outside. You just remember to stay inside the hotel. It won't be hard. The Brown Palace is one of the good ones."

The food arrived and Leo signed for it again with his left hand. He'd been a hermit for five years, but the impression he made with the undisciplined scrawl was the signature of a gregarious man. Which he was not.

They enjoyed the meal in silence, with Joanie knowing full well why Leo wanted her to drive across the country alone. He had to be assured she wasn't still into heroin, even occasionally, or depending on any other addictive drug such as methadone. He could see her eyes were neither pinned nor glazed with dope, but that was just for now. There was no point in his simply asking her if she was clean, because her answer would be yes. And yes was just a word used instead of no.

It would be maybe all the way. At least until she drove across the continent and arrived in New York. Then Leo would believe she was probably healthy. Afterward he'd have her examined by a doctor to confirm she was certainly healthy. Following that would be the constant possibility of her not remaining healthy. The answer to the question would always be maybe.

The strange part was that Leo's concern didn't run too deep. He seemed to know Joanie was clean and would stay clean. He had that shrewd measuring of people and motives found in older ex-convicts. The cross-country drive was his way of making sure Joanie understood she had a definite role to play in the caper. She was a partner.

But Joanie only thought of the task as a test. A Naline test. Considering her track record in narcotics, she felt it was surely justified. She also felt hurt.

She gulped down the wine and blurted, "What am I always gonna be, the worm in the apple?" She refilled her glass. Leo wondered why she was getting ruffled.

"Anything wrong?" he said.

"What about Sage?"

"What about him?"

"He was a junkie. A down junkie!"

Leo understood everything at once and all too clearly. He turned Joanie off and tabled the question with a rare explanation.

"Shaddup! Just listen. And carefully cause I'm saying this one time. No more.

"Sure it matters Sage was a junkie. But it matters more who, what kind of character he was before he used dope and how he landed after he quit using.

"Well, he landed on his feet. The guy can stand anything he's gotta stand. He plays it the best way. With brains and guts. Guts enough to commit the crime. And tough enough to do his time without telling someone else's story to get a lighter sentence.

"He's a self-taught pro. A career thief who always shoots square. As straight as ace-deuce-trey. And smart. Keeps his eyes open. It was his eyesight spotted the mark when it came to the surface. The caper I've been rooting after for years.

"My whole life, I always lost in the end. All that fucking bread I scored went for bail bondsmen, attorneys' fees, payoffs, fixes. You name it. They got most of it. But no more. I'm too old for that pace. This time I'm gonna get to keep what I get.

"This time I'm gonna play for the whole sweet roll. But it can't be played alone. So I gotta play with them that plays with me. And Terry Sage and his partner are good playmates. You don't have to worry none about that, understand?

"And understand another thing. What you've done, you've paid for and been paid for and that's that."

"OK, Leo."

"OK. Bring the butter with you to bed."

TERRY DREW himself up onto the sill and sat by the window, smoking a cigarette, drinking his malt whiskey, and staring down at the Sure Enuf Saloon on the other side of the street. DayDream appeared in the entrance, her opaque eyes looking up, her arm waving for Terry to come over. She'd never done that before, which meant something had happened or was about to. He studied her for a sign, but her gestures were as difficult to read as her eyes.

He threw on his jacket and went out the door, down the stairs. It was easy for him to care for DayDream because she took care of herself. A woman who was more than just two letters of the alphabet bigger than a man. She was a special mystery. An all-daring enigma. Never afraid to go anywhere or try anything. Yet never revealing. With a cool as strong as her passion she was the kind of woman men wanted to keep, but the type who couldn't be pinned down. Terry never tried. He left well enough alone. Which was why they lived together. The child was also a woman. The man was also a boy.

"What's on?" Terry said.

"Stalebread asked for you," DayDream said.

They walked into the saloon and its sounds of glasses rattling against glasses and clattering against wood, of the rums talking at the bar, words being slurred together in a raveled noise. The music slouched from the jukebox with Dr. John Creaux singing lyrics that hovered over it all.

Your Cadillac ain't no hipper than my bus stop.
Your champagne ain't no better than my soda
*   pop.*
Your sharkskin ain't no better than my levis, Jim.

Terry passed by the backs leaning on the bar and stepped to the side of the room where tables and benches were set within chest-high wooden stalls. The air was a gray cloud of smoke. He went to the corner booth where smoke was coiling from a Havana cheroot.

You may find me down skid row with all the
bums.
May seem sick. May seem dumb.
But that don't mean you know where I comin'
from.

The man kept the cigar in his mouth and let it wag while he spoke. It was so long it looked like a baton when it moved.

" 'Lo, Terry. Treat yourself to a seat," he said.

The man was Stalebread Charley Stein, a comptroller for a neighborhood numbers bank who got his nickname from habitually eating stale bread so as not to forget the severe poverty of his childhood.

All I got is some common sense
The best teacher being experience.

DayDream slid inside next to Terry, who still didn't know what it was about. He looked down at the finished plate of gumbo with a napkin crumbled in it, and let his eyes crawl sidewise from the table, checking around for a possible hint.

Your education ain't no hipper
Than what you understand.
You better watch out for I'm comin'.

Stalebread flirted his forefinger at Cobez indicating a round. The drinks were carried over by a deaf-mute called Bascom who was the only one of the barflies permitted regular access to the booth area. The occupants of the booths never associated with those who stood at the bar because they were a total bust. Failures who were of no use to them and who were also considered dangerous for the way booze turned the normal stupidity of their lives into blabbering foolishness. Bascom's inability to hear or speak therefore made him the exception. He was also appreciated by the booth-sitters for his other primary attribute. He was born blood-simple. As a waiter, his job was guaranteed.

> 'N I'm comin' up fast
> 'Cause I'm qualified.
> Qualified to last.

The table was cleared and the drinks set down. Stalebread raised his shot glass and nodded his head. His guests returned the acknowledgment. Terry twirled the ice inside his tumbler. Stalebread momentarily stared at it before asking, "What's the name 'a that whiskey again?"

"Glenfiddich."

"What kinda name's that?"

"Scotch."

"Didn't know it was Scotch."

"It's unblended Scotch. A malt whiskey."

"What's the difference?"

"It's better."

"Me, I like ryes."

"And I like to know what's going on."

"Where?"

"Here."

"You don't know?"

"No."

"He don't know. You gotta be puttin' me on, you don't know."

"What am I supposed to know?"

"He really don't know. He *really* don't know."

"Goddammit, Charley. Don't run no games."

"Hey, hey. Cool it with that feisty shit."

"OK, I'll go out, come back in, and we'll start from scratch."

"Relax. Just thought you was tryin' to put me on, is all."

Terry muttered something and glowered at the table. DayDream sat there with nothing in her manner to show that she had any personal interest in what was being said. Stalebread cracked up, almost biting his cigar in half, his chunky body heaving with abrupt laughter.

As cold as dry ice, Terry said, "What's funny?"

"You don't know *is* funny."

"Terrific."

"Believe me, it's funny."

"I believe."

"Try believin' four-one-five."

"No shit."

"You bet a number 'n you don't know it hit. Where you been?"

"Preoccupied. I forgot."

"He forgot. Well, remember Stalebread Charley Stein's on the square with his action. Anybody else woulda let you go on forgettin' forever."

"You didn't know I didn't know."

"What difference what I knew? You just lucky you played with an honest man's all."

"Right."

"You betcha right. 'N here's what you get when you deal with a man who's straight with his customers. Paid."

There was a rubber band around the bills Stalebread tossed under the table into Terry's lap. Moving the money to his pocket, Terry flashed a brief smile and said, "Thanks, Charley."

"Thanks is right."

"Look, here's twenty. Three-five-nine combination for tomorrow."

"It's already tomorrow."

"I mean Monday."

"OK. Three-five-nine combo. You got it. 'N you remember it too, 'cause I ain't gonna go around lookin' to hand you the kinda coin you'll win, you hit one a these numbers. I mean there's a limit on honesty."

"I'll remember. Want another drink?"

"All I'm wantin' is to go to bed. Take care, Terry. Dream."

"You too, Charley. You too."

The pair remained seated and watched Stalebread Charley Stein move his thickset self down the line of booths, exchanging good morrows with those in each. When he left the saloon, DayDream switched to the bench on the other side of the table. Terry motioned for another round. His lips curved in a thin but irrepressible smile. He felt good, almost merry. He directed his pleasure at DayDream. A brief playful glint came into her face that her eyes had nothing to do with.

"Your lucky night," she said.

"Luck was only part of it."

"What's the other part?"

"An area code."

"What's that mean?"

"It means I not only hit that number tonight, I also dialed it."

"Four-one-five?"

"Frisco."

"What'd the man say?"

"Soon."

"How soon?"

"Within a week."

"The car too?"

"No."

"No when?"

"Two, three weeks."

"How'd he sound?"

"Good."

"Together?"

"We'll have to wait and see."

"Babe?"

"Yeah?"

"What happened to your ear?"

"What ear?"

"Your right ear."

Terry fingered the sore lobe, his eyes shifting to the double glazed doors that were swinging open to the street outside. He let his smile drop, returned his eyes to DayDream, and said, "Nothing."

13

THE BELLS in the Church of Saint Augustine were ringing the Angelus, while a pink-cheeked, reddish-haired, bobtailed man in his adolescent twenties sat in a catty-corner apartment across the street and listened.

His spirit exalted by the chimes, Billy Jamaic flung himself to his knees. In his ecstasy, he forgot that his feet were soaking in a bucketful of hot water. His face hit the linoleum ahead of his knees. The steaming water splashed between his naked legs, flooding the tiny room.

Near frenzy, he tried furiously to kick free of the bucket. It was no use. His feet were jammed inside it. He rolled to get away from the scalding pool. But there was no place to roll. He struggled frantically to push himself up with his arms, only to have his hands slip on the wetness and split his arms spreadeagled and his feet stuck in the pail for the better part of half an hour.

Billy Jamaic wasn't used to the rough-and-tumble. Which was why he immersed his feet in a bucket of water in the first place. He was trying to soak away the blisters that were the aftergrowth of his long dash through Prospect Park in pursuit of Sage. It'd been quite a lot of running for someone who disdained exercise.

Coming to in a daze, he could taste the epsom salts in his mouth, as well as the copper-penny flavor of burning pain. Since he earlier opened the window to better appreciate the music of the Angelus bells, the water had become ice cold. When he turned over on his back, the freezing puddle almost made his heart jump out of his chest, sitting him straight up.

31

He began to shiver uncontrollably. Leaning forward to get at the pail, he opened his legs and the scorched sack containing the pair of hard-boiled eggs that was his scrotum dropped inside his soggy briefs. The moment they flapped in the water, Billy Jamaic leaped into the air with a shrill gasp. He landed in the armchair where it all began. His fingers caught the rim of the pail and held it while he tugged his feet loose.

Shaking, he rose from the chair, shut the window, and hobbled into the glory-hole that had been his father's bedroom. He peeled off his sopping underwear, wrapped himself in flannel pajamas, and lay down on the bed covering up with a quilt.

Billy Jamaic was in grief. He stared at the blank sheet of paper neatly framed on the wall. It was a poster of Saint Augustine and it was blank because no one knew what he looked like. This fact warmly consoled Billy and, as always, renewed his faith in the anonymity of the monastic life he shared with no one inside the small hermetic apartment where he now rested in a room made to resemble a garden. A lifeless nursery in which all the plants, shrubs, flowers were stillborn. A botanical patch tilled in plastic that required little more than occasional dusting.

It was in this wax evergreenery that Billy Jamaic lay racked with misery, thinking of himself. Of how he was ignorant of his body. And of how his neglect of that ignorance made him guilty. He promised to push himself into better physical shape in order to be of greater service. With these thoughts, he ejaculated himself to sleep.

THE TRAIN from Montreal pulled into New York at
eight o'clock on a Thursday morning. Leo Warren was
on it. He hadn't expected to be. But during the time
he'd spent inside the penitentiary, the railroads had
discontinued the passenger lines that ran directly from
San Francisco to Chicago, which left him only schedules jumbled with jigsaw options. He used the Amtrak
rail service to travel from San Francisco to Seattle and
on to Vancouver, where he boarded the Canadian
Pacific to Montreal. There he made another Amtrak
connection for the last leg of the trip. The rail ride
took five days. Five days that Leo employed coolly re-
adjusting himself to the regular mores of the society
of which he was once again a part.

There were just two moments along the route that
were disquieting: the brief layovers at the border
crossings into and out of Canada. But he covered
them nicely. Before leaving the West Coast, he had
the footlocker that was his tool chest delivered to
the Fairmont Hotel from the storage company where
his former attorney had placed it. Besides the specially designed equipment in the metal case, there was
a kit containing blank passports, driver's licenses, and
other means of identification, as well as stamps to
validate them. The task of drawing himself an identity
on those bare pages was more than worthwhile. It
was absolutely necessary. Since the Hearst girl had
been kidnapped, the whole Bay area was burning with
heat. There was no way Leo could have arranged for a
set of papers through normally simple channels without the possibility of a rumble. Every cop's mind was
like a dogcatcher's. It was odds against tomorrow

for anyone out on the street who couldn't prove he was somebody. Fortunately, Leo had everything available he needed to homemake a credible package of identification which established him as a distinguished citizen from Bismarck, North Dakota, whose business was public relations. An occupation that required nothing more than a smile and a clean shirt.

He was wearing both those accessories when he stepped off the train at Grand Central Station. His smile broadened as he walked down the platform and began to taste the hard-edged flavor that is New York. The sole city in the world that touches everyone everywhere in some way every day and leaves its mark. An indelible style that is a people who call their cops the finest and their crooks wise. God may bless America, but the devil is afraid of New York.

When Leo Warren reached 42nd Street he began keeping his smile to himself. He melted into a crowd crossing over to a cafeteria where he used the pay phone. He dialed Terry Sage's number, letting it ring once and hanging up. He did this three times, which was the prearranged signal that he had arrived in the city. Terry responded by dressing quickly and going downstairs to the phone booth on Flatbush Avenue. While waiting, he skimmed through what was left of the Yellow Pages. There wasn't much, since some kid had torn most of the book to bits, which is a juvenile pastime inspired by Charles Atlas for those who always think they're about to get sand kicked in their face at the beach.

Terry answered the phone in midring.

" 'Lo."

"What's happening?"

"Where're you?"

"You know the Lincoln Building on Forty-second?"

"Across from the Grand Central?"

"That's it. I'm having coffee in the cafeteria."

"We'll pick you up this side of an hour."

"Who's we?"

"Me and her."

"Good."

"In a while."

An icy rain was falling as DayDream shouldered the BMW curbside. Terry was sliding from the car when he saw Leo standing in the lobby waving him back. He opened the rear door and Leo hustled from the building through the downpour, tossing his suitcase and himself onto the seat. There was a quick exchange of greetings, with Terry introducing DayDream. She shook Leo's proffered hand firmly before putting in the gear lever and pushing the car into the eastbound traffic.

An intent, almost studious look came to her face as she drove with her right hand high, moving the wheel, and her left low, locking it. Leo watched her smoothly weave a path through the clogged street, shifting down the gears, seldom using the brake pedal. She handled the gray metallic BMW securely and her graceful expertise relaxed any apprehensions Leo might have had. He sat easier and turned to Terry, who was asking, "How'd the trip go?"

"Went fine," Leo said, "just fine."

"Lotta snow in Canada this time of year," Terry said.

"That country's fat with snow," Leo said. "You ever been there?"

"Montreal a few times," Terry said.

"Yeah," Leo said. "Did my stuff arrive?"

"Yesterday," Terry said.

"Good," Leo said.

"Man, that footlocker must weigh five hundred pounds," Terry said. "Those fucking Greyhound porters at the bus terminal did nothing but moan and groan about hernias. Had to lay ten bucks on a pair of them to get it into the car. They dropped it in the trunk, the front end almost rose off the ground."

"Where is it now?" Leo said.

"At the loft," Terry said.

"What loft?" Leo said.

"Well, actually there're two," Terry said. "See, we rented the top floor of this warehouse and divided it. One part we fixed up like an apartment, the rest we left a work space."

"How'd you get the locker up there?" Leo said.

"That's the real beauty of the place," Terry said. "It's got a freight elevator. One of those strong old jobs with ropes and a wooden gate. And a steel door that opens onto a back alley. We just drive the car in, pull on the rope, and it lifts us right up to the workshop."

"Who else uses the building?" Leo said.

"No one," Terry said. "It's in the process of being sold to Long Island University. They want the site for some dumb urban renewal project."

"When's that gonna happen?" Leo said.

"Not for at least a couple months," Terry said. "They're waiting on a federal grant to come through."

"Who's the landlord?" Leo said.

"A savings bank," Terry said. "The original owner used the place as collateral for a loan he never paid. I got to know the branch officer who's handling the sale. I pay him a thou a month rent. He pockets the cash and no one's the wiser."

"Sounds a little dicey," Leo said.

"Not really," Terry said. "His brother's a stand-up character. Top shelf. He hipped me to him. It wasn't for the extra ten bills a month, the guy would be embezzling from the bank just to make ends meet. His wife had triplets last year."

"A real family man," Leo said.

"Yeah," Terry said. "Hey, how's Joanie?"

"She's doing OK."

15

JOANIE PAID her bill and walked through the fading elegant lobby of the Brown Palace Hotel to where a lean-faced, weather-beaten man with a big hat, boots, and a shirt with pearl snap buttons was standing.

"Enjoy your stay?" he said.

"Well, there's nothing like spending two solid days in the stately luxury of a bedroom, alone, is there, sweets?"

"Guess not. Here's the keys. Car's all set."

"Where is it?"

"Right outside. Come on."

In front of the hotel, Joanie's aqua-pale eyes searched the street for the Toronado. She was bewildered.

"What'd it get, towed away?"

"What you mean?"

"I mean, I don't fucking see it anywhere."

"You're standing next to it."

The car had been stripped down and painted a dull, neutral green color. Its make was no longer easily identifiable.

"Jesus. It looks like a goddamn DeSoto or Hudson or something."

"Exactly. Get in."

Behind tinted windows through which it was practically impossible to see inside was an interior equipped with a strengthened standard stick-shift gearbox and a police radio concealed in the glove compartment.

"See this switch on the dashboard here?"

"Yeah."

"Don't touch it. It's the supercharger. You flip it and you'll wake up dead."

"Delightful."

"OK. Everything else Leo wanted's been done. So drive carefully and watch them speed limits or he'll never see what he paid for. Good luck."

"Thanks. Thanks a lot. Hey. . . . Shit."

He was already gone before Joanie could ask him the best way out of Denver. When the bellhop appeared with her valise, he gave the proper directions. A few hours later, she was cruising along Interstate 80 in Nebraska with the needle on the gas gauge nearing empty.

She pulled off the highway and turned into the town of Ogallala, driving down Front Street past a Cowboy Museum, a Boot Hill, and unopened service stations. A strong prairie wind was blowing the crust from the frozen snow banking the deserted sidewalks. It was late, very cold, and the streetlamps just brightened the dimness of the chicken-colored stores that were rolled up for the night.

Joanie Brown began to feel uneasy as she approached the far end of the town with no sign of anyone doing anything anywhere. There had to be a motel or at least a bar open, she thought. After all, the place was some sort of tourist attraction. But it was also out of season. And a tourist town out of season is like a well-dressed corpse.

She figured there was about enough gas for her to take one more swing through the main street before she became desperate and blew her cool, as well as the horn. In the middle of the U-turn, her headlights discovered a small single-pump garage hiding behind a parked tractor-trailer. Inside there was a guy working on a snowmobile.

"Well, shine on harvest moon," she sang, and drove up alongside the darkened front window.

Her clothes were suitable for the winter, but the hard bitterness of the cold north country sliced into her as she rattled the garage door. The guy took his time unlatching it and letting her enter the coal-oil warmth of a shabby officelike room.

He looked at her with a steady expressionless gaze and didn't speak. Joanie complained about the obvious weather, using the moment to give him the once-over.

He was a balding fat boy wearing greasy Levi's that were too tight for him and an orange sweat shirt with a stars-and-stripes caricature of Evel Knievel embossed on the front. She made him for a goon.

When she said that all the service stations were closed and she needed gas, his mouth partly opened in a loose grin and he continued staring. What she wanted to say next, she didn't. Instead, she tried running a line.

"Listen. Please. You have to help me. I'm all alone and my mother's dying in Chicago. I just have to get there before . . ."

"What happened to your mother?"

"I dunno. My father hit her over the head with a Waring blender. Lookit, I'll give you twenty-five dollars to fill up my tank. OK?"

"Don't need no twenty-five dollars."

"How about fifty?"

"Don't need no fifty neither."

Joanie knew then what he needed all right. But she asked him politely anyway.

"Be a nice fella. Tell me what you need."

"Don't need nothin'."

"Well, is there anything at all you want?"

"Yup."

"What is it?"

"You."

"Terrific. Go filler up."

"Nope."

"Hey, man, enough with the charades. You just go out and give the car all the gas it needs. Then you come back in and I'll give you all the pussy you want."

"How do I know?"

Joanie opened her lynx coat, pulled up her skirt, slipped off her silk panties, and handed them to him. She only gave him a brief but expert look at what he wanted. It was enough to nearly erect his penis clean through his jeans, but not enough to excite him into a frenzy. She didn't want to be raped. She just wanted to buy some gas.

Fat Boy was outside in double time, pumping fuel into the car. Joanie watched him through the fogged front window and listened closely to the bells registering the number of gallons being poured. She was satisfied he wasn't playing any tricks, especially when she saw gas overflow from the tank.

While he hurried to lock the nozzle back up on the pump, she took a quick look around the funky office for something she might have to use. She found a ball peen hammer on the cluttered floor and propped it against the side of an oily armchair. She then carefully hung her fur coat on a rack and sat down.

Fat Boy returned simultaneously latching the door and unzipping his pants. He was balls-ass naked in seconds. Joanie had her legs spread with her thighs

straddling the arms of the chair. Her soft white belly
arched upward as she swept saliva from her mouth,
carrying it below her hips where her fingers moistened
the dry lips of her vagina, making it pucker with spit-
tle. Fat Boy knelt before her, above the juicy scent.
His forearm of a cock brushed along Joanie's smooth
thigh, curving beneath her firm ass. Before Fat Boy
knew what had happened, he exploded a pint of
sperm all over the back of the chair.

"Shoot! I came 'fore even got in! Hurry up 'n put
it inside ya, girl! There's plenty more left in the load."

"Come once, come all!" Joanie murmured as she
slapped Fat Boy upside his head with the ball peen
hammer, knocking him cold to the floor. She then
carefully climbed from the chair, flung her coat on
her shoulders, and clearly marked a twenty-dollar bill
before hiding it in the top drawer of a make shift desk,
The money was her insurance. If Fat Boy screamed
bloody robbery, she'd easily prove rape.

She hustled out to the car and drove back toward
Interstate 80, leaving her silk panties clutched in Fat
Boy's grubby hand and wondering whether the chump
would have them framed after he woke up. If he ever
did.

16

THE LOFT setup, with its private freight elevator,
workshop, and separate living area, impressed Leo.
The place was an arrangement to steal. Everything
there was equipment, from his unopened footlocker
of select tools to Terry's library of periodicals, trade
journals, confidential papers, locksmith's and factory
reference books, to DayDream's blown-up photographs
of buildings and complete road maps tacked on the

walls. It was a factory to produce grand larceny. Theft rather than robbery. There were no guns. The workers of this plant were craftsmen. They preferred to go on stage cold, singing a cappella. Leo cut the ribbon and they opened for business.

"Good layout. Real good," Leo said. "The deal this good?"

"We think so," Terry said. "I'll run it down to you over some coffee."

DayDream brought in the cups and lounged on the huge pillows piled by the window. Leo kicked off his shoes, undid his tie, and sank into the sofa. Terry poured the coffee and crouched as he talked.

"The deal is two million cash. Half on deposit in front. All on delivery. The buyer's a Czechoslovakian who's middling for either an Arab who wants to be a sheikh, or for some organization I don't want to know about. All I do know is they want to sneak all the way. No heist with shotguns blasting. Just a nice quiet lift. They want to be long gone before the grab's discovered and the biggest shit in history hits the fan. That's why the man came to me and me to you. It's exactly what we talked about five years ago in the LA County."

"Maybe somebody was listening," Leo said.

"Yeah," Terry said. "Fate."

"Tell me about this Czechoslovak," Leo said.

"There's not much to tell. . . ." Terry said.

"Then," Leo said, "tell me not much."

"Well," Terry said, "he ain't one of those Intertel-CIA-KGB assholes. He's a straight businessman. Only in it for money. Just like us."

"How do you know?" Leo said.

"Same's she knows," Terry said.

Leo turned a gradually exasperated look at Day-Dream, who was looking out the window.

"How do you know?" he said.

"He's my father," DayDream said.

The unexpected was something that Leo knew how to handle. Quickly. Alone. And in silence. He tilted his head back until his eyes watched the ceiling. He became like a wild animal with a brain. Chasing his thoughts.

Sifting for the question his experience taught him was the only valid one to ask about someone entering his world. A world where you seldom trusted anyone you worked with and never trusted anyone who hadn't spent time in prison, or time trying to stay out of one.

"Your father," Leo said. "He ever done any time?"

"Nope," DayDream said. "Never even been busted."

"Was there ever a reason why he should've been?" Leo said.

"Not until now," DayDream said.

Leo shifted his stare at Terry and waited for a very good answer. He wasn't kept waiting.

"I know what you're thinking, Leo," Terry said. "But I already thought it through six months ago. The guy's out of the picture. His only contact with us is by Dream. And let's forget their relationship. When we have to, we've been calling him 'Czechmate.' OK. Now, as far as his personal history goes, he worked for thirty-two years as a clerk in a brokerage company, until one Saturday morning about a year ago he got a telegram saying he was fired. It was a shit job but he liked the people he worked with. They were his friends. His wife's been dead six, seven years and his only child was doing a short bit for grand theft auto. He was alone. Then he became lonely. So he takes what savings he's got and splits for an indefinite visit to his hometown in Czechoslovakia.

"When he left New York, he was sad," Terry said. "But when he returns here six months ago, he's all smiles. Not the least nervous about nothing. Got a whole new attitude. He visits his daughter at the institution and tells her everything's gonna be all right from now on.

"When she graduates, he picks her up in a rented limo, asks her if she knows anyone who can get him what he wants without lotsa noise. She says maybe and comes to me. I contact you. Joanie Brown gets back to me with your answer. Czechmate is told yes. Dream and I set up shop together and get down to the work we've been doing these past months. Clean and simple."

"He don't know from Adam about us, about anything," Leo said. "Is that it?"

"That's it," Terry said. "He's just waiting on her to tell him when and where."

"What've you two been using for money all this time?" Leo said.

"The same I used to fly to the coast and meet with Joanie," Terry said. "Mine."

"Yours?" Leo said. "What were you, the beneficiary in someone's will?"

"Lighten up, Leo," Terry said. "Just let me lay it all out. Knock off the questions, till I give you my answers, OK? *Now,* the bread we've been coasting on came from a score I pulled early this fall. I hit a brownstone on the Upper East Side.

"A few weeks later DayDream shows up to see if I'm interested in what Czechmate has in mind. I give her a possible, fly to Frisco, see Joanie, blah-blah-blah, and there you are."

"Yeah," Leo said. "Here I am."

A long pause followed, with Terry stretching his legs around the large enamel-white room; Leo's eyes again uninterestedly regarding the beamed ceiling; Day-Dream still staring out the window at whatever only she could see. There was no particular tension. No strain. Just a breather. Some moments to soften down the kinks in a renewed relationship and reaffirm roles.

For Terry Sage this interval was unnecessary. But, at thirty, he was still young with miles yet to go. Leo Warren was running out of miles. He had one good one left in him and he was going to set the pace. He took his time and Terry waited to answer what he knew he'd be asked.

The questions that were to peg it all down were not long in coming.

"Terry," Leo said, "tell me about exactly how this Czechmate plans payment?"

"He doesn't," Terry said. "We do."

"On the Friday afternoon, right before the holiday weekend we go on the caper, him and Dream rent a safety deposit box at the South Brooklyn Bank on Atlantic Avenue. Near closing. Each fills out separate signature cards, so either can enter without the other. In the box, Czechmate's gonna put twenty thousand fifties. All these bills have already been laundered and got no consecutive serial numbers. I asked for fifties 'cause, you know, they're the hardest to counterfeit and the easiest to spot when they are queer. Anyway, Dream will spend enough time counting and checking to make sure there are two hundred stacks of five thousand real dollars. And she'll keep doing it until the bank closes. Then he goes his way and she comes our way. Each with duplicate keys."

"So," Leo said, "you're saying he don't know nothing about the South Brooklyn Bank, or when, or how, or anything. Just one mill in clean fifties is all he knows, right?"

"Right," Terry said. "But he also doesn't know something else. We've got a large deposit box rented there for months. So, after the caper, early the following Tuesday morning, Dream picks up Czechmate somewhere near Atlantic Avenue. Say, around nine forty-five. With him will be another million. This time all hundreds, and all laundered with nonconsecutive serial numbers the same's the fifties.

"Now," Terry said, "he'll probably be expecting some sort of quick exchange. The money for the goods. If so, Dream will calmly explain the difference between the minors and majors. She'll do this by driving to the South Brooklyn Bank and parking in a space we'll vacate for her. They'll enter the bank, go downstairs to the vault room, where the teller not only inserts his submaster key in the box rented on the Friday, but also disengages the backup lock on our deposit box, into which Dream transfers the stacks of fifties, slipping her duplicate to the other box in one of the bundles. Czechmate is told to refill the other deposit box with the stacks of hundreds. These she won't bother to check thoroughly 'cause there ain't gonna be time. Just a quick look, and she'll summon the teller to engage the second lock on each of the deposit boxes. Then they split to the drop near one of the Gowanus Canal basins where a sample of the goods will be stashed in the trunk of a car. The Toronado we'll have dumped by then.

"Now," Terry said, "while Czechmate's satisfying himself that the stuff is McCoy, I'm inside the South Brooklyn Bank emptying the fifties from our box as well as the duplicate key to the other. That's one million made ours. It's also protection for Dream 'cause we gotta figure whoever's putting up this kind of bread ain't about to let Czechmate walk around alone with satchels full of it. So, in front we gotta assume he's got a heavy tail watching him. The catch is that Tuesday they'll be thinking Czechmate has the keys to ALL the money, not just half, and all the goods. So if anything goes down at the canal basin like some people showing up saying thanks for the favor, now go take a swim, Czechmate has more reason to stop their play. Mainly, they're already out half the bread and maybe all, since Dream can only come up with the right key to the wrong deposit box. Plus, there's only a pinch of the stuff they want, or don't want to pay for. And by then, time'll be running out fast. For them, not for us. That'll leave them no choice but to follow these instructions: DayDream back to us in fifteen minutes with the rest of the bread safe and sound, while whoever you people are, just remain nearby that particular phone booth until I call you back upon Dream's arrival to let you in on the secret that what you just paid two million cash for is inside a garbage can three feet away from you, asshole. Good-bye."

"That it?" Leo said.

"Almost," Terry said. "Finale's an angle I figure we oughta draw. See, I been thinking this through step-by-step for half a year. Read a lot about a lotta things. One thing always comes across. This stuff's poison in anybody's hands. And I ain't about to put it into nobody's. Specially strangers may wanna fuck up with it. Rather pick poor men's pockets the rest of my life than hand people the kinda misery this can bring down."

"So?" Leo said.

"So," Terry said, "when they turn to look at the garbage can, they're gonna see a hundred of them. All lined in neat rows, the way they always are for Tuesday morning's collection. Next thing they're gonna see is about a dozen private sanitation trucks pulling into the basin's lot—begin hauling away the garbage out to the dump in Canarsie."

"Then what?" Leo said.

"I call this priest I know, don't know me," Terry said. "Got himself locked in the slam once, he wouldn't reveal some guy's confession to the DA. Said he gave him absolution. Really believes in the sanctity of the confessional, this Father. So I ask him to hear mine over the phone. Make him swear to uphold his vow of secrecy. Don't really matter, he does or not. But it'll sound better, when I hip him to what one of those big green trucks is carting through the streets of Brooklyn. Ask him to forgive me my sins. Give him the OK to do what he can about what I'm really sorry for. Priest's whole family's cop. Think his mother's even an auxiliary. He'll know what to do. By the time he does, we'll be in the wind. Let Czechmate, the others take what comes. They like it or not. Just a miscalculation, a mistake is all. The end."

"Don't you believe it," Leo said. "If these guys ain't on the square, what you just ran down's got too many rough spots. Especially the spot she'll be in. Also there's the bank. What if some people do make an appearance and couple of them decide to hang around the bank that second morning, while the others follow her and Czechmate?"

"They'll be removed," Terry said.

"How?" Leo said.

"An anonymous tip to the local precinct," Terry said. "About a couple of dangerous radical aliens with automatic weapons progressing to rob the South Brooklyn Bank. Which means they'll be splattered all over the pavement 'cause one thing's certain—these folks ain't paying two million to put their hands up."

"Maybe. Just maybe," Leo said. "We're gonna have to fine down the details. Speaking of details, how much bread we got to work with?"

"I got little more than a thou left," Terry said. "You?"

"More or less the same," Leo said. "It's not enough."

"I know," Terry said. "But Czechmate's willing to bankroll the operation. . . ."

"You know fucking well I won't go for that," Leo said. "His fucking money's no good until payday."

"I know. I know," Terry said. "Just wanted to hear it. Time has a way of changing. . . ."

"Well, I ain't time," Leo said. "So quit the horseshit and tell me what you got lined up to get us financed, enough to cover, bail us out of any binds."

"We worked out a pretty tight plan," Terry said. "Get us to the caper. Bag what Czechmate wants to buy."

"How long's this plan take?" Leo said.

"Entirely up to us," Terry said. "The plan itself's got thirteen steps."

For the first time that morning, DayDream spoke without being addressed. "They say if you count thirteen backwards thirteen times, a miracle happens."

Leo turned and thought of a miracle. He was standing at a crap table, shaking the dice, trying to make his point. His point was thirteen. To throw that devil's dozen would indeed be a miracle play.

"Then start counting," Terry said.

17

"ONE-TWO-three-four. One-two-three-four. One-two-three-four," was the cadence Billy Jamaic huffed aloud while bungling the job of keeping his limbs in rhythm with the numbers. For even though he'd inherited a firm-boned, bantamweight frame from his late father, the awkward patter of a pigeon-toed body had come with it, directly descendant, he was sure, from his mother. Whoever she was. It was surely her spastic genetic lineage that deprived him of his father's facile, nimble ways and marked him with the cross of the physically clumsy. The cross under which he diligently sought to persevere in this series of exercises: Jumping Jacks for Jesus.

As he paced to and fro across the floor, relaxing his breath, he could feel the tone his body was already taking. Its idle flimsiness was quickly shaping into slender sinew. It was becoming more aware of itself, as he was of it.

He snatched the .32 automatic from the top of the bureau and his pace changed to a sort of prance. He was amused by how light the gun seemed in his hand. The workouts were not lost labor, he thought, as he twirled the .32 with him into the bathroom.

He plugged the bathtub drain with a rubber stopper and opened only one faucet. While the hot water splashed and rushed to fill the porcelain tub, Billy Jamaic removed his blue sweat suit with PROPERTY OF SAINT AUGUSTINE ACADEMY emblazoned in orange across the cotton shirt. He did this before a full-length mirror that covered the inside of the closed bathroom door. He did it slowly and without shelving the automatic. He also did it ungracefully, which bothered him enough so that he didn't watch himself doing it.

Once undressed, he stood straight, gun in hand, and regarded his naked form with a keen eye. His sharpened look searched for the slightest, the newest details in his tightening physique. His eyes permitted no illusions and, in fact, none were really necessary. His body had changed. There was a certain definition appearing in his slim muscles, and ridges were beginning to form on his two-by-four stomach.

He would have murmured a pleasant "alleluia" if the steam hadn't misted him from the mirror, nor the bath overflowed. Instead, he yelped and charged the tub, plunging his hand into the hot water to unplug the drain. Unfortunately, the hand he chose for the task was the same which held the .32 automatic, and the instant the fingers of that hand merged with the scalding water, they flinched and the trigger jerked off a round. Hand and weapon recoiled simultaneously from the bath. The bullet mushroomed in the rubber stopper, popping it from the mouth of the drain.

Billy Jamaic had no clear idea of what really happened. His brain was too stunned by the resonance of the deafening report echoing in the tiled bathroom. As the ringing subsided, he shut off the tap, then looked curiously at the shrapneled stopper dangling from its beaded chain and was saddened that the bullet had been unable to reserve itself for its rightful target.

18

"TERRY," DAYDREAM said, "take a look."

He went to the window, caught sight of what she pegged, and motioned Leo over.

"You see that guy walking down there?" Terry said.

"Terry," Leo said, "I see a lotta guys walking down there."

"No," Terry said, "I mean the guy with the raincoat, wearing rubbers. Across the street, with the umbrella."

"Yeah," Leo said. "I see him. Who is he?"

"Name's Skidmore," Terry said. "At least, that's what he's called."

"And?" Leo said.

"And he's step number seven," Terry said.

They became quiet and watched the lanky, grizzled-looking figure mosey along the rain-soaked pavement, his gawky feet negotiating puddles, his gangly legs worming the way to the Sure Enuf Saloon. Before entering, he collapsed and furled his umbrella. He wore no hat and Leo was surprised by his thick shock of gray hair. He figured the guy for bald.

Leo left the window and walked through the loft

into the workshop. He bent over his footlocker and dialed the combination to the padlock. The lid propped open, he found what he wanted and returned to the front. He was carrying a pair of glasses. The glasses were Tasco 20 x 60 binoculars. He wanted a closer look at this stringbean, and the Tascos would clap his eyes right on him. He pulled down the shade and knelt against the sill with Terry.

DayDream retired to the sofa.

In the City of New York there's a law which states that every house licensed to sell alcoholic beverages to the public be required to have a windowpane at street level permitting an unobstructed view into the premises. The Sure Enuf Saloon adhered to this regulation, but Joe Cobez's interpretation of "street level" made it impossible for anyone who wasn't either seven feet tall or wearing stilts to see inside. Only the uppermost part of his windows offered a clear view of the barroom, while the rest of the front was coated with a muddy gold paint.

This was all the opening Leo needed to get an eyeful of the action. He kept his glasses on Skidmore and said nothing. Just watched.

Inside the saloon, Poley Grymes was cashing his welfare check and swallowing his first round of the day. A double Fleischmann's with a short beer back. He scooped up the dole money Cobez laid on the bar and began counting the bills, snapping those that were brisk. It made him feel good to count cash. He put a five back on the bar and folded the rest into his trouser pocket.

Skidmore stepped up to the rail alongside him, and Poley shouted for Cobez to give the man his usual. He was buying. He forgot that Skidmore's usual was an extra-dry double martini, though he quickly remembered when he saw Cobez rinsing the cocktail shaker. He tried fast to come up with a reason to cancel his offer, but it was too late. Skidmore was already expressing his gratitude.

"Thank you, Mr. Grymes. Thank you, indeed."

"Yeah, sure," Poley said, as he cursed himself,

watching Cobez ring up a dollar for the double rye and two for the double martini.

"Do you realize, Mr. Grymes——"

"Sure lost that fuckin' round. Two for one. Can't break even."

"Is something amiss, Mr. Grymes?"

"A miss? Yeah, I missed. Missed up. Do me a favor, willya."

"Certainly, Mr. Grymes."

"Knock it off with that Mr. Grymes. Name's Poley. No more Grymes, OK. Just Poley. Call me Poley."

"As you wish, Poley. As you wish."

"I wish."

"An unusual name that. . . ."

"Well, you won't find too many Skidmores in the phone book either, y'know."

"Suppose not. Cobez, could you please give Poley here a refill."

The bar soon became crowded with the lushers exchanging their welfare checks for another day in the life. Another day spent in the dense warmth of a noisy packed saloon. A snug way to die.

The others also began to show, sitting down for their lunch-time breakfasts of coffee wet with whiskey, and opening their booths for business. They interested Leo. He shifted his glasses from Skidmore and the barflies to scan the array of characters. Terry gave him a brief rundown on them and what their games were.

Stalebread Charley Stein was hunched over his corner table listening indifferently to one of his runners complain about how he was hurting and needed to handle more action to get out of debt. Stalebread nodded and told the kid he would try to steer him some longer money.

A sharp-featured black dude in a full-length beige leather coat appeared from the men's room, smoothing his moustache and his nose at the same time. His name was CoCo Robicheaux and he tipped Bascom well for serving his Bristol Cream on the rocks. He sat coolly nursing it, as if he were waiting for eternity to expire. He retailed pure cocaine by the quarter, the half, and the ounce.

Leila Russell was one of his better than regular buyers. She was also a brassy, hard-boiled, thin-lipped, implacable middle-aged madam who operated a quintet of mother-and-daughter prostitution teams. These pairs were wired to her by the purest coke and the righteous profits. Two of her stable prosses were chatting over too hot cups of coffee, eager to break luck, anxious for Leila to tell them where to turn the first trick of their workday.

A pale man in his forties with a hawk nose and a long chin slid into the booth behind them. Known as P.B., his full name was Pinckney Benton Stewart. He was an independent shylock who financed his loan sharking with the five thousand dollars his mother paid him to stay away from her home in Marietta, Ohio, which was where he was born.

Sitting across from him was a huge, battered head with two lumps of skin for ears. Beneath the head was an enormous body and fists as big as melons. The usage of these fists gave the gorilla his name, Typewriter. As a professional pug, he had taken so many dives that the Boxing Commission had finally revoked his license. He had then found an even easier occupation collecting the vigorish from persons who borrowed moneys from P.B. The previous night his boss had sent him after a guy who was welshing. Asked what happened, Typewriter said his favorite and often-repeated line, "Evbody sucker fer sumtin, a lef', a right." After he stopped laughing at his own joke, he told P.B. that the welsher would pay, as soon as he got out of the hospital.

An olive-oil-skinned Latin gambler named Ray Ray padded over to a booth and plumped down on the bench. With his $300 suit under a $100 hat, it was difficult to tell he'd been floating with a crap game for three solid days and nights. Only when he raised his head to mouth an order at Bascom for some food was the sleeplessness of his eyes made obvious. There was nothing in his face to say he'd won or lost. Just that he was tired and in his thirties.

A shrewd, shifty, unpleasant little nickel-nurser of an old gink entered as if he was about to begin scattering pennies around the barroom. He was a small-time fagin who set up marks for others to score. By always speaking in a creaky undertone, he acquired the name Squeaker. The greed in his aging, hollow eyes brought a grin of recognition to Leo Warren's face. He stood up, stretched his arms, and said, "There's one thing I'm sure about that saloon."

"What's that?" Terry said.

"I sure enuf ain't never going in there," Leo said. "Specially with lying sacks of shit like Squeaker around. He'd make me in a second and trade me in a minute. That cocksucker's been dropping dimes on people for twenty years. Beats me how the fuckin' snitch is still alive. Why they let him work outta there in the first place?"

"He only turns up low-riders now," Terry said. "Punks shooting up a delicatessen on their first heist. Rapists. Shorteyes. Quiets down the neighborhood to get those kind off the street. Anyway, I think it's part of the package Joe Cobez, the owner, had to accept from the sergeants' club at the precinct when he first opened years ago. A good enough deal. I never seen a cop near the place since I been back. On or off duty, in uniform or out. Never saw one come anywhere close to that front door. And no one in there's taken a fall in over a year. 'Cept of course for all them deadbeats gettin' rousted for drunk and disorderly. But nothing else has ever gone down with the law. Nothing.

"I still think you're right, though, about you not going in there. Shit, can you see the two of us walking in and sitting down together. . . ."

"Yeah," Leo said. "I can also see us in bracelets pictured on page three of the *Daily News* the next morning too. With all the harness bulls from the local precinct who're never supposed to go near the place standing round us in a circle jerk, smiling their jive asses off. That I can see very well. Which means we can't be seen together, anywhere. I'm not going to leave this loft until post time."

"Gotcha," Terry said.

"What the fuck those characters down there think you do, anyhow?" Leo said.

"They think I live off women," Terry said.

"And they think I'm the woman," DayDream said to no one in particular.

Leo laughed and returned to the window. He leaned his strong, patient body against the frame, his elbows resting on the sill, his hands around the glasses. The tone of his voice was unflattering.

"Nonsense," he said. "Nonsense."

19

ARTHUR SKIDMORE peered at the photograph hanging over the bar, as if its presence was a surprise. Hie eyes grew dim contemplating the familiar tintype of the classic scene: a New Orleans parade led by the famous Eagle Brass Band playing Dixieland with a march beat while a group of kids stomped along behind, mimicking the instruments. These kids in the photo, marching behind the band, were known as the second line, and although they'd try to play the same music the Brass Band was playing, it always came out looser, more lively, better.

Arthur Skidmore knew this. He also knew that he'd give every day of every week of his entire life to be any one of those kids for a single hour.

Since this was impossible, he bleared the vision and returned to listening to Poley Grymes talk about people, using their names as though it mattered.

"For instance, take what Myrtle, Myrtle Wilson, said to me. She said, 'There were no gloves.' Now, Ulric always had on some kinda gloves. Then, you got Etta telling me the big Bertha May woman got it the same way's Ulric, only in an alley 'stead of a doorway. I mean it's weird. You know what I mean. Persons getting murdered. Shot in the fucking head. For what? A pair of gloves? She was here, she'd tell you they weren't there. 'They were gone,' she said. And Myrtle don't lie. You know Myrtle Wilson, dontcha Skidmore?"

"Don't believe I do, Poley. Don't believe I do."

"Anyways, you must a seen her around here. She comes 'most every day. Funny she hasn't been in lately. Must be sick or something, huh?"

"Possibly."

"Cobez, you seen Myrtle Wilson?"

"Nope."

"Hey, anybody seen Myrtle?"

A burly slob down at the end of the bar yelled back, "I seen Myrtle. She was humpin' a turtle 'cross the Brooklyn Bridge. 'S that Myrtle, always doin' the turtle!"

The mug slapped the wet bar with his big, fleshy hand and laughed so hard he began choking. The gagging sounds he made as the capillaries in his face were breaking had everyone rollicking back and forth, cheering for epilepsy. When he began to recover, the crowd quieted and someone grunted, "Shit." They were all very disappointed. Especially Poley Grymes, who kept mumbling something hopeful like "Hemorrage, motherfucker, hemorrhage."

Rash Cohen, a frail elderly man, was muttering into his Manischewitz. He spoke only Yiddish. "Az men ken nit aroyf, muz men arunter. Az men ken nit ariber, muz men ariber."

The paradoxical phrase startled Arthur Skidmore, but he showed no sign of having heard or understood it. He simply drained his glass, bid farewell to Poley Grymes, and walked quickly outside. The rain had ended. He looked up at the darkened sky and traipsed along the avenue, thinking about Rash Cohen's ironic words. "If you can't get up, get down. If you can't get across, get across." It was the sort of expression that made him feel good. Good to be a Jew. No, that's the gin talking, he thought. Good to *have been* a Jew was more like it. Yes, his attitude toward human existence could no longer be considered Jewish. His pessimism was too profound. A Jew's was general. And a Jew was skeptical, whereas he'd become narrowly cruel and inwardly destructive.

The alcohol pumped his blood, rushing it through his veins. His thought babbled on. He drank more for his cirrhosis than to decay his brilliance. He wanted his liver to harden in a final contraction. A lasting contraction that would take the rest of his life. An overly self-indulgent, merciless act of contrition. A personal misconduct penalty for shunning the law of Moses. Fuck Moses! Ha! Wonder what that unshaven pork-faced Irisher cop on the corner really thinks about his Yahweh.

"You won't find too many Skidmores in the phone book either," he said to me. True, Grymes. How absolutely true. You won't. And neither will the Justice Department's ISD, FBI, or the Department of Defense. Not to mention the Airily Eliminate Concern Commission, which I see is now guised as two agencies. Energy Research Development and Nuclear Regulatory. Wonder which one handled that Crescent, Oklahoma, woman's automobile accident. Wonder if anyone cares about the little lady lab-technician besides her union, and they'll settle with money. What about scientists who fall out of grace by refusing to eradicate the mysteries, the harmony of nuclear science. What would occur if they discovered Arthur Skidmore was actually me? . . .

Skidmore didn't see the bus. He slipped on the wet metal of a manhole cover and went flat down on his back. The driver jammed both his feet into the brake pedal with such force that the wheels locked, jerking the bus to an abrupt stop and hurling three dozen passengers forward in a screaming mass collision with the windshield. The stunned red faces of the mass were pressed together, bouncing back and forth, bobbing up and down. Their infuriated, anxious eyes wet and clouded with fear, yelling to crash out of the packed heap.

A neatly dressed librarian slumped unconscious over the exact-fare coin box with four of his ribs snapped

by the crush of the frantic crowd. A bloody body rolled
down the two or three steps to slam against the front
doors and just lay there. Her bloodied head quivering
slightly in one corner of the glass-strewn stairwell. A
cute, spanky six-year-old sat on the floor directly beneath and between the spread legs of an enormous
fat lady whose back was embedded in the shattered
windshield. The little boy looked up the darkness of
her dress and saw what her panties could not hide.
He shoved his hand into her crotch and, using all his
body weight, yanked out a brillo pad of pubic hair.
The fat lady bolted, screaming one scream after another after another, and shoved all the others over
backward as she lunged toward the rear of the bus,
where she fainted with a resounding thump. A scrawny
Puerto Rican junkie wearing a yarmulka scrambled on
his hands and knees through the mess of spilled gro-
ceries and broken bottles searching wildly for a
postage-stamp-sized glassine envelope of heroin, tear-
fully hollering: "I dropt et! Muzza focka, I dropt et!"
The bus driver, his feet still frozen on the brakes, was
vomiting violently and not at all hearing the golden age
couple who were leaning on the impaled librarian and
shrieking hysterically, "You crazy! You almost killed
us!" over and over, while the cop who'd been standing
on the corner was now beside the driver's window,
beating on it with his nightstick, shouting for him to
open the goddamn doors that were jammed by the
bloody body and bent into malfunction by the panic of
the mob seeking to exit from the rear. A pair of high
school lettermen began cheerfully swinging on the overhead aluminum handles and kicking out the emergency
windows through which no one had any serious intention of climbing, especially after a clearly sensible Nor-
wegian carpenter lifted the body up away from the
front doors, and then let it fall out onto the asphalt
after they sprung open which triggered a yowling
stampede by the battered passengers, clashing to
bloody the body more with their feet, using it as they
would a curb.

After the passengers had fallen over each other
and spilled into the street, heads began popping out

of windows and doorways and peering from slowly moving cars to observe the riotous mass that was spreading and swelling around the Flatbush Avenue bus whose driver was enduring more nausea crawling around his stomach, until the corner cop entered and poked him with his club and pulled him from his seat and told him to come on outside quick which he did, after heaving his guts up on the nape of the cop's neck, splashing it chicken-noodle-soup warm, with the frost-bitten cop stiffening as the warmth trickled down his spine so smoothly that it relaxed his bladder completely and he took a thoroughly comfortable piss in his pants beneath his closed rain slicker.

There was a secretory sigh of a smile on the corner cop's face, wheen he turned to watch the driver crouch below the bus to look for the man he thought he killed. Leo Warren, Terry Sage, and DayDream were also watching. As soon as Skidmore had walked in front of the bus and Leo spat, "Fuck!" they'd been riveted to the window awaiting the obvious outcome of their step number seven.

They'd already scratched him when he suddenly amazed them. Clutching his umbrella, Arthur Skidmore belly-crawled out from under the back end of the bus, scampering as quickly and inconspicuously as he could to his feet, mingled with the periphery of the growing crowd for a moment or two, and gradually sauntered off in the direction of the single-room hovel that was his home, without anyone the wiser. Except for those to whom he was still considered the seventh step of a plan.

After nearly sticking his head right through the windowpane at the startling appearance, Terry dashed down to the avenue and hustled over to watch Skidmore walk down Sterling Place. He watched carefully, and by the time Skidmore entered his rooming house, Terry was satisfied by the man's brisk pace that he was alive and well and unhurt. But he hung around for a short while just to be sure an ambulance wasn't called or whatever.

Inside his cluttered room, Arthur Skidmore finally managed to close, lock, bolt, and chain his door.

Then he took the only medicine he'd ever want or need again. He spun off the top and wrapped his mouth around the neck of the bottle, gulping a substantial swig, before easing himself onto a rumpled bed. He sat with the umbrella across his lap and chugalugged the gin, trying to erase the grease-coated filthy horror of having opened his eyes to see the entrails of a bus. A bus that rolled over him. A bus that squatted over him. A bus, he thought. Ingenious! Run over by a mundane bus. Simple. Quick. No crap. No questions. Just answers. Brilliant! Hit by a bus. Not by a half-dozen nine-millimeter bullets from a double-action automatic. A bus! Yessir, the contract on Dr. David Leigh Rabinovitch aka Arthur Skidmore was filled today by our man from Teamsters Local 007. A perfect hit, sir. He used a bus. Hit him with a plain old city bus, Splat!

The noises in his brain soon became muddled with swallows of gin, and he lay back on the bed exhausted to perhaps sleep and continue hoping that his whereabouts were unknown.

20

TOOLING DOWN the highway, half whacked out of her skull on Quaaludes and Dexamyls she'd copped from an attendant servicing a station in Moline, Illinois, Joanie Brown was listening to a Merle Haggard tune on the radio and enjoying the isolation of the car against a midnight rain storming outside, when she came up behind a twin-trailer rig, boll-weeviling the lanes of Interstate 80, hogging the road somewhere in Indiana.

She went to pass him, but he swerved to the left, blocking her. The driver was either toying around, tired, drunk, or crazy, she thought, tailgating him at

less than forty miles per hour. She pressed on the horn
and flicked her beams, but the truck jockey wasn't
hearing or seeing, only interested in playing.

She cursed him and damned him, and after fifteen
minutes at thirty-seven, -eight miles an hour, Joanie
Brown was fed up. Then she got hot. Drawing the
twin trailers over into the left lanes with a feint, Joanie
punched the Toronado hard to the right, passed his
blind side, and smoked the cowboy.

An hour or so later, Joanie crossed into Ohio and
was no longer angry. She was depressed. The gas gauge
was running empty again. "Goddamn," she thought,
"goddamn."

She turned off the highway and pulled up in front of
the neon-lit Hundred Mile Coffee Pot Cafe. She parked
the Toronado near one of a dozen different trailer rigs
lining the gravel-paved lot. It was when she got out
and was locking the car that she saw him. A young,
husky guy sitting on the running board of a tractor cab.
She thought it was a funny place to sit, especially with
a shotgun cradled in your lap. Some folks sure take
their duck hunting serious, she was thinking, as she
walked into the flat white fluorescent glare of the diner
to discover that ducks were not what was in season.

Inside, there were two thousand pounds of men leaning on the counter and lounging around the stools.
There were no tables. Planted by the cash register was
a gigantic hulk who easily accounted for a fifth of the
assembled weight. There was a .357 Magnum Colt
snub-nose nestling in the palm of his hand. All the
others had some sort of firearm, either tucked loosely
in their belts or propped beside them. Everybody was
silent. No one moved.

Joanie didn't know whether to shit or go blind or do
the Charleston. The drugs and the driving and their
staring and the quiet had her wishing she could do
something sensible, like faint. Instead she almost
jumped out of her ninth pair of panties in five days,
when the Hulk grunted for someone named Woodchuck
to search her.

A short round ball with no neck and a leer for a
mouth and beads for eyes waddled over and rummaged

through her purse very fast, announcing the contents, until he satisfied himself and the Hulk that neither a weapon nor a badge nor a press card was concealed among the pills, the cosmetics, the money, the odds and ends of paper, and the many more pills that were loose on the bottom of the bag which he carefully laid on the floor, before slowly running his rough callused hands up and down the inside and out of her legs and under her coat to pat the front and back of her body and slide over her sides and arms and shoulders quite professionally.

He finished with a quick nod to the Hulk, indicating that the lady was clean.

Joanie felt rage and wished briefly for a derringer to make a cyclops out of the round-ball Woodchuck. Picking up her purse, she shot a throwaway line at him instead. "What do you wash your hands with, sand-paper?"

The tension in the diner snapped like a dry bone. Bellies shook, eyes watered, hands slapped thighs, and mouths guffawed with horse laughter at the blushing Woodchuck, who even managed to snort a churlish chuckle. A loud fart kept everyone laughing and then someone else belched and the hilarity soon dwindled to a wide, fearless smile on the Hulk's thick-jowled, inquiring face.

"Anything I can do you for, lady?" the Hulk said.

"Maybe. I dunno." Joanie said. "Tell me, you guys expecting an invasion or something?"

"Oh, you mean this thing here," the Hulk said po-litely, tossing the Magnum around in his hand like a candy bar before placing it on a shelf beneath and be-hind the register. "No, lady, nothing like that. You just drove up on us so quick, we'd no idea. Apologize for scaring you an' all, but we just can't be too careful. You see, we're all independents. Independent truckers, that is. What with the inflated fuel prices and bullshit speed limits, we can't barely make ends meet. Pay off the banks for what we owe on our rigs an' donuts an' everything. So, with things being what they are, we can't even afford to work. Even if there were big enough loads to haul. May sound silly, but a man can't break even with the cost an' all. All these utensils you saw when you came in are to show we mean business. Our particular business at this time is to see no rig, large or small, rolls on that road, not even if it's hauling postholes. 'Cause we're being forced outta business. And our business is driving trucks, hauling freight over roads, like that one you came off of. We need that road, but they won't let us afford to use it. OK. We don't use it. Nobody uses it."

"And anybody who tries is gonna get utensiled," Joanie said. "Is that it?"

"You said it, lady," the Hulk said. "Not me."

"The reason I asked," Joanie said, "is there's a clown about a half-hour or so behind me hogging that road of yours with a double trailer I'm sure's hauling more than what you call postholes.

"Before I came in here," Joanie said, "I just figured him for another cowboy. Now I know better. The son of a bitch is nothing but a crummy scab."

Within minutes, every man except the Hulk was outside taking up positions along Route 80. A few were crouched atop an overpass. Others squatted low in the brush shouldering the highway. All of them waiting with open-eyed anticipation, looking forward to greeting the big rigger.

The Hulk was behind the counter, leaning his massive head toward Joanie as she sat on one of the stools.

"You weren't kiddin' us about that twin trailer, were you, lady?" the Hulk said.

"Come on, big boy, who'd kid about a thing like that," Joanie said. "Now, how's about giving me some of that hundred-mile coffee of yours."

The Hulk placed a saucer on the counter and poured her a large cup of coffee that was as black as any native pictured in *National Geographic*.

"Anything else I can getcha?" the Hulk said.

"That depends," Joanie said. "What you got here besides this mud coffee and food?"

"Beer and pills is all," the Hulk said. "But from what Woodchuck was saying, guess you don't need no pills. And you're already drinking somethin'. . . ."

"I don't need no more uppers," Joanie said, "but downers I could use."

"Could you now," the Hulk said. "Well, let's see. I still got some redbirds and yellowjackets. And a few of these little white pills some fella left with me. Don't rightly know what they are. Supposed to put you to sleep though. I think he called them footballs."

Joanie spat a mouthful of coffee back into the cup and asked to see them. He handed her the tiny plastic bottle and her heart pitter-pattered at the lovely sight of her dearest darling favorites of morphia, Dilaudid.

"D'you know what them footballs are?" the Hulk said.

Joanie lied. "Yeah, they're a type of tranquilizer made by the Knoll Pharmaceutical Company. Don't remember the exact name. But I like the way they work. Very relaxing."

"Don't say," the Hulk said. "Where'd you learn so much about drugs?"

"Medical school," Joanie said. "How much for the reds, the yellows, and these?"

"Red an' yellows go for a dollar," the Hulk said. "Those'll cost you two bucks apiece."

"How come?" Joanie said.

"Went to medical school myself a while back," the Hulk said.

They both laughed and Joanie counted out thirty-five dollars and put the three plastic bottles of sleeping pills in her purse, just as the gunfire sounded in the distance outside.

The Hulk began switching off lights and was telling Joanie she'd best be on her way before the state troopers arrived, when she told him her gas tank was dry.

"Lady," the Hulk said, "you mean you were deadheading when you rolled up here?"

"If that means running empty," Joanie said, "yeah."

"Shit," the Hulk said. "We gotta get you on outta here. Go an' pull that car a yours round back. Got a saddle tank in my pickup fulla gas. Hurry on up, now."

"How much gas can you give me?" Joanie said.

"Give you a gallon to get you back on the road,"

the Hulk said. "But it'll cost you twenty for me to fill
your tank, this time a night."

"A deal," Joanie said. "Filler up."

Joanie backed the Toronado around to the rear of
the diner and waited and watched as the Hulk siphoned
the fuel into her car. It took several slow-passing minutes before the mouth of the tank brimmed full. She
bent down to smell the fumes and then looked at the
needle on the gauge tilting "full" and replaced the gas
cap tightly, satisfied it was gasoline that filled her tank
and not kerosene, or cow piss.

Slapping two tens into his oversized hand, Joanie
tried to jump up and kiss the Hulk's moonface, but
bumped off his mammoth belly and there was no more
time. So she settled with a grateful wave of her hand
and a "Thanks a lot, big boy," as she shifted into gear,
and snaked the car through the lot toward the service
road, paralleling Interstate 80, and away from the approaching sirens and the neon of the Hundred Mile
Coffee Pot Cafe that promptly blinked out.

21

APPROACHING THE corner, Terry Sage took a few
deep breaths and relaxed his insides. His eyes were
alert, but silent. His face blank. He neither feared nor
hated anyone, anything. His mind was unclogged and
as clear as a Trappist monk's. He was cold and calm.

He turned the corner slowly and kept walking. There
was no one loafing nearby. Across the street men were
loading trucks. On the sidewalk in front of him, a
tough old messenger coughed, marching along with a
package under his arm. There was much noise. Industrial sounds of engines, horns, slamming doors. He
heard it all without listening.

A few yards farther was a scuttle. The flat metal
cellar doors were opened at ground level onto a basement. Dangling freely from a hasp was a short-shanked
padlock made of case-hardened steel. It was the same
brand and type as the one in Terry's hand. He bent
casually, switched them quickly, and continued walking
at the same gait.

Whistles began blowing and time clocks were punching out cards and people were filing from the buildings. The work week was over and they crowded
around the bus stop chatting about the things they
wanted to do and some parties planned for the weekend. Terry stood among them and watched a heavyset
man close the cellar doors and clasp the padlock firmly
shut. His partner keyed an alarm and pulled a corrugated aluminum shutter down over the front, covering
the windows and a stenciled sign that read HABER &
BROMBERG PLUMBING SUPPLIES.

A bus came and people started packing themselves
into it. Terry waited. The heavyset man swung a bur-
gundy Cadillac out of a parking lot from across the
street, picked up his partner, and drove past the bus
in the direction of the Queensboro Bridge.

Another bus arrived and Terry got on it. He found
a seat and read in the *Daily News* about some rabbi's
nursing-home empire. It was a story about greed and
graft and great profits and pain. He rode the bus until
he finished the article. He was still in Long Island City,
which is in that borough of New York known as
Queens, when he got off. He walked for a few blocks,
then went into a movie. Inside the theater he phoned
the loft. DayDream answered on the second ring. She
heard Terry say, "Post time," before he hung up and
sat down to watch a film about a big tub of guts with
a Texas mouth chase Chinese around Hong Kong in
search of an acupunctured statue. It was 6:00.

An hour later, Leo Warren pushed through the turn-
style at the Lafayette Avenue subway station and
boarded a GG train. He was wearing a hat, an overcoat, a turtleneck sweater, and trousers that were all
as dark as his shoes. He placed a large shopping bag
on the floor beside his seat. It had been a very long

time since he rode the subway, and he wasn't enjoying the experience. The train rattled from side to side, tossed him around the plastic seat, and generally made him uncomfortable. He stared at the newspaper in his hands and counted the stops to Long Island City.

Pulling the BMW off the Brooklyn-Queens Expressway, DayDream rolled along Northern Boulevard and then through a course of streets to be sure no alternative routes were blocked in case of pursuit, or any other emergency.

Satisfied that all was as it should be, DayDream parked the BMW near the west-side corner of a relatively deserted street facing south. She left the key in the car, attaching it to a magnet beneath the dash. She then doubled back two streets on foot and unlocked the door of a stolen Ford LTD which she had curbed there earlier in the day. She adjusted her naval deck jacket and tightened her gloves by rubbing her hands against her blue-jeaned thighs.

She looked at her watch. It was 7:30. She drove the Ford to Northern Boulevard. Leo was coming up the stairs when she pulled over to the 36th Street station. He got in beside her and immediately began to peel off his clothing, as she wound the car through vacant avenues to the spot where Terry was planted.

When Terry climbed in the rear, Leo was already wearing a thick work shirt, coveralls, four pairs of socks, crepe-soled work shoes three sizes too big, a knitted wool cap, and clear rubber surgical gloves beneath a pair of dark, thin leather gloves. The clothes he'd worn on the subway were now stuffed in the large brown shopping bag. Both sets of clothing were new. Terry changed into an outfit identical to Leo's. Except his work shoes were only one size bigger than his normal.

Nothing was said, until the changing of clothes was completed and the shopping bag thrown into the trunk of the parked BMW, and a large canvas satchel taken out. DayDream was turning east at the corner when Leo asked her about the phone booths.

"The first one's coming up in a coupla blocks," she said. "There. See?"

"Yeah," Terry said, "I see. Nice and outta the way."

The Ford sided to the curb and Terry walked over to the telephone. He dropped in a dime, dialed a number, and listened to it ring a few times. He then jammed a celluloid splinter beneath the cradle to prevent an accidental disconnection and cut the coiled wire from the side of the box, tossing the receiver into some shrubbery. He returned to the car and they drove off.

The number was one of two at the plumbing supply company. The line was used as an inexpensive alarm system, known as a "dialer." When the alarm was activated by an intrusion, it was set to automatically ring a secret precoded telephone number at both partners' nearby homes with a recording stating that a burglary was occurring on their premises. Terry had easily deactivated the system by occupying the only free line on which the dialer could operate.

The other system, which Terry had witnessed being keyed earlier, was a silent alarm hooked up to a remote panel at a centralized private security agency. It would relay a warning over a leased telephone line, whenever activated by the breaking of an electric circuit that flowed through magnetic foil taped on the windows and metal contact devices on the doors. This protected the ground-level perimeter of the plumbing supply company.

The deactivated dial alarm system was only arranged to cover the basement area, which had no staircase or any other access leading directly to the interior of the office above. This was because the two business partners had something definitely hidden in the cellar: lots of stolen copper pipes and tubing. There was also plenty of tax-free money stashed to buy what they sold for quick, huge profits.

DayDream drifted the Ford along the streets of the industrial area. Their eyes peeled the night, searching for anybody, anything that didn't belong in the dark. No one was afraid or excited or worried about cops. They were unplugged from their emotions, clinically eyeing the shadows; the car rolling them toward the mark. The first step of their planned thirteen.

His eyes still traveling outside, Leo spoke to Day-Dream. His voice was consciously monotonous.

"Park the car, motor running, lights off, on that side street six blocks down with the booth on the corner. You'll be able to see the front of the place from there. Ring the loft to make sure the phone in the booth works. Then dial the first six digits of the plumbers' other number and hang in there like you're having a conversation.

"You see a definite rumble about to happen, dial that last digit. Listen to make sure you get a ring, then leave it ringing, jump into the car, no lights, and pull it two blocks north and back this way six blocks. You don't see us running down the street or nothing, you back it into that driveway as planned and wait. We don't show in a few minutes, kill the engine and wait some more. Wait until whatever's happening's over. Or we show. Sure you got some dimes for the phone?"

She took her hand off the wheel for a moment and jingled the coins inside her jacket pocket.

"OK," Leo said. "Terry, got the key?"

"In my hand."

Leo glanced at his watch. It was 8:15. He looked hard at the streets once again. Nothing felt wrong. Everything was calm. Quietly he said, "Now."

DayDream crawled the Ford alongside the curb a bit past the plumbing supply company. Terry slid out the rear and onto his knees. He opened the padlock and laid it on the sidewalk, leaving the key in it. He lifted one of the metal doors and held it for Leo, who moved down the steps, carrying the satchel in front of him into the blackness.

DayDream watched the area. Terry quietly lowered the metal door over himself and disappeared into the basement. DayDream pushed the automatic shift into park, scrambled out the passenger side over the sidewalk. She slipped the shank through the hasps and padlocked the cellar doors before driving off. She parked and entered the phone booth with the key to the padlock still in her left hand. She slipped it into the watch pocket of her jeans.

Terry cupped the beam from the flashlight with his gloves, narrowing it on the unzippered satchel. Leo snatched up an aerosol can, shook it roughly, and sprayed black paint over the only window in the basement. The window was a rectangle cut high in the back wall directly below the ceiling.

When the glass was thoroughly black, Leo turned his attention to the steel barring the inside of the window. Terry uncupped the mouth of the flashlight and set it on its end on the floor so that the beam bounced against the ceiling to brighten the entire space.

Snapping the lid back on the aerosol can, Leo shoved it in the canvas bag with one hand and pulled a light automobile jack out with the other. Terry pushed a heavy wooden crate against the wall directly below the window. Leo stood up on it and placed the base of the jack against the bricks framing the inside of the window and the upper end of the jack against the first of the four steel bars. He worked fast. Pumping the short handle on the jack, mindful of not breaking the window with a sudden jerk, Terry crouched on the rim of the crate, stretching to hold the base of the jack firmly in place.

The sound of the pumping almost drowned the constant ring of the dialer alarm phone upstairs. Both men were aware of its ringing, but were unconcerned. They would listen only if it silenced, or the other line rang. Until one or the other occurred, they'd continue working and never talk. Voice-activated tape recorders had put more than a few loquacious thieves in prison.

The vertical steel bar spread, cracking and loosening the masonry. Terry tucked his neck into his shirt as chips and pieces of mortar and brick bounced down on him from the ledge. The sprinkle from overhead soon grew thick with dust. Leo tapped Terry on the shoulder and motioned him around to the other side of the crate, where the process was repeated. The spreading and dislodging of the second bar was done much more quickly and easily than the first, since the ledge was crumbling. For the two remaining, Leo placed the jack between both vertical steel bars and they popped out the entire middle of the sill.

Terry took the small auto jack, put it in the satchel, and joined Leo back up on the crate. Grabbing hold of each steel bar, they bent one at a time upward, until all four were practically flat with the ceiling. Finished, they stepped down and looked at their watches. It was 8:50. Half an hour spent creating an emergency exit for themselves.

The two men shared a towel, mopping the sweat from their faces and necks. Copper pipes were crowded beneath several tarpaulins that covered more than half the cellar floor. Behind them, slightly concealed in the rear far corner, was the safe. Leo lifted the bag and Terry followed with the flashlight. Picking their way through the draped piles, they stepped toward the box.

DayDream coasted slowly by the plumbing supply company. Several blocks farther she turned sharply onto a side street. A figure appeared in her headlights. She anchored the brake pedal, skinning the tires. The Ford jolted and stopped. The figure froze in the middle of the road about five feet from the car. He was a young guy. Short. Slightly built. DayDream felt she'd seen him somewhere before. She flicked on the brights to get a better look at him. He didn't seem to like that very much, because he flung his hands up in front of his face and dashed around the car onto the sidewalk and off into the night, running toward Northern Boulevard.

Dimming the lights, DayDream drove away. She thought about the young guy's face, trying to place it. She didn't think she knew him. But she was certain she'd seen his face before.

A few streets later, DayDream swung westward and turned on the radio. Dylan was singing a ballad of lost love, and all her thoughts about the young guy's face drifted away as she headed for a quiet spot where they sold coffee all night long, to wait for her next pass by the plumbers'.

Terry stood with the flashlight alongside Leo, who was squatting in front of the safe. It had them both a bit confused. It was an ordinary square-door box with a dial in the center and a handle on the left middle of a single door that opened from left to right. It was also very old. So old that the rivets seemed crystallized. It wasn't exactly the sort of box either of them expected to find sitting out in the open. Something was wrong.

They tried moving it from where it sat flush against the corner walls. It didn't. This struck them as strange because it was neither bolted nor imbedded in the cement floor and should have weighed much less than it did.

Kneeling in front again, Leo decided to try punching the box. With a small sledgehammer, he knocked the numbered spindle off the dial and studied the remaining pin that held the tumblers in position. He then placed a metal punch against it and drove the pin into the interior of the safe. As soon as he hit the pin, the tumblers fell down and Terry simultaneously opened the door with a tug on the handle, before a possible locking device could permanently freeze the locking bars.

Swinging the door wide open, they could see there was no such locking device. They could also see the box was completely stuffed with large coin sacks. Terry pulled one out and ripped it with a knife. It was filled with pennies. The two men looked at each other and took the rest of the sacks from inside the safe, cutting into each one, finding only pennies, and dumping them in the opposite corner.

There were more than a hundred thousand copper pennies strewn on the floor behind them when they finished. Both men were thinking unkind thoughts about Haber & Bromberg's fetish for anything copper, when they attempted to move the safe again.

This time it moved. They pushed it across the floor, until it was jammed up against the mound of pennies. Leo examined the ground in the corner where the safe had been. Set in the concrete was a large round steel ball known in his profession as a niggerhead keister. It was also known to be a difficult nut to crack. Terry had never seen one before. But Leo had and he remembered the labor involved in busting one apart.

They stared at it, with Terry waiting for Leo to decide, while the dialer phone kept ringing upstairs and the sweat poured from their bodies, soaking their clothes. They gulped some water from a canteen.

It was nearly ten o'clock when Leo took the cold chisel from the satchel and they both began taking turns breaking up the concrete to pound apart the niggerhead keister for what they could now smell it contained.

An hour later, DayDream drove past and saw a white plastic strip sticking out from under the metal doors. She made certain there was no one around before parking the car and removing the padlock. She got back behind the wheel as Terry pushed up one of the doors, held it open for Leo, and closed it, replacing the original padlock he'd taken that evening.

In five minutes Leo and Terry were sitting in the BMW watching DayDream park the Ford farther down the block. They were tired, dirty, and wet. The towel was in the trunk with the satchel. After climbing in and starting the engine, DayDream pulled another towel from under the front seat.

The men were still drying their faces as she drove on to the expressway back to Brooklyn, where they counted the $29,000 from their first step and showered and bedded down in the loft to get the sleep they would need to take their second, later that Saturday night.

22

IT HAD been a bad day for Billy Jamaic. An awful day that began many hours before on Friday afternoon. Along his way to deposit the insurance check bequeathed him monthly by his father's union, he had suddenly seen his runaway prey walking down the stairs of the IND subway station.

Surging with missionary zeal, he skipped after Terry Sage. He followed him with anxious discretion, boarding the same GG train but standing in another car. He watched and waited, not knowing where it was taking him.

Having never ventured outside his neighborhood without his misguiding father, he found the subway ride an interminable journey. He was nervously relieved when Terry finally got off the train and ascended to the street. But his relief was short-lived. For when he stepped out of the subway onto the sidewalk, he was stunned by the strange unfamiliarity of the area. Everything was misplaced, unexpectedly odd.

Unable to apprehend the surroundings, he was nearing hysteria as Terry Sage disappeared around a corner. It was at that moment Billy Jamaic began to change. Like a divining rod, he stalked the nearby streets and avenues of Long Island City, no longer caring where he was, only concerned with the whereabouts of the gadfly whose mere existence had become an agonizing threat.

It was this new determination, this total commitment to locate and dispatch Sage that carried Jamaic through the darkness of the night and into the middle of a road where he barely escaped being run down by a car. Its bright lights startled him into retreat, back to Brooklyn where he now stood in a doorway on Lafayette Avenue, waiting for Terry to emerge from the subway, until the cover of night receded and the approaching dawn forced his despairing return to his hermitage.

23

THE SOUND woke him and he listened to it grow louder. A muffled pounding, rhythmic slapping coming from the opposite side of the room. The light, squeaky bounces of the hideaway bedsprings accompanied by a steady thump-thumpa gradually became a crescendo pierced by small female cries and hmm-a-hmm-ahs of a male voice and the slurpity-slurp slaps of sweat-sweetened flesh against flesh and then a long loud delicious screaming delight that slowly turned into a soothed whistle.

Leo turned over on his side and lit a Camel. It was nearly sundown, but there was still enough light for him to see across the roomy loft. Terry was lying squarely atop DayDream, his well-muscled body almost concealing her, his head against her shoulder. Their glistening bodies were beautiful, he thought.

DayDream blinked her eyes and glanced over at Leo. They smiled and she said, "I thought you were a gentleman."

Lifting himself around, Terry smiled his smile and echoed, "We both thought you were a gentleman."

"Let you finish, didn't I?" Leo said, beginning to feel the stiffness and ache from the previous night's back-breaking labor. He walked naked to the shower stall and let the steam ease what it could.

DayDream playfully fingered the cock hanging half rigidly between Terry's legs and said, "Leo's a good-lookin' man."

"Oh, yeah? What am I, Howdy Doody?" Terry said.

"Ah, Terry booby, you're my favorite forever, handsome," she teased, as she kissed his thighs and put his cock in her mouth for a moment, then dragged him over into the shower.

Leo cooked steaks and eggs and the three sat around, eating the hearty evening breakfast, and discussed the night's schedule. Satisfied their timetable was correct and pat in their minds, they left the empty plates and began.

DayDream took all the clothes used on the job the preceding night, including the shoes, and disposed of them in the incinerator of a nearby building. She returned and studied official New York City police maps of upper Manhattan, the Bronx, and Yonkers, while Leo and Terry dressed in fresh khaki outfits, putting on several pairs of socks to fill their new, oversized workshoes.

Leo checked the equipment in his large tool satchel carefully, making sure it contained everything they'd need. Terry folded two more sets of brand-new work clothes, socks, shoes, gloves, and hats into a large brown paper bag. He stapled it shut and placed it in the trunk of the BMW. Leo slid onto the back seat with his tools, and DayDream put her maps in the glove compartment before starting the engine. Terry switched off the electricity, stepped into the freight elevator, and pulled on the rope which carried them down.

Leo lay flat in the rear as DayDream backed the car into the alley and Terry turned a key, closing and locking the warehouse elevator's steel-plate doors. The car rolled out and finally left Flatbush Avenue to cross the Brooklyn Bridge. Leo sat up and slouched back in the seat.

They felt easy. Their conversation was light. They talked about how great the skyline looked and, no matter how fullashit corny, that statue had meant liberty to a lot of people, and about all the good-time swims in the East River, and then on up the F.D.R. Drive, avoiding the Triborough Bridge tolls, to cross the Harlem River and joke along the Cross Bronx Expressway about how Haber & Bromberg would each always think the other did it because there was no sign of forced entry, only four bent bars on a window never opened. They laughed about the two plumbing suppliers who'd never trust one another again, until DayDream turned onto the Grand Concourse toward Fordham Road, and they quieted down to the business at hand.

She drove slowly up an east-side street in the Bedford Park section of the Bronx, passing residential buildings and the doctors' offices that were the mark. There were no lights on in the Medical Center, just some kids playing nearby. She circled the block.

It was 7:30 when the kids moved on, and she double-parked next to a narrow, tree-lined alley bordering the Medical Center. She watched the street, while Terry and Leo walked calmly into the alley and disappeared under the cover of the trees. She pulled away to keep circling the surrounding blocks for the fifteen minutes it would take the two men to deactivate the alarm and make their entry.

The exterior of the center resembled a fortress. The windows were not only barred, but covered with a steel wire mesh. There were two doors. The one in front was the patients' entrance. The side door opened onto the alley. The front door was firmly bolted from the inside. It was through the side door the doctors privately entered and exited, relying upon the round-threaded housing of the door's mortise cylinder lock to keep out intruders and on the passive security of a vibration alarm system to detect a presence, if someone should manage to gain entry.

With a pair of pliers, Terry inserted a key blank into the lock and placed pressure on it by twisting the pliers. A telltale outline formed on the blank and he went back beneath the trees to cut the first impression with a file. He returned to the lock several times for new impressions which he continued to file into the blank. The lock had more pins in its mechanism than he figured. After cutting the eighth impression, he reinserted it into the lock and his sense of touch told him that the blank was now shaped into a duplicate of the real key. He waited.

Leo was behind the building, kneeling over a utility grate. A combination padlock lay open on the ground beside him. It was opened because a few weeks earlier, DayDream had copied the serial numbers stamped on its exterior and Terry located them in his locksmith's reference books, then cross-indexed the numbers to find the factory-set combination which Leo simply dialed to unlock the grate and get at the alarm's self-contained switch enclosed in a small weatherproof housing unit.

He worked slowly and with extreme care. Opening the unit to disconnect the detection device was easier than Leo anticipated. The difficult part was in deactivating the circuit itself. He couldn't use a flashlight for fear of being seen from one of the hundred-odd windows that lined the apartment buildings overhead. He settled his eyes into the darkness and waited to see.

It took perhaps a minute for his sight to adjust, until he saw the small pendulumlike weight being held under slight spring tension in contact with the switch's other contact, maintaining a closed electric circuit. If the contacts separated, the current continuity circuit would open and activate the alarm, transmitting a signal over a direct wire connected to the Police Department and the central station of the security company that installed it. Leo did not want this to happen.

He made sure it wouldn't by slipping his fingers into the unit and gently pressing them onto the pendulum, holding it firmly against the other contact. He sealed them tightly together with a patch of gaffer's tape, thereby disengaging all the microphones attached to the surfaces of the walls, floors, and ceilings surrounding the safe inside the offices.

He closed the utility gate, replaced the combination padlock, and quietly walked to where Terry stood between the trees. He told him there'd been no tamper device to bypass on the deactivated alarm system and asked about the entrance. Terry said it felt right to him. Leo gave the go-ahead and Terry stepped casually over to the door. He inserted the shaped key into the lock and, guiding it softly with his touch, soon opened the multipin tumbler lock, then the door.

Once both had entered, Terry relocked the door

from the inside, leaving the key inserted. He used a desk phone to call DayDream at a phone booth on the nearby Fordham University campus. When she answered and no one spoke, it meant they had made their entry and she was to stay where she was until it rang again for her to come and pick them up.

Leo was examining the safe. It was a hybrid box combining the features of fire and burglary-resistant money safes. He knew he couldn't risk punching it. There was probably a metal plate welded to the back of the steel door, and the pin would mushroom against the plate and block the tumblers. He'd have to peel it open.

He took the big cold chisel from his satchel and placed it in one corner of the first layer, in the crack between the safe door and the frame into which it was fitted. The box was well constructed and it was difficult for him to get a start. He worked the chisel hard, while Terry stood alongside with the flashlight cupped in his hands.

It was 9:00 when Leo got into the first little ridge of the front plate and drove the chisel inside and pried it loose. Then he took a large pry bar and began ripping the rivets that were welded there. Once he got started, it was just a matter of minutes. The door was thick, but there was only about a quarter-inch of steel on the outside and the hollow of the inside was filled with asbestos fireproofing.

After he tore open a large crack in the upper left-hand corner, he stuck his arm down inside and tripped the locking device, releasing the locking bars and freeing the door. Then he pried loose a small steel money chest that was bolted to the interior and dropped it into the satchel along with his tools.

The room was filled with the white dust of the asbestos torn from the innards of the safe. The powder hung heavily in the air like a cloud, sticking to their sweaty faces and blanketing their soaked clothes. Terry shone the flashlight through the dry mist, scavenging inside the safe, searching for whatever else might be there.

A tiny cardboard carton tumbled out. He opened it

and smiled. He showed the contents to Leo: six sealed ounces of MERCK pharmaceutically pure cocaine. He did a brief, joyful jig before placing the carton in the satchel and phoning DayDream.

While waiting, the two men made their job on the safe seem amateurish by needlessly demolishing the entire box and tearing its walls to pieces. They also ran through the adjacent offices, emptying desks and quietly scattering debris about the rooms.

DayDream revved her engine as she passed, and the two men made their exit with Terry relocking the side door before joining Leo under cover of the trees to wait while the BMW circled the block. Both knew the word that was going to be repeated by the doctors on the following Monday morning. "Cyclone," they would say. "Cyclone."

They almost said it themselves when they climbed into the car, but there wasn't even time for that. They had to go through a clothes change and be on the roof of a supermarket before the last of nine races was trotted at Yonkers Raceway. It was nearing ten o'clock.

On the west side of Woodlawn Cemetery, Terry tossed the stapled brown bag into the graveyard. Leo stashed the steel money chest and the MERCK carton inside a compartment beneath the rubber-matted floor of the trunk. DayDream drove the BMW slowly north, between the cemetery and Van Cortlandt Park.

It was damp and cold, but there was nothing to be done. The two men stripped and toweled themselves down as best they could in the dew of somebody's burial plot. They dressed quickly and put on the necessary socks to fit into the different pairs of irregularly sized work shoes that wouldn't match up with the prints left behind on the dust-laden floor of the Medical Center.

Finished dressing, with his wool knit hat pulled over his ears, Terry packed the dirty clothes and shoes into the brown bag and walked briskly with Leo to the north end of the cemetery, where he shoved the bag down into the noisy waters of a large sewer drain,

leaving the contents to be carried out to sea by way
of the Bronx River.

They hurried into the gladdening warmth of the auto
and relaxed while DayDream drove to the Thruway.
It was a bit past 10:30 when they came off the ramp
of the second exit, circled around Yonkers Raceway,
and approached the parking lot of a shopping center
whose supermarket would make "three."

The BMW mingled with other cars parked in the
lot by trotting fans. They sat for a few minutes, scout-
ing the area to be certain all was clear, and listened to
a race being called from the track. Satisfied there was
nothing and no one around to bother them, DayDream
positioned the car sidewise to the corner of the shopping center and the two men got out, walked quickly
behind the one-story building.

After reparking the car in a spot facing the supermarket, DayDream shut off the engine and smoked a
Salem. She would remain there until the races were
finished and the fans returned to drive home and the
lot was empty. Then she also would leave, and would
check into the room she had reserved at the Yonkers
Motor Inn a short distance away. She'd stay in that
room, watching the all-night movies on television and
perhaps reading a few magazines and not sleeping a
wink, while waiting for the phone to ring the signal
to check out, which would be sometime before Sunday
dawn.

Terry was weary and wishing for a few good snorts
of the cocaine he scooped from the Medical Center.
But it was a wish he wouldn't dare fulfill during a
score. He always had a healthy sense of disaster
when working on a job, and he certainly didn't need
to increase it by coking up his imagination with fan-
tasies. So he continued stacking wooden skids against
the rear wall of the corner building without any me-
dicinal aid, while Leo watched the vicinity from the
dark.

The building housed a ladies' apparel shop, and it
took less than a dozen wooden skids to gain access to
its roof. They climbed the stack as they would a ladder and crept over the rooftops of the shopping center

until they were crouched on the tar paving of a super-market that had been robbed many times, but never burglarized in the two decades of its operation.

This was due to an elaborate alarm system that covered the entire perimeter, but which Terry discovered could be bypassed through an entry made in a particular section of the roof where the ceiling had been left unwired for a proposed skylight that had never been constructed.

He had garnered this knowledge during the prior burglary of an engineering company, by xeroxing some filed drawings and flow sheets. He tape-measured the exact distances indicated by the old drawings and marked the spot.

The walls of the supermarket were so high they hid any visibility of the roof area. Leo used a carpenter's brace, an expansion bit, and a pocket-sized keyhole saw to cut a small hole in the center of the square chalked off by Terry. Through this hole he inserted a long, thin umbrella which he opened by pulling up on the handle until he heard the catch click. The umbrella was to prevent plaster from crashing to the floor and creating a dust storm that would easily be seen by anyone passing the front windows of the market's well-lit interior.

The two men heard the loudspeaker announce that the ninth race was about to start. They had to move fast to get inside before the crowd left the track and a hundred or more or them returned to the shopping center for their cars. They paused briefly to eye each other and then rushed to work on the asphalt-covered wooden roof. The plaster was soon falling from the ceiling inside as Leo bored a string of holes approximately one inch in diameter and about six inches from center to center in a square pattern as wide as him-self.

Leo held the umbrella while Terry inserted the key-hole saw into the first hole and cut completely to the second and on to the next, until he had finally sawed out the entire black-tar square, which he lifted away and rested in the shadow of the rear wall. They knocked the remaining plaster from the ceiling into the umbrella, which was then lowered inside the market from a nylon rope anchored with a slipknot around the towering leg of an aluminum ventilating tank. After using the same rope to lower themselves and their tools, they slipped the knot free and pulled the rope down to where they were squatting, behind a meat counter, drinking cans of soda, waiting for the people to clear their cars from the parking lot outside.

It was well past midnight when DayDream flicked her headlights twice to let her partners inside the market know she was leaving for the Motor Inn. Everyone had driven away and all was clear and right for them to take off the money accumulated during the past twelve business hours.

A long maintenance ladder was carried from its place adjacent to a janitorial closet and laid flat on the floor behind the meat counter. If all went well, it would be used to exit through the hole in the ceiling. In case of an emergency, they'd simply cut the noise wires of the audible local alarm and escape through the fire door that was locked by only a panic bar. They didn't care about the silent alarm that the opening of the fire door would relay to the central system because, with any luck, they'd be long gone from the scene by the time the police arrived.

The store manager's office was a glass-and-wood paneled enclosure set in the right rear corner overlooking the entire supermarket. It had no exterior windows. The two men sat on the floor behind the wood paneling of the office, silently studying the safe.

It was a large round-door box with laminated steel walls and 1½ inches of steel thickness for a door. There was also an Underwriter's Laboratory label on the front of the box, guaranteeing it could withstand damage and was quite burglarproof. The label was scratched and faded and almost made Leo smile. But he knew better.

He decided the only practical way to gain entry was to crack through from the rear. Moving it out from the wall, however, was an enormous struggle. It wasn't anchored to the floor or bolted down. It just weighed about eight hundred pounds and had probably never been moved from where it was set flush against the plaster. Both men strained themselves to finally budge it; then, using sheer strength, they managed to turn the box and expose its back.

Leo sat on the floor to take a needed breather. Crawling on his hands and knees, Terry got a six-pack of ginger ale from the market's opened cooler. The two sipped from the cans of soda and rested away a few minutes, toweling the sweat that flooded their eyes.

Thankful for the management's evident dislike of Dobermans and all other breeds of guard dogs, Leo remembered the time in Florida when he was a kid, breaking into a welding shop for some needed equipment and not believing the sign on the entrance that said, BEWARE OF SNAKES!, until he was halfway inside and heard the hissing and rattlelike sounds. Ever since, he believed what signs said, unless he could prove otherwise, as he was trying to do with the Underwriter's laboratory label by drilling into the box it guaranteed.

When the drill bit deep, Leo became aware of something he'd not expected. The back of the box had been rebuilt. Reinforced by several more layers of steel added to the rear wall. This was going to make it a lot tougher. What normally would have taken an hour or so was to take much more time. He looked at Terry and frowned. Terry replied with a shrug of his shoulders, his lips forming the question, What?

Leo answered by returning the drill to the satchel and picking out the cold chisel and the large pry bar with a nail-puller on one end. It was useless to continue drilling, now that he knew how long it would be and how dangerous the shrill sounds became with time. They'd have to peel off the whole back to open the box.

Leo began to force the chisel beneath a sheet of steel whose corner he'd bored with the drill. Once he raised its edge, Terry jammed the nail-puller end of the pry bar under and ripped at it. Leo continued on to the next layer, repeating the process, until several whole sheets of steel were torn away to reveal a thick section of concrete which walled the interior metal plate of the box. They dug out the concrete and pried loose the weld to peel free the plate of metal and finally bare the inside of the safe. Three grueling hours of labor had left the box in a shambles.

DayDream answered the direct-dial telephone in her motel room and listened to Terry snap his fingers twice into the receiver before both hung up. She left the night table light on, the television off, and the key on the bed. She slipped into her coat and adjusted her tight pigskin gloves. The contents of the ashtray flushed down the toilet, she went outside to the BMW, whose engine gradually warmed during the short drive to the shopping center.

She made her approach slowly, ever aware of patrolling vehicles, and watching for any unusual movement in the winter darkness of the deserted area. It was 4:30 in the morning. She was about to pull into the wide driveway surrounding the rear of the various shops at the center when she heard the siren blare and saw the red light spinning in her mirror. A prowl car was coming fast from behind. She kept driving at normal speed. Two blocks away, the prowl car was joined by another, and then another. They swerved out from a side street to fill the night with screaming beacons, strobing closer and closer. She continued at normal speed, driving along the right side of the avenue hugging the curb. The squad cars were on top of her in less than a minute, and flew past her in split seconds toward some destination.

DayDream was unruffled by the episode as she turned back to the shopping center. Her partners were lying low beneath a loading platform at the rear exit of the driveway. She entered with her lights off and the men jumped out to put their gear satchel and the swollen sack of money into the trunk. They clambered into the car and began to feel the exhaustion their bodies could no longer deny.

Leo dozed off and Terry smoked a cigarette, thinking thoughts of cocaine, while DayDream wheeled the BMW along the thruway toward the rising sun and away from the gutted wreckage they had left for the police to find.

24

THE BURLY mug, who, days before, had nearly choked on his Myrtle-the-turtle joke was lying on a gurney in the crowded emergency room of Kings County Hospital. A tall detective named Sid Struve was leaning over him, pressing his ear close to the dying man's mouth, listening to his final words. There were a few mumbles, then the blood gagged in his throat and he died.

The detective seemed preoccupied by what he had heard. He walked over to where his stocky partner, Tomas Canales, was handling the identification papers found on the man and standing with the uniformed patrolman who had discovered him slumped against the cornerstone of Brooklyn's Central Public Library.

"Is he dead?" Canales said.

Struve nodded that he was and listened to his partner read aloud from a worn ID plate. He said the man was "Terrance 'Keel' Maroney, born July 28, 1909, Caucasian, Boston, Mass., et cetera. There's about a dozen different addresses. Probably all as dead as him. He tell you anything, Sid?"

"I don't know," Struve said. "Maybe."

"Well," Canales said, "what'd he say?"

"Said, 'From behind. Someone. No see. Voice say "Godspeed." Head hurts,'" Struve said. "Then he died."

"He say anything about the voice?" Canales said. "Male, female? Young, old?"

"Nope," Struve said. "Just 'Godspeed.' "

"Godspeed," Canales said. "Jesus—H—Christ."

"Looks like we got ourselves a holy epidemic," Struve said. "Somebody's out there waging their own personal Inquisition. We'll know when the lab compares the slug with the others. But I'm almost positive."

"I was thinking all the time it was juvenile," Canales said. "A gang initiation type thing. Jesus!"

"Remember the oil on the last two," Struve said. "Specially the hands of that Ulric what's-his-name. They first called us in, I thought it was kids myself. But I saw the report on the guy's hands and how they were clean, except for some oil. . . ."

"And I cracked a joke about how the old guy was probably a Catholic," Canales said. "Must've tried to give himself the Last Rites."

"We should've stopped laughing long enough to see the next one coming," Struve said. "Now there's another lying over there. I'll bet he's all greased up for the great beyond, too. Officer, what's your name."

The rookie patrolman told Struve his name was "Paul Miller, sir."

"OK, Miller," Struve said. "You stay with the body. Don't leave till the lab guys tell you. And don't breathe a word of what you heard to anyone. Newspapers get hold of this, they'll run wild. See you back at the station."

"Yessir," Miller said. "I'll keep everything on the QT. Won't let Maroney outta my sight."

"I'm sure he'll appreciate it," Struve said. "Let's go, Tomas."

"Back to the squad room, Sid?" Canales said.

"Nope," Struve said. "To church."

"You mean Catholic church?" Canales said. "To Sunday mass?"

"Not my fault our shooter appears to be a practicing member of your faith," Struve said.

"You implying he's Puerto Rican?" Canales said.

"Just saying he probably don't worship in synagogues," Struve said. "If he worships at all."

"You're prejudiced," Canales said.

"I'm not," Struve said. "The evidence is."

The two first grade detectives were veterans of well over a decade in the Homicide Division, where they'd been paired as partners. Known as "Mutt and Jeff" among their colleagues because of their contrasting physiques, they continued sparring about the possible ethno-religious background of the killer. Recently assigned to the Brooklyn South Homicide Zone, they specialized in the investigation of puzzling cases. More than a few of these cases remained unsolved, the suspects still at large. This was the overriding reason Sid Struve wanted the murders kept under their hats and out of the press. There'd be less pressure on them, no spotlights brightening the failures of their careers.

But the pair of detectives had already failed. Failed to notice the rather inconspicuous hospital orderly who was beaming over the phone, tipping an editor at the city desk of the New York *Daily News* to his embellished story of a maniacal holy war being waged on the streets of Brooklyn by some Spanish-Catholic nut who whispered "Godspeed" to the victims of his private Inquisition, before he shot them in a series of killings that were under investigation by the famed "Mutt and Jeff" homicide team, and "please spell my name for me once, so I'm sure you get it right in print."

25

DAYDREAM DID a little two-step on the staircase to let them know it was her returning from the incinerator, where she had burned all the clothes and shoes encrusted with the cement and embedded with the fine steel splinters which were the residue of the peeled supermarket safe, the box whose door the Brinks'

guard would open early the next morning, hoping not
to find what he would: rubble.

The front of the loft was filled with midafternoon
sun. DayDream sat in its rays on the floor between
Terry and Leo as they finished counting the bills that
were stacked in three piles. Leo fingered each as he
added up the scores.

"Plumbers—twenty-nine. Doctors—sixty-three.
Market—thirty-one," he said. "Evens out to a hundred
twenty-three thou, plus the few hundred bunched on
the side there. And this wad of queer here. You know,
the market took over twelve hundred in counterfeit,
probably yesterday alone. Somebody's robbing the
place blind."

Leo wasn't trying to be funny, just commenting.
They all laughed nevertheless, even DayDream, as
the fake notes were torn in half and half again, tossed
into a large pail, doused with kerosene, and burned
to ashes that easily flushed down the toilet.

Terry and Leo talked about a Manhattan attorney
and what was to be done with the money.

"How's the Honorable Donald Stewart MacDonald's law practice these days?" Leo said.

"His firm's doing fine, as I could see," Terry said.
"Reception room's fulla felony beefs. I've been in contact with him ever since I came back east."

"What'd he have to say?" Leo said.

"Same story," Terry said. "But a little steeper, cause
of the inflation, recession, depression, family's two extra
mouths to feed, and blah, blah, blah."

"How much does the Scotsman want?" Leo said.

"He only knows about me," Terry said. "He quoted
a thou a week, his price for being on retainer for the
four of us. That's two hundred fifty per, excluding fees
for any court appearances. For stashing any cash, he
wants five percent of the amount. Even he just stores
it for an hour. Told you, same story."

"But a little steeper," Leo said. "Man's Scotch to
the bone."

"Yeah," Terry said. "And he don't know you're
around yet. Wonder if he'll get a feeling, he reads the
newspapers?"

"He may," Leo said. "Might even check to see I'm released from Folsom. But I doubt it. He's straight. Never meddles, brings down heat. Long's he's paid, he don't give a shit."

"I say put him on retainer," Terry said. "Let him hold a hundred thou. Anything goes wrong during the next stages, the fall money'll only do its work in somebody's hands. That's what it's for. Won't do us no good buried someplace where we can't get hold of it for bail."

"What about you, Dream?" Leo said.

"For it," Dream said. "He's step six."

"OK, Terry goes retains MacDonald tomorrow and stashes the hundred thou with him," Leo said. "Only question, what the fuck we gonna do with the bread tonight? Can't take it along. . . ."

The answer to the problem was in the single ring of the telephone that was followed by a double ring and a triple, then silence. Joanie Brown was in the city.

"Finally," Leo said. "Finally."

Scooping up a loose handful of fives and tens from the odd pile, DayDream announced she'd go down to the booth and answer the phone and take a cab to wherever Joanie was. "I've gotta handle that Toronado," she said. "Specially we're gonna use it tonight. Those streets and lanes downtown are tricky 's murder. Gotta go over them a couple times and route a few good courses in case we get involved in a race."

"Watch the time," Terry said. "We got a date in a few hours."

"Dream," Leo said, "don't forget the password."

"What password?"

"Butter."

DayDream simply smiled and was gone.

The two men laughed and Leo said, "Funny woman. Spoke more in that minute than all the while I been here."

"Cars are what she's good at," Terry said. "She gets off behind them."

"Why don't she drive stock cars?" Leo said. "Seems good enough."

"Thinks racing round a circle track's boring," Terry said. "Told me she'd rather beat cops and their radios, anytime. Knows how. Together woman."

"Sure got her act together," Leo said.

"Takes care of herself, too," Terry said. "Same's she takes care of business."

To Joanie's chagrin, DayDream was doing just that through downtown Manhattan.

The area was deserted and she easily wheeled the Toronado back and forth, across and around streets with names like Gold, Cedar, William, Pearl, Pine and along the waterfront where Joanie began bitching about having been inside "this fucking wagon for a week," until DayDream flipped the supercharger switch, wrenching the Toronado forward in an immediate surge, throwing them both back in their seats. She only let it blast the engine a short distance before switching it off. The noise quickly dropped and she slowed the car, circling it toward the bridge and driving the quieted Joanie Brown to Brooklyn.

Terry rolled the BMW from the freight elevator into a space in the workshop of the warehouse. He was about to resume discussing step five when Leo made a cautioning signal with his hand. The elevator lowered and they heard the motor running smoothly on step four, being lifted into their scheme.

Handing Terry the large photo he was examining, Leo spread open his arms to catch the happiness of Joanie's rushing across the floor and leaping into him. They held on to their embrace, with Joanie planting kisses all over Leo's face and neck, while DayDream leaned on the car and Terry against a wall, watching.

Leo looked at both of them and said, "I thought you were gentlemen."

They laughed and left the couple to finish what had just begun. Terry carried a paper bag with him downstairs. The bag contained the shredded metal of the doctors' money chest taken from the Medical Center. He dropped the flattened pieces down a sewer in the back alley, then joined DayDream for a meal at the Sure Enuf Saloon.

Joe Cobez told them Ray Ray was out gambling,

so they sat in his empty booth and slowly ate the bouil-
labaisse, fashioned into a spicy Louisiana gumbo by the
Creole chef. They ordered whiskey which they didn't
drink. Squeaker was seated nearby and Terry didn't
want to give the little snitch anything unusual to pon-
der, such as their not normally drinking while they ate.

Surveying the bar, Terry didn't see Skidmore in the
room, but he saw and heard Poley Grymes loudly crying in his beer, moaning about how someone named
Myrtle was dead, and how the corpses were piling
up fast, until Cobez told him to "shut the fuck up."

It was dark and 8:00 when they returned to the
top-floor loft of the warehouse. Joanie was sleeping
soundly. Leo was already wearing a black cotton business suit, charcoal rayon turtleneck, black shoes and
socks. He had on thin leather gloves and was holding
a pair of crepe-soled shoes that were two sizes smaller
than his normal. The toes were cut out of them.

Terry dressed differently, in casual clothes that were
the same deep-blue color as the navy pea coat he
put on.

The large photograph with a slim nylon line attached to it was placed in the trunk, as were a suction-
clamping device and a set of picks and jimmies. These
tools were all they would need. The satchel was left in
the workshop, the money and the attorney's name and
number with Joanie, whom Leo had instructed on what
to do in an emergency.

Ten of the twenty thousand dollars Leo was carrying he gave to DayDream, as she coasted the
Toronado toward the district of Manhattan called
"downtown." This money would be used to buy their
way out of a pinch, if the police should tumble on to
them during this fifth installment of their plotted bak-
er's dozen.

DayDream liked the feel of the car being pulled
around corners by the front-wheel drive shaft and the
sturdy sound of the standard shift whenever she
changed gears. It was an average vehicle transformed
by a skilled mechanic to seem even more ordinary,
but properly equipped to become deftly extraordinary

at a given moment in the expert hands of a cracker-
jack driver, which she was.

The light inside the glove compartment was enough
to enable Leo to fiddle with the radio, searching the
range for frequencies on the band to finally locate
the correct wavelength on which they could listen to
the district's police talk mostly in numerical codes
that DayDream studied and understood.

The Toronado drove through the skyscraper can-
yons and Terry reassured Leo that he watched the company supervisor dozens upon dozens of times, using
field glasses to be certain he saw what he did, and
"I tell you, the guy never twirls the combos. He just
leaves the dials on day-lock. Always. There's salesmen
going and coming at all hours and they gotta have
quick access to the manuals in an emergency.

"Maybe the guy's eccentric. Figures rolling it over
by the front window, lighting it up, is enough protection. They never been hit. I mean who'd wanna break
in a showroom fulla brand-new safes, is the way I
think he thinks."

"OK, then," Leo said. "Let's give him some second
thoughts for breakfast."

DayDream curbed the Toronado briefly, and Terry
hopped out to sneak up to the second floor of a building under construction on a site diagonally across
from the safe company. He'd remain there on point,
perched in the shadows with a tiny transmitter to
buzz Leo a signal in the event of trouble.

After circling the street, DayDream dropped Leo
in front of a building adjoining the safe company and
left him to pick the locked door. Within thirty seconds,
he was standing inside the ground-floor hallway, waiting for her to return with the photo and the tools. A
minute later, she arrived and carried them into the
building. Then she drove to a spot within sight of the
company to listen to cop talk and wait until either
the job was done, or the Toronado was needed to
kidnap the safe, if it wouldn't open, or to supply Leo
with a getaway in case of trouble. Trouble which, she
thought, could easily be eluded by her masterful driving.

After jimmying open a door behind the hall stairwell, Leo toted the photo and tools downstairs to a basement where he used a pair of alligator clips to bypass the electronic alarm protecting the company's basement door, before he jimmied the lock and climbed another staircase, emerging on the floor of the showroom crowded with safes.

Leo had three minutes to do something he'd never done before. He set the tools down a moment, waiting for his center to calm. Within ten seconds, he was walking across the well-lighted interior to the front of the showroom. He stepped atop the safe which was centered near the window and clamped the suction device to the ceiling directly overhead, so that the transparent nylon line suspended the matted photograph blown up to the exact size of the company safe it pictured, and in front of which it was now hanging.

Firming the back edge of the photograph to the floor with gaffer's tape, Leo had sufficient space to work between it and the actual safe. Anyone patrolling by would assume all was well. The photograph provided that very illusion behind which Leo was squatting on the pair of toeless shoes and ignoring the sweat that dripped from him to form tiny pools on the floor.

He turned the first dial leftward a click. The second dial he clicked to its next position. He repeated this movement each way on both dials, until he discovered Terry Sage was correct about the safe always being day-locked and the dual combos never twirled. On the fourth sequence, he struck the combination and the door opened.

Cramped by the limited space, Leo held the door ajar and reached inside, emptying the box of a dozen sales and maintenance manuals that contained the precise measurements and locking specifications to every safe and vault ever manufactured or designed by the international safe company. He carted the books to the rear of the showroom where he hurriedly dumped them into a hefty plastic garbage bag.

Watching from his spot across the street, Terry saw Leo release the suction clamp from the ceiling, remove the photograph, and disappear into the basement. He immediately left the construction site, hearing Day-Dream turn over the car's engine a block away as soon as he became visible.

The three arrived simultaneously at the hallway entrance. Terry opened the trunk and helped Leo hustle the goods and the gear inside before climbing after him into the Toronado. DayDream calmly pulled north through the silence of the downtown streets and returned to the warehouse at midnight, where they found Joanie startled awake by a nightmare, she said, "was about a drunk pulling a body from a casket in a funeral parlor, dragging it outside, and trying to stuff it down a sewer after he hears some cop cars. That's what woke me up. Sound of them fucking sirens. How'd it go?"

"Went fine, just fine," Leo said.

"Great! How's about a party?" Joanie said. "Crossing the whole goddamn country's got me up for some real high play."

"Well, coming through this weekend's got ME down for twelve end-to-end hours of solid sleep," Leo said. He promptly removed himself from his clothes, tossing them into a paper bag along with the shoes whose toes were cut away, and said good night, adding, "Changed my MO so many times the past forty-eight hours, can't remember what size shoe I really wear."

They all laughed and said they'd see him in the morning. A minute later, they could hear his comfortable snore.

"At least he's enjoying himself," Joanie said, and kept on about partying somewhere for a while.

Terry also felt tired, but then he remembered the carton of MERCK. He unsealed one of the jugs and spooned some coke out onto a mirror, forming a fluffy mound of sparkle-white flakes that were soon drawn into lines which they sucked into their nostrils through crisply rolled hundred-dollar bills. The party was on.

They drifted over to the Sure Enuf Saloon, where the unfamiliar Joanie Brown caused some attention, but not enough to bother them in their drinking and their continual wandering to the washrooms to snort more coke from a jug passed between them. Then DayDream realized she'd forgotten the brown paper bag and left to burn Leo's clothing in the usual incinerator.

While they were alone, Joanie made Terry promise secrecy and revealed the two Dilaudids that remained from the several she copped at the highway cafe, telling him to drop one of the pills with her because the high lasted longer when you took them orally, and anyway Leo would flip if he ever discovered she was using a needle for anything other than to sew.

Soon DayDream returned to listen to Joanie's tales of her cross-country trail that was littered with lechery and wild perversions.

"From the time I left Frisco," she said, "it was a giant gang-bang. A fucking daisy chain alla way. Shit." She kept on talking until the Dilaudid began to mellow the cocaine and she felt nothing more was important enough to say.

Terry caught himself nodding and went directly to the men's room where he sat in a stall, blowing coke from the ounce jug that was nearly half-empty. He rejoined the women, passing them the jug, and sipped at his rock-filled glass of Bristol Cream while they were busy in the washroom maintaining their high. The high that all three floated on outside to Flatbush Avenue, when Joe Cobez closed up the Sure Enuf Saloon after four A.M.

It was cold, but dry and with no wind in the air. The coke and the booze had DayDream wandering her peculiar wander, and the added Dilaudid made Terry and Joanie impervious to the weather. Mentioning this, Joanie went on to complain about how long it'd been since she used her feet on anything besides the pedals of the Toronado.

"Come on," she said, "let's go for a walk in the park. The sun's coming up soon. Just for a few minutes. I haven't walked in weeks. Then we can drive out to Nathan's Famous in Coney Island for some clam chowder. Come on, let's take a fucking walk."

Terry was so stoned he didn't care either way. But DayDream seemed to think it was a good idea. She went to get the BMW, saying she'd meet them in Grand Army Plaza. Joanie was glad about it all, as she slipped her arm under Terry's and the two of them marched along the avenue to the speedball beat of their high.

They had just entered the plaza when DayDream appeared and curbed the BMW. The three strolled arm in arm over the path into Prospect Park. Joanie shuddered, "Brr. 'S gettin' colder," immediately before Terry saw the flash and felt her spin from his arm to slump on the pavement and he heard the sound of the gun as it flared again in the darkness behind a clump of bushes.

Terry bent low and charged toward it, only to stumble from the drugs and the booze and fall.

Kneeling beside Joanie, DayDream saw the figure step out underneath a lamp post. The light revealed his face as he aimed at Terry, who lunged forward. The gun misfired and Terry almost had the runt, but he slipped and fell again, allowing Billy Jamaic to dart away with his automatic jammed and his mission unaccomplished.

The bullet had exploded into Joanie's left breast. She wasn't dead, but Terry could see that she soon would be. He cradled her on his lap in the rear of the BMW as the elevator lifted them inside the warehouse. Then he eased her onto the floor. DayDream woke Leo. He didn't ask or say anything, but motioned for the two of them to leave the room. Then he knelt by the woman who had earned her rights long ago. Especially the right to deal with her own death.

A warm body wrapped in a hard shell, Joanie Brown had taken everything the streets had without batting an eye. The eyes she now opened to play it her way, till the end. She stared pleasantly at this man, Leo Warren, who was hers, and managed to curl her lips in a smile that remained after her mouth moved to say, "I just got here," before she died.

Terry was surprised when DayDream said she'd seen the Prospect Park shooter that Friday night in Long Island City, while he and Leo were taking off the plumbing supply company. "Almost ran over him. He walked right in front of the Ford."

"You shoulda," Leo said, taking a cigarette, sitting on the edge of the bed. Terry gave him a brief account of what had happened, and also told about the morning when the same runt tried to shoot him. He would have continued in more detail, but Leo stopped him.

"Empty my footlocker," he said, "wipe it clean, use it for a coffin. Cops find her body, they'll connect me. Know a place where she can be buried, left in peace awhile?"

Terry said he knew a spot, and DayDream helped him hurry to complete what was necessary, before it became too light and too late.

She drove the BMW to the Coney Island Creek which led into Gravesend Bay and Terry opened the trunk, sliding the footlocker into the water, sinking Joanie Brown in the sea.

Leo still sat naked on the edge of the bed, smoking cigarettes. He looked tough without being interested in toughness. He simply wanted to bury certain feelings and keep them buried in order to survive through the approaching holiday weekend, George Washington's Birthday, and the caper.

He heard the lurching sound of the elevator as it rose. Then, the rapid footfalls of Terry Sage who burst into the loft with a Monday morning edition of the *Daily News* in his hands. The headlines blocked on the front page read:

"GODSPEED MURDERS TERRORIZE BROOKLYN"

26

"NO COMMENT," snarled Tomas Canales as he shoved past the handful of reporters to enter the drab, unwashed dankness that was the precinct station, temporarily housing the Special Homicide Task Force of the Brooklyn South Detective Command. He hurried up the warped staircase to the shabby second-floor offices and the gloomy squad room where Sid Struve was hunched over a desk patiently responding to their chief on the phone from police headquarters.

"Yessir . . . my partner and I fully realize . . . yessir . . . we certainly will . . . right sir. Understood."

The one-sided conversation completed, he stared briefly at the silent receiver, then slammed it into its cradle.

"Chief's really burning, huh, Sid?" Canales said.

"Yeah," Sid Struve said, "you could say that. He said they're trying to excommunicate him from the Catholic Church. Said half the priests in the diocese phoned to complain about us implying one of their congregation's a religious fanatic. Said even the Knights of Columbus called his Irish ancestry into question. Said the Anti-Defamation League was demanding a retraction on behalf of the city's Latin community for us insinuating the homicidal maniac's Spanish."

"I'll go along with that," Canales said.

"You'll go along with something you'll much better enjoy, Tomas," Sid Struve said. "You go get on the phone and shake that uniform, Miller, out of the sack, or off of whatever duty he's on, and tell him to run a make on that faggot hospital orderly, until he comes up with something. Then tell him to bust the scum-pit bastard's ass. Or we'll have his. Hole and all."

"Then what?" Canales said. "Back canvassing the Borough of Churches?"

"Later maybe," Sid Struve said. "First we gotta check out this report on a probable shooting in Prospect Park. Seems around four this A.M. an anonymous called in, saying she heard gunfire. A car investigated, found blood on the pathway entrance, but no body. Hospitals are being checked for gunshot victims. . . ."

"And we gotta locate possible witnesses," Canales said. "See if the shots, the stains, and God knows what got anything to do with our shooter."

"And we should be so lucky," Sid Struve said.

27

IN THE Sure Enuf Saloon, the bar was aroused and the booths were amurmur with talk of the Godspeed killings. The sitters were huddled around adjoining stalls, concentrating on the obvious effects any prolonged manhunt or dragnet in the area would have on their various business affairs. Since the newspapers were already screaming, squeaked the Squeaker, the neighborhood would probably be overflowing with reporters sniffing around for good copy. Especially if the mad Holy Roller kept the pressure on by eluding the coppers. Knowing this, they agreed on using their collective means and manpower to assist in turning up the Godspeed freak as swiftly as possible for the betterment of all their own best interests.

The informal meeting concluded with Typewriter cracking the walnut knuckles of his cantaloupe-sized fists and volunteering to personally surrender "duh boid ta duh bulls, afta foist bustin' his snout wit foeh, five rights 'n lefs." His laugh was sliced to the quick by CoCo Robicheaux, who personally thought Typewriter's status as a pretty tough boy was highly overrated and sneered, "We gotta turn the punk first, Mistah Tush Hog."

Anger would easily have flared violent and the challenged rating instantly been decided in gore had not Poley Grymes exploded the malevolent silence by hollering his way through the front doors.

" 'Nother one! They think there's another! Cops all over the fucking plaza. Roped off the entrance to the park. Those two from the Special Homicide Task Force, papers call 'Mutt 'n Jeff' are there. Guy told me they heard some shots inna park this morning, early. Found bloodstains onna pavement, couldn't find no body.

"The late edition a the *News* names those the motherfucker's shot. Here, says at least eight known murdered. Four victims onna list were from here. From right fucking here where I'm standing. The last four: Bertha May Williams, Ulric Svensen, Myrtle Wilson, Terrence Keel Maroney. All a them regulars at this bar! And who the fuck knows whose blood's over inna park.

"Shit. 'Godspeed,' he whispers. The motherfucker. All four a them regulars. I told ya Cobez . . ."

"No, I'm telling you," Cobez said. "You don't shut that yap, you ain't regular no more too. Clam up, or you're eighty-sixed. Which?"

"Jesus, Joe . . ."

"Which?" Cobez said.

"The usual. Gimme the usual."

28

UNLIKE THE mixture of shabby and modern decorating most of the law firm, Donald Stewart Mac-Donald's extra-private office was a carefully conceived inner sanctum. Painted a powerful blue with all its furniture casually positioned to the direct disadvantage of his classier clients, the windowless room enabled the attorney to display the power he obviously enjoyed. The large antique clock on the wall behind him warned he was a busy man whose time mattered.

Built like a keg, the lawyer sat enclosed by an enormous oak desk and wasted little of his precious time counting the money. Satisfied the stacks of wrapper-sealed bills amounted to a hundred thousand dollars, he raised his head and bowed his eyes in congratulation.

Standing on the thick-carpeted floor in front of this man whose round cheeks were lined with little veins broken by whiskey. Terry Sage thought to himself: Six down, seven to go. Then he proceeded to place the attorney on retainer with a thousand-dollar fee. He didn't bother explaining their quartet had been reduced to a trio. It was none of his business and would change nothing, especially the price. He simply got the lawyer's assurance that he'd remain on twenty-four-hour call, until otherwise instructed, and that the cash would be securely stored and always available for prompt delivery on demand minus, of course, his 5 percent surcharge.

When the financial arrangements were settled, Terry told MacDonald the password by which his partners would be able to identify themselves, if something should happen to him.

"The code's 'Butter,' " Terry said.

"Butter?" The attorney smiled.

"Yeah," Terry said. "Butter. The stuff you spread on bread."

"Why not margarine?" MacDonald said.

"Butter's natural."

"Not these days. Hardly tell the difference."

"Don't kid yourself," Terry said.

"Anyway," MacDonald said, "I'm on a fat-free diet."

"You're not getting paid to eat it, counselor. Just listen for it. You hear the word, you follow the instructions. We understand?"

"Sure, anything you say."

"No! Not anything I say. The word's———"

"Butter!" MacDonald said. "I know. Not margarine. Butter! I hear 'Butter,' I move. Relax, Sage, for crissake. What the hell you so uptight about? It's just a word."

"You're right," Terry said. "I'm a bit edgy is all. Didn't mean nothing."

"Forget it. Don't worry. I'll remember. 'Butter.' OK? Satisfaction guaranteed?"

"With you, counselor, always."

"Now, that's more like it. Learn to ease up a little, Sage. Things go lighter. There're enough hassles."

"Right," Terry said. "I just need some rest. Appreciate your handling all this business."

"My pleasure entirely," MacDonald said. "We'll be seeing each other again soon, I'm sure."

"Do my best, counselor. Bye. And thanks."

"Anytime. Take care."

Terry exited the same way he had entered, through an exclusive door that opened directly onto the emergency stairwell of the building. He walked down the flight of stairs without anyone knowing he had visited the attorney. DayDream was sitting down the street in the parked BMW, waiting to drive to their prearranged meeting with Middle Vincent in the neighboring Red Hook section of Brooklyn.

The appointment was kept and the transaction went smoothly. Terry paid Vincent well for his silence in middling with a dealer from whom he purchased a

.22 Magnum revolver with a nine-chambered cylinder and a box of soft-nosed bullets to reload each chamber many times. The gun was still packed in Cosmoline for storage, which meant it was brand-new and only factory-fired. Its mere presence, however, meant much more. If the police happened to stop them on their return to the loft and tossed the car, finding the gun, it would mean Terry Sage's death certificate was virtually signed. From then on, he'd always be considered "armed and dangerous" by the law and they'd blow him up with "justifiable" cause if they ever surprised him during a job.

This was the main reason he and Leo, and pros like them, never carried a gun on a caper. The other reason was subtle, but nonetheless reasonable. By carrying a weapon along with them to work, they knew they'd eventually grow dependent on it, rather than trust completely in their senses, their awareness. Most characters could take off the same places they did, through the stark intimidation of armed robbery. But that craft involved a clumsy web of risks, not the least of them being the eyewitnesses. It was this point of never being seen, never leaving conclusive traces for the police to follow directly, that made professional cracksmen and high-class burglars extremely difficult to apprehend.

Never on a score, but only on rare occasions, as when some character had to be thoroughly convinced of something, was a gun reluctantly used for persuasion. And for protection in exceptional, dangerous matters like the situation that faced them in the anonymity of Billy Jamaic. It was his menace that prompted Leo to suggest the gun purchase and had him easily fashioning a clip-brace in the workshop, when the BMW rolled safely from the elevator into the warehouse.

He had just fitted the Toronado with a set of brackets to hold the .22 Magnum so that its butt would be hidden beneath the dashboard, though readily handy on the driver's side. While Terry cleaned off the Cosmoline and loaded the revolver, Leo firmly secured the other clip-brace to the underside of the BMW's

dash in a similar position where it would be immediately accessible for defense against the maniac about
whom DayDream was reading in the evening paper.

She skimmed through the story, recounting only
what they did not know about the freakish runt's
prior victims and how the reported gunfire and discovered bloodstains with no corpse further puzzled the
already baffled sleuths of the Special Homicide Task
Force. Then she went on to another article, detailing
the "unrelated" burglaries of the Bronx Medical Center and the Yonkers supermarket for which the police
had rounded up several prime suspects. The addicted
son of one of the doctors whose office was "totally
ransacked" was also being sought for questioning in
the belief that he had duplicated his father's key,
since there was no visible means of entry. There was
no mention in the press whatsoever of either the
plumbing suppliers or the safe company. They obviously shared like motives in their rejection of un-
wanted publicity. Both definitely needed to stay out
of the news in order to stay securely in business.

After Leo showed her how to fasten and remove
the revolver from the gripping brackets in each of the
cars, DayDream retired to the loft for a shower and a
nap. This was the first time the two men had been left
alone together since Joanie Brown had arrived in town
the day before to die. Terry glanced at the contents
of the absent footlocker, arranged atop the thick
wooden surface of a workbench attached to the warehouse wall. Leo rested against it, smoking a cigarette.
He betrayed neither tension, nor anger, nor disap-
pointment. Terry looked for some sign to appear in
the calmness of his face. Leo's flat, hard style revealed
nothing, not even when he asked, "You OK?"

Terry shrugged in reply and pulled a cigarette from
his pack. He searched his pockets for the matches
he knew were inside the BMW. With the cigarette
thrust in his mouth, he continued patting himself down
and waiting. Waiting for the move that would clarify
what was to become of their relationship which suddenly appeared tenuous. The moment dragged on almost to the point of slapstick, before Leo tossed him

a matchbook and said, "You forget about the booze and the dope and your keeping what we should've been told a secret. You forgot about it all. So will I."

"Done," was the only word Terry immediately thought to say. He stared through the fluorescent glare of the overhead lights, watching for some reaction to his abrupt acceptance.

There was none. It was over. His instinctive reply was correct. As for Leo, nothing was owed. No debt to pay. Just a three-way split, instead of four. The matter was buried in cold water, never to be surfaced by them again. As for his own regret, Terry knew there was no remedy.

They then talked for a while about the religious phantom and how their precision timetable automatically canceled any possible digressions, such as the tracking down and the disposal of the dangerous lunatic. There was no choice but for them to continue as scheduled and simply remain on the alert to prevent his uncooking the score. They'd let the hundred-odd cops assigned to the area handle his case.

Easily committed once again to their course, they realized it was getting late. Mentioning that tomorrow was not only tomorrow, but also the seventh step, they went inside the loft apartment to discover DayDream lying snow-white naked on the pillow cushions, invitingly bunched in the center of the dimly lit room. On a tray beside her were an opened jug of cocaine and tubes of various fruit-flavored vaginal jellies.

They undressed.

BILLY JAMAIC risked a stroll through the Botanic Garden across from the east side of Prospect Park. Under the watchful eye of a grounds keeper who knew him only for his black thumb which wilted every petal it ever touched, Jamaic moved along the flower beds in the nursery.

Always rendered insensible by the floral conservatory, his usual flowerpot stupor was whiz-banged to distress when he exited at Parkside corner and saw the headlines of the newspapers he never read. A stout man stood with his back to him, reading aloud from a page and talking excitedly with the news vendor. The man was Poley Grymes and the words spilling from his mouth had Billy Jamaic reeling.

The incomprehensibility of the scene almost crippled him and he swooned past the men by the newsstand, dazed. A look that the woman in the familiar candy store where he bought the newspapers might have immediately recognized if she had not grown old watching the young Billy Jamaic grow dead.

WITH LEO remaining at the loft to study the safe company manuals for the exact specifications of a newly constructed fire vault, and with DayDream already out casing the routine activity inside a Manhattan skyscraper, and with his own role thoroughly rehearsed, Terry Sage prepared to hustle Arthur Skidmore for information that could prove essential to their success in lifting the goods for which Czechmate would pay them two million cash on delivery.

Adjusting the .22 Magnum to fit snugly beneath his belt at the base of his spine, he picked up a thick manila envelope and went downstairs to walk the few blocks to Sterling Place where Skidmore roomed. The revolver's four-inch barrel moved in rhythm with his jaunty pace. He soon became too conscious of it, wanting to touch it to be sure it wasn't loosening. But he knew that would be a dead giveaway to any alert, experienced eyes that might be watching. He hadn't packed a piece in a long time and hadn't wanted to this afternoon; however, the others insisted on it to protect himself and defend their invested schedule from being interfered with again by the maniacal punk who'd blown away one partner enough.

He quit thinking about the muzzle riding his rump when he stopped at a liquor store to buy a bottle of Tanqueray Special Gin, an extra-dry vermouth, and a bag of ice cubes for Skidmore, who hadn't been outside in six days. Ever since he escaped from beneath the Flatbush Avenue bus on the previous Thursday, he had remained holed up in his room where his silhouette was eyed, moving behind the closed shade of his large, single window fronting the sidewalk. Terry was confident he'd enter the ground-floor room through the use of his wits and on the strength of the trump card that was the manila envelope.

This confidence stemmed from the tempered realism of years spent smooth-talking his way in and out of situations which most men who lacked his silver-tongued Duke of Cork artifice would've found impossible to handle without the assistance of an ambulance. Always known for his feistiness, Terry only employed this other artful stratagem when there was no recourse, as there was none now, stepping inside the tiled foyer of the building and thinking, Seven come eleven, to himself.

Arthur Skidmore was wildly awake with the jim-jams, the sponged-dry shakes which he knew were only a prelude to the distempered horrors his parched gin-drinker's liver had contracted to perform in the ferocious spectacular of delirium tremens. Absolutely convinced the bus had not been accidental, but a down-right attempt on his life, his paranoid fear prevented his venturing into the open to purchase the ardent spirits he now desperately needed to revive his corpse-like body—the body which was weakened beyond control and could do nothing more than shimmer at the vacant stock of emptied bottles.

He was dreaming of placing a generous order for a quantity of alcohol over the telephone he did not have, when he heard the knuckles rap twice on his door.

Torn between suspicion and thirst, he cowered in his bed and thought how it might simply be the land-lord knocking, or a pointless salesman, or perhaps a cub scout selling cookies, or possibly one or more of those from whom he sought escape and refuge. Since he certainly had a leg in the grave already, and by sole fortune it could be a passing good Samaritan, he was prepared to take the gruesome chance. When the knuckles rapped their sound again, he burst, *"Who?"*

The feeble shrill of the cry told Terry that he couldn't have come at a better time. It was the rickety tremble of a voice he'd often heard weewowing from the drunk tanks and hospitals in county jails across the nation. He had never seen or heard anything so cruel and devastating as a person coiled in the tortured snakedom of the DT's. Not junkies withdrawing cold; not addicts with drugstore habits rolling in the bile of their barbiturate-deprived stomachs; not the babbling frenzy of amphetamine freaks or the twisted apparitions of the hallucenogenic overdosed. None of these sicknesses was comparable to the delirious pathos which is a compulsive alcoholic drying out an irreparably wasted body and a scar-tissued, damaged brain.

This was why Terry Sage knew he couldn't have arrived at a better time.

"A friend," he hinted positively in response, removing a thin folder from the manila envelope and breaking the seal on the Tanqueray Gin.

"What do you mean, 'friend'?" was Skidmore's unsteady plea.

"I mean this," Terry replied in a matter-of-fact tone, pushing a FOR OFFICIAL USE ONLY coversheet underneath the door and continuing, "this means more than that," as he slid another coversheet stamped CONFIDENTIAL across the floor and said, "this means more than both" while shoving another, marked SECRET into the room. Sprinkling the next with a splash of gin, he concluded, "And this means more than all," slipping a TOP SECRET coversheet inside. He listened to Skidmore crawl over by the door and heard him sniffing and soon lapping at the drops of gin on the paper.

Terry knew if he were thus to tease a street-smartened addict with a few specks of his drug habit, the junkie would probably snarl back that he'd kill him, even while he lay flat on his face in the full-out sickness of withdrawal. But rarely an alky riding the shakes, about to tumble into the abysmal throes of the spidery blue-Johnnies. Terry was certain of that, even though he had no other feelings at all about it.

Straightaway, there were anxious whimpers: "Why're you doing this? What do you want? Who are you?"

Terry was both firm and soft in his reply.

"I came around to help you, and return these papers you gave me for safekeeping. All I want is some advice. If you look through the peephole, you'll recognize me from the Sure Enuf.

"Honestly, I'd no idea you were sick," Terry said. "I just happened by and thought you'd like your things back and maybe a couple martinis is all."

"Where'd you get my papers! What advice are you talking about! Stand away from the door, so I can see you!"

Terry complied, stepping from the door. But feeling the .22 Magnum move, he suddenly flashed that Skidmore might also have a gun, or a rifle, or something, and he was in clear line-of-fire view and what to do was quickly remove the green bottle of Tanqueray from the bag and visibly hold it up, so it would drop from his hand and smash to the floor along with him.

It proved effective. The door was not splintered with bullets, but fumbly opened as wide as the chain latch permitted. On his knees, Arthur Skidmore reached up and out through the space with a trembling arm, while his red-rimmed eyes watered and his mouth begged.

"Please, please. Give me. Let me and go away."

Slowly approaching the crack between the door and its frame, Terry was not the least aggressive. He did nothing at all assertive, like using his shoe to block its closing, or snapping the chain from its latch on the wall. He had to be invited inside. Unwelcomed or not, his role demanded he portray a guest seeking help from a helpless man. A man he'd have to put upright, but keep off balance with pleasant firmness in order to have an informative chat.

"Please, Mr. Skidmore," Terry said. "I explained I need some advice. You, we can't talk with me standing out here with these papers you gave me and——"

"Gave you!" Skidmore said. "I never——"

"Please!" Terry said. "Yessir, you gave me. How, I'll explain. But I can't, standing here in the hallway with this bag of ice melting all over. I think it'd be better if I returned when you're feeling well enough. You should get back in bed. I didn't mean to disturb your rest. I'm sorry."

"No. Wait!" hurried Arthur Skidmore, as he slammed the door to unlatch the chain, reopening it instantly with a furtive gesture that was thirst over-coming suspicion.

The stale stench of decay inside was heightened by the steam-hissing radiator that overheated the room. Terry felt like he'd just stepped into a combination shithouse and sauna. Nauseated and a bit faint, he wanted to open the front window, but it was too early to initiate such action. First, it was get-acquainted time and until that was taken care of, he'd keep his breathing shallow and his nausea to himself.

"Now," sighed the rapidly sagging Skidmore. "What is it you want with me? What in . . ."

"Just a brief, pleasant visit, Mr. Skidmore," Terry said, handing him the full manila envelope and quickly mixing the driest martini he knew how. Using a large empty Polish-pickle jar as a cocktail shaker, he filled it with ice, brimmed it with gin and droplets of ver-mouth. With his fingers acting as a strainer, he poured half the chilled liquid into a pair of smeary glasses and turned toward his involuntary host, whose mouth was loosely agape at the eye-opening libation.

A once-expensive, tattered flannel robe draped the lanky meatless bones that jerked and twitched in the spastic manner of a skeletal puppet bobbing out of control. Arthur Skidmore let the manila envelope fall to the floor by the crumpled coversheets, braced him-self against the closed door, and extended his limp, forbearing arms to clasp his quaking hands around what Terry Sage dispassionately gave him.

Realizing he had not only arrived at a favorable time, but also in the nick of time, he watched without feeling as Skidmore strained to totter the nectar to his lips. He waited a long few seconds, before calmly as-sisting the man.

Carefully easing the glass to the man's mouth, Terry rested the rim on his lower lip and nursed the gin into him through a slow transfusion of slight sips which took a full minute to complete. He then made some comfort-ing remarks about how all would soon be better and everything right again, while he delayed giving Skid-more the second glass as long as he possibly could. He was waiting for the alcohol to filter his bloodstream, lessening the chance of shock. He also began thinking about food. He'd have to go get some, or the man would just become hopelessly drunk and utterly useless.

"Here we are, Mr. Skidmore," Terry said, proffering another cocktail, forcing him to move and circulate his blood. He steadied the cool, transparent gin into the man's hands and eyed the pastel color creeping into the skin of his otherwise hueless face. "Easy does it, now," was all he instructed. His protective grip on the glass, however, made the words an order, enforced by his firm unspoken control over the rate of the drink's consumption. He couldn't let him gulp it all in one swig. Not yet. Not until he was practicably revived and able to distinguish what Terry wanted him to understand.

Unhanding the nearly drained glass, Terry was about to bend down when the revolver pinched his back, and he straightened up instead to squat. He shuffled the rumpled coversheets inside the envelope and, exchanging it for the quickly emptied glass said, "I've always wondered why they're called 'manila' envelopes. Suppose it's got to do with the color, or some other racist implication."

He turned away from Skidmore, stepping over to the improvised cocktail bar, and waited to hear his voice. He listened to the sound of crinkling paper go with the sluggish footfalls padding across the floor toward the corner bed. Sweat began streaming down his spine past the pistol he wanted to shift to the inside pocket of his raincoat. The strong-smelling stench of the reeking room added to the discomfort of the silence that finally broke with the cranky noise of the bedsprings.

"There's nothing derogatory, nor racially discriminating, about the usage of the word 'manila' in that context," Skidmore stated with a mild degree of manic excitement, resulting from the normal overactivity of his brain. "It's a valid adjective whose root stems from the simple historical fact that the durable buff-brown paper in this type envelope was originally made from Manila hemp, a fiber obtained from the leafstalk of a banana peculiar to the Philippine Islands, known also by its native name, *abaca*."

Having poured another martini, Terry was about to say something, when he returned to see Arthur Skidmore dumping the arranged contents of the envelope in confusion onto the squalid bedding and heard him mutter, "Der mentsh iz vos iz, ober nit vos er iz geven."

"A man is what?" Terry said.

"Yiddish," Skidmore said. "You speak Yiddish? You . . ."

"Only a bit," Terry said. "I understand some. My mother used to use it."

"You're Jewish," Skidmore hoped.

"Not exactly," Terry said. "Almost."

"How so?" Skidmore said.

"My mother was," Terry said. "My father was Irish Catholic. A great marriage. Brought me up in a good home. Fine family life. Always together. When she died, it got lost. My father collapsed. Later, he killed himself. Couldn't live without her. I still miss them. That's why, when I heard your Yiddish, I remembered and asked. You can understand?"

"Of course," Skidmore said. "And I'm sure your mother would have understood my meaning, 'A man is what he is, not what he used to be.'"

"I see," Terry said, handing the fresh martini to his reluctant but gradually relaxing host.

"Yes, I suppose you do," Skidmore said, fingering the papers, picking a bound volume from the pile. "I assume you've read through these, including my journal. I gave you to safeguard, was it?"

"For safekeeping, yessir. You remember . . . excuse me, Mr. Skidmore, but you mind me taking my raincoat off? I'm sweltering," Terry said, and proceeded without awaiting approval. Swiftly undoing the buttons he moved smoothly. His right hand clasped the revolver, slipping it from the waistband and holding it beneath the coat behind his back. He collapsed his left shoulder to let the sleeve slide from his arm which he extended rearward, enabling him to slip the pistol inside the vest pocket and swing the coat to his right side, removing it without ever revealing the lining he casually overlapped to hide the .22 Magnum he certainly knew would panic the man who was watching him closely without eyeing anything unusual.

There was only one straight-backed chair in the grubby room cluttered with newspapers, worn books, discarded clothing, and empty bottles. Neatly folding his raincoat, Terry placed it on the dusty sill of the shaded window he'd wait a while longer to open.

He then went to work on this man who chose to call himself Arthur Skidmore. Like Tiger Balm, he slickly waxed his story as he would a salve, rubbing it evenly and well into affected parts that were easily shaped by his lie. Arthur Skidmore listened in wide silence to how, on a cold December dawn, Terry Sage discovered him unconscious and freezing on the street outside and carried him into the warm safety of this room, where he then massaged him back to life and where he now kneaded that truth with the yarn of how, once awake, he told Terry his real name was Dr. David Leigh Rabinovitch, a former Atomic Energy Commission physicist who had fled their employ and was being hunted by government agents to prevent his damaging disclosures of nuclear research profiteering from billions of tax-subsidized dollars being used mainly to camouflage the incredible dangers inherent in modern technology's inability to control the scientifically unknowable caprice of the fiendishly toxic alchemy endemic to the nuclear power industry whose intended production of plutonium-fed fast-breeder reactors would necessarily grind to a halt upon publication of the classified documents that he'd given to Terry for safekeeping, until such time as he regained his health and was able to properly use the evidential facts compiled in the dossiers to prove beyond question that the AEC purposely misled the public about nuclear safety standards, resulting in the accidental release of huge amounts of radioactivity which would undoubtedly lead to an unparalleled catastrophe, unless the United States completely ceased nuclear power-plant construction and redirected its interests to the intensive development of inexpensive, harmless but equally powerful solar and geothermal energy resources.

Impressed by the lash of words, Arthur Skidmore was nonetheless stunned at having told this young man these frightening truths and appalled at having given him his secrets documenting not only the collusion between the nuclear power cartel and the AEC but also the private journal of his own personal involvement.

The vigor of Terry's rhapsodic account was indeed persuasive and his delivery quite believable, since he had garnered much of the information during months of his own research, prior to obtaining the data contained in the folders of the manila envelope, the package Skidmore was aghast at having handed over to another. He sucked his martini in silence, daunted by what he believed he'd outrageously done.

It hardly mattered that he hadn't done it. It was too late. For he *was* revealed. Betrayed not by himself so much as duped by a hustle baited with truth. He swallowed hook and line, but not yet the sinker that was the weight-result of groundwork that had begun when he first appeared at the Sure Enuf Saloon.

As a regular at the bar, Arthur Skidmore seemed to be some type of hoax to Terry Sage, who'd casually wondered what put such a presumably erudite man on the tramp. It was long after he and DayDream occupied the warehouse loft and were preparing the caper that he spotted something very strange about this man. Something that eventually led him to the discovery of his true identity.

It happened late one afternoon in the last week of that December. Terry was sitting alone in Stalebread Charley Stein's corner booth waiting for Bascom to serve him a drink and a plate of food. The booths were quiet, but the bar was crowded and busy with panhandled money supplying the Yuletide action. Skidmore was by himself, standing at the rear end of the bar decorated with potted palms and directly parallel to where Terry sat. The Cajun fiddler, Doug Kershaw, was on the jukebox, sawing wildly through "Diggy Diggy Lo," his swamp-magic version of "Dixie."

Everything was as usual along the rail of the saloon's hell-bent bayou with the fuddled elbow benders squandering their vagabond lunacy, lurching to the music.

A big drunk started to carouse up front, clapping, stomping, hooting, and knocking over glasses of other hard drinkers. Joe Cobez rushed forward to chase the bum out before a riot ensued. He shouted for the guy to "SCRAM!" in his loud accented drawl, and each time he did, Terry watched Arthur Skidmore become more noticeably ill. This struck him as sufficiently curious, for not only was Skidmore far removed from the eruptive scene, he had also witnessed, in Terry's memory, many previous barroom brawls whose severe violence had never made him visibly sick, as he was by the sound of Cobez yelling "SCRAM!"

His routine insouciance nudged, Terry was further pried when Skidmore returned from having obviously vomited in the washroom and hurried outside the saloon, leaving a freshly poured martini untouched on the bar. This perplexed Terry, and for some reason he was unable to disregard Skidmore's overwrought reaction. Whatever upset him was surely more than met the eye, and Terry couldn't figure out what it could possibly be. Something inside him seemed to feel he should.

He quit the booth to check if Skidmore was simply taking a breath of air. Once on the sidewalk, he spied the gangly gray-haired man double-timing it a block away. This bothered him enough to make him follow and nearly break into a trot, when his man turned up a side street. Terry reached the corner in time to see Skidmore climb the stoop of a house on Sterling Place. He immediately ran down to the building and caught sight of him unlocking and entering a front room on the ground floor. He nosed about for a moment wondering what to do next, as well as wondering why he was doing anything at all. He soon decided it was enough that he knew the guy lived someplace and where he could be found whenever, or if ever, whatever was bugging Terry about the gent became distinct.

Terry returned to the Sure Enuf Saloon feeling somewhat like a tout who expected to share the prize on a horse scratched from an unscheduled race. Not relaxed by the malt whiskey, he ate the boiled shrimp and crayfish without his usual gusto. He was annoyed and sensed, if he kept on drinking, he'd become angry and provocative. He stopped.

At the warehouse, he tried to dispel his annoyance by immersing himself in the mound of confidential and technical information he'd acquired through the public relations departments of various corporations and certain divisions of federal government agencies. The loft was soon scattered with books, booklets, pamphlets, transcribed speeches, memos, brochures which did little to abate his increasing agitation. He was having a definite hunch without knowing what the hunch was at all about.

He felt exasperated and was ready to burst by the time DayDream showed with a batch of enlarged photographs. She looked around the mess of books papering the floor and said, "You lose something?"

"Maybe. Yeah. Maybe my fucking mind," Terry blew, choosing a glossarial encyclopedia at random from the haphazard pile and leafing through it. "Cross-referencing all these goddamn terms to find out what the fuck their definitions mean is driving me nuts. It's all space talk. Fucking moon language. Listen to this shit."

"Betatrons, bremsstrahlungs, Cerenkov radiation, Doppler effects, epithermal neutrons, gamma rays, muons, neutrinos, neutrons, pions, protons, roentgens, scram. . . ." Terry paused and stared long at the word, with every cell in his brain realizing the hunch was paying off.

Rising slowly to his feet, he continued to read in a voice taken by surprise.

" 'SCRAM—the sudden shutdown of a nuclear reactor, by rapid insertion of the safety rods, or by the Core Cooling System. Emergencies or deviations from normal reactor operation, such as accidental cracks or overheating, cause the reactor operator or automatic control equipment to scram the reactor.'

"Scram the reactor," he repeated in muffled tones as the revelation crept to his eyes and finally reared in his head.

Goddamn . . ." Terry said. "No wonder I'd so fucking much trouble understanding this motherfucking terminology. They don't want nobody understanding these jive definitions. They're running a game on me. How do those cocksuckers mean, 'scram the reactor.' Shit!"

"But," Terry said, "I bet bottom dollar that guy, Skidmore, what's his name, knows. I bet he's even been somewhere when it happened. Inside a nuclear installation someplace, you know."

DayDream didn't know anything. She was a spectator, listening to Terry realize whatever it was he seemed to know and was beginning to find funny. She passed him a joint and he toked on the grass, until the smoke got him high and steamed up a frolicsome array of images.

"Sure," Terry said, " 's why he panicked this afternoon. Cobez screaming 'Scram' made him remember. And what he remembered made him puke. 'S gotta be it. 'S why he's on the tramp. He scrammed a motherfucking nuclear reactor. He's probably still scramming, for crissake.

"He was like just standing around," Terry said. "Like at the bar today, doing research in some laboratory. Everything nice and quiet. Then, alla sudden, WHAMMO! Some operator presses the belly button and over the PA system comes a tape-recorded announcement ordering everybody to 'SCRAM the reactor!' Every five seconds 'SCRAM!' Get out! Get away! Beat it! Blow! SCRAM!

"Shit. 'S gotta be it. Something to it anyhow. Got a gut feeling about that guy. What time's it?" Terry said, tossing on a jacket, seeking out his gloves.

When DayDream told him it was 5:00 A.M., he said he'd be back and left down the staircase, rushing along the frost-bitten avenue to Sterling Place, where he found Arthur Skidmore slumped on the pavement, unconscious from swacking his mind blank with an overdose of schnapps.

Terry didn't bother checking for vital signs of life. He just scooped this man whose body seemed to weigh less than his clothes and carried him the short distance to the building he'd obviously collapsed trying to reach. Once inside, he quickly picked the keys from a pocket and hurried the drunk into the grubby room. He stripped off the rain-wet outer garments and shoes, before bedding the man down to snore his sleep. Then he searched the place with the expertise of a thousand steely hours committed to flat burglary.

His aroused suspicions were gratifyingly confirmed by what he discovered hidden between the folds of an indiscernible Sunday *Times* gathered with scores of other newspapers into a confused, dust-veiled cluster crowding in a side wall. A single glance at the cover-sheet contents in the envelope made his eyes narrow, his mouth cluck. He left with the documents, locking the door from outside and sliding the key back underneath to the center of the floor where it rested beside the wet overcoat.

The dead-drunk Arthur Skidmore awoke hours later to feel nothing more apprehensive than a howling hangover, an ache he cured by going on a pie-eyed binge that lasted until the incidental Flatbush Avenue bus discontinued his pot-valiant jag, forcing his present retreat indoors and leaving him at the mercy of this bewildering young man whose face he knew but whose name he had to ask.

"Dennis," Terry said, refilling Skidmore's glass with a newly mixed martini and contenting himself with the watery dregs thinned by the melted cubes of ice.

"Dennis . . ." Skidmore mused in a mellow, open manner that told Terry the time was nearing for him to pitch the sinker. He'd only have to be patient while the man drifted tipsy into the batter's box and up to the plate, ready or not, to play ball.

"Dennis . . ." Skidmore continued, "yes, yes, I do seem to remember something of the circumstance under which it appears you found me. Must've been a strange day.

"An alcoholic I utterly am," Skidmore said, "but I seldom get totally sloppy. That particular day I seemed to experience something quite unnerving. Upset me. Though I can't recall what it was exactly. . . ."

"The season," Terry abruptly interjected, not wanting Skidmore to be panic-struck again by the memory of the simple word "Scram." "Holiday season. New Year's and all. Everyone merry with fake joy. Depressing time of year. Who invented Santa Claus anyhow?"

"He wasn't actually invented," Skidmore mechanically replied. "In the fourth century, there was a Saint Nicholas from Asia Minor who became known as the patron saint of mariners, merchants and children, and as the heavenly guardian of Russia. That is, until he was more or less abandoned for the good of Communism. Dismissed during the Bolshevik Revolution. But long before then, the American colonials had made him the bearer of presents on Christmas and, with the success of the American Revolution, had corrupted his name to Santa Claus. An amusing paradox."

"What's that?" Terry said.

"Revolution," Skidmore said.

"I dunno," Terry said. "I sort of take it seriously myself."

"Is that why you don't remove your gloves?" Skidmore said.

"Well no," Terry said. " 'Course not." He'd forgotten all about them and bought a few seconds by suppressing his surprise with an embarrassed chuckle. "It may sound silly, but I got this thing. This phobia . . ."

"Dermatophobia?" Skidmore said.

"Exactly," Terry said, jumping at the word. "I'm afraid to touch things barehanded, you see. Guess it's psychosomatic, but my skin is very sensitive, especially my palms. I get these terrible rashes. My mother, she was always bringing me to doctors when I was a kid. All they ever said was it's an allergy. Never anything precise. So whenever I can, I wear gloves. Only medicine I know works. Tried everything else prescribed. Nothing.

"And it's nothing to me," Terry said. "If it'll make you feel any better, I'll take them——"

"No, no please. Not at all," Skidmore said. "I just noticed them and wondered. It's irrelevant. Believe me, irrelevant. You've indulged me enough as it is, returning my papers, reviving me with a generosity of spirits. Since I do entertain a basic skepticism toward life, I must admit I find it a bit odd someone would bother about anyone like myself. Trouble themselves so, without reason. I don't mean to sound overly cynical, you understand. . . ."

"I understand," Terry said, and he did. He understood he was being put on the defensive by Skidmore's drifting away from, rather than close to, the plate. He also understood that if he lost control, or balked, he'd forfeit this seventh base on balls to booze. He began his delivery.

"I understand I'm one of a vanishing breed."

"Vanishing breed?" Skidmore said.

"Yessir," Terry said. "You see, we're all human beings. Some of us just don't feel condemned by that fact, is all. We help people 'cause we are people. I was bred to respect my fellow men, regardless. What's cynical about that?"

"Nothing," Skidmore said. "It is surprising. . . ."

"Surprising there're some who're not afraid to love others. To help others. To trust others," Terry said. "You have to trust someone sometime."

"Sometimes there's no choice," Skidmore said.

"No choice *is* a choice," Terry pitched, dropping the sinker across the plate, and watched Arthur Skidmore gulp in the sound of reality striking home.

With his man again vulnerably raw, Terry was careful not to force the play. To ease the mounting pressure and cancel further debate, he changed pace by politely asking to open the window slightly to freshen the room with a breath of cool air.

"I suppose . . . a crack," Skidmore said. "But not the shade. Please, not the shade. Leave the shade."

"Sure thing, Mr. Skidmore," Terry said. Switching his raincoat from its place on the sill to the floor, he went behind the drawn shade to open a window that had been painted shut for years. He tugged at the multicolored latch, until the paint chipped and released the lock. Its frame tightly sealed with layers of thick lacquer, the window itself wouldn't budge.

He feared he might break the pane if he put much more heft into the struggle. But it was too late for him to leave it shut. Given permission to make his move, he had to open it. He listened to Skidmore nervously slurping the martini. Confidence and trust were not built by failing to complete such simple tasks as the opening of a stubborn window. In order to thoroughly and successfully convince, Terry thought it best to chance the risk. The sweat washing out his every pore also strongly advised it was either the window or the toilets.

Running his fingers up along each side of the wide frame, his eyes looked for nails. There were none. He placed his hands flat against the top edges of the horizontal wooden framework and slid them slowly down the front to a point even with his chest. His elbows relaxed, he began increasing tension until his entire body was shaking its energy into his taut hands. The window began to tremble. The shade fluttered noisily. Arthur Skidmore rattled, "What? What's happening? What?"

The vibrations strained in a rising controlled violence, till Terry felt the intensity cresting and sharply bent his knees to simultaneously stress his gloved hands, pressing firmly upward, cracking the window loudly ajar with a whip-bang sound that split the still air of the dusking afternoon like an ax.

Holding an aerosol can of antiperspirant and considering whether to shave or grow a beard, Billy Jamaic casually shifted his eyes from the mirror to glance in the direction of the racket disturbing the normally quiet Sterling Place where his second-story, hermetic apartment cornered Sixth Avenue. What he saw made him leap naked through the bedroom and unwittingly spray his mouth full of deodorant.

Diagonally across the street below was the prime target of his avowed concern, raising and lowering a window. He watched in dismay with his eyeballs ex-

panding at the flabbergasting sight of Terry Sage working a window up and down and up again, then leaning
his unmistakable face outside for several soothing
breaths of refreshing air. Seconds later, Terry pulled
his head back into the foulness of Arthur Skidmore's
room, gapping the window slightly at the sill before
disappearing behind the drawn shade.

Terry Sage's sudden exposure in the ground-floor
window of the nearby building had Billy Jamaic in a
frenzy. He raced around his patch of plastic horticul-
ture, excitedly gathering his clothes from the bed.

Freshly bathed and quickly fully clothed, Jamaic
was itching to descend. But he knew he'd have to wait.
There could be others, too many others, inside the
shaded apartment. He did, however, hope the girl was
there. The girl who also saw him in the park that
dawning Sunday night he shot and missed and hit
another.

Wearing his overcoat, he stood set in anticipation
and watched a yellow glow kindle the interior of the
room against the evening's blanketing darkness. The
soft light silhouetted a murky shadow across the
surface of the window blind, a shadow whose movement Billy Jamaic hard-eyed in a fever that trickled
his barely stubbled face moist with sweat. Like a
statue, he did not fidget.

"That's absolutely correct," Arthur Skidmore said.
"In conquering nature, these technocrats choose to
ignore death, thereby violating its very logic."

A slim winter breeze fanned beneath the shade
while Terry enjoyed a cigarette's relief. Content to
have ably steered the conversation away from his
unlined leather gloves and such, he felt at ease watching Skidmore become assured and stimulated by the
discussion of ecology. A thorough reading of the papers
contained in the manila envelope had provided the
clue. This man deeply cared about a single thing:
corporate political corruption destroying the environment.

Skidmore's voice no longer sounded furtive.
Propped up by the gin, it was eager. He began to speak
rapidly, too rapidly, the words leapfrogging one an-

other to gild the lily of his past hopes as a scientist concerned with nature's survival.

Terry listened, and the more he heard, the more confused he became. He moved the straight-backed wooden chair from beside the window and sat to light another cigarette. He looked carefully at Skidmore's aging, saggy face, at his yellow-gray, veiled eyes gleaming with a sudden cheerfulness. A sparkle Terry made as easily as a paper doll. He also saw that without food, the aroused man would soon fade behind the liquor.

The first match flicked out in the cold, thin draft slicing through the gapped sill. Terry struck another, cupping it in his hands. He pulled on the cigarette and coiled the smoke with his tongue. Arthur Skidmore raised his glass and practically wrapped his mouth around it.

Shit, Terry thought. Shit.

Billy Jamaic, his eyes still intent on the drawn window shade, became tormented by the sudden absence of the silhouette. The shadow had stopped moving behind the blind and disappeared.

His red hair was matted wet, he was soaked in the sweat of nervous exhaustion, but he didn't dare remove, or even unbutton, his wool overcoat for fear of again missing another God-sent chance. He stayed firmly posted against the wall of his darkened bedroom, staring down at the front of the building diagonally across the street. Ready and set, he waited in pent-up fury.

His rigid face strained to control the throbbing pulse beating inside his temples. But the more he tried, it worsened. There was nothing to be done. Billy Jamaic had what he'd never had before, a headache. He began to pray for it to go away, just as the shade was jostled by the reappearance of the figure in the window frame below. He watched Terry Sage shut and latch the window, and then go beneath and come up behind the shade to form the familiar outline of his silhouette, moving strangely in place.

The projected image resembled a sailor signaling by semaphore, jutting his arms every which way in a stiff fluidity of choreographed motion that greatly confused Jamaic, for he had no idea that what he was seeing was simply Terry Sage donning his raincoat to go purchase an abundant supply of food and grog to revitalize the dwindling Arthur Skidmore.

Handing a freshly stirred and chilled but watered-down martini to his bed-resting host, Terry was cordially obliged with the keys to the room. To ensure against this newly courted friendship wilting in his absence, Terry flexed his leg into the side of the makeshift cardboard carton table, sending the full and final contents of the Polish-pickle jar splashing to the floor, leaving not more than a measured liquid thumbnail at the base of the green bottle of Tanqueray Special Gin. Which was quite enough to keep Skidmore still, perhaps to doze, while waiting. But not at all sufficient for an impulsive drunken stupor.

Terry apologized for his clumsiness and said he'd hurry right back, then left, closing the door and keying the double locks that safely sealed up Skidmore inside the room to indeed await his quick return.

His feelings wary about the pace with which he was taking this seventh step, Terry was otherwise rapt by his obvious success in pampering the man's weakness and firmly inspiring confidence and trust through sympathetic familiarity. The rummy Mr. Arthur Skidmore seemed finally to be relieved that someone else actually knew he was also the good Dr. David Leigh Rabinovitch, the noted nuclear physicist whose initial motive for solitude was to accomplish his work. Since there was now no purposeful meaning to his loneliness, it had grown rapidly malignant with complicated, empty doubts and booze-nourished, endless fears until he became a bottomless bum, a ruined shell of shattered ego in total, impersonal despair.

"Fucking dumb gun, stay still," Terry said to himself, buttoning his raincoat in the musty-black hallway. He adjusted the .22 Magnum beneath his belt and walked from the building into the night outside. On the brownstone stoop, he stood for two shakes of frosted air and bounded down the steps, cutting slantwise across the pavement toward Seventh Avenue.

Billy Jamaic blinked his wildly rolling eyes and started in pursuit, only to be spun to the floor by his waterlogged feet and stiffly sleepy legs. He groped to the bedstead and pulled himself up, arousing a thousand pins and needles as he lurched through the apartment and bumbled down the staircase, then wobbled back up again to lock the door he had forgotten to even close.

He finally stumbled out the entrance way and rushed his sopping self around the corner of Sixth Avenue directly into a westward wind blowing up Sterling Place. This chill factor swept away his headache, but also caused undue sensation in his bowels. He tightened up his asshole quick.

On the balls of his sneaker-shod feet, Billy Jamaic trotted headlong over the sidewalk with his legs bowed to keep his fuming rectum pursed beneath his late father's moistened flappy overcoat of worsted Irish wool. By the time he reached the stretch where Seventh and Flatbush avenues intersected, he looked like a steambath running a furlong over frozen tundra. The plain cement was leveled even flatter by a dull fluorescent fog cast by paled neon signs.

His buttocks clinched together, Jamaic scanned the plate-glass-windowed fronts, looking for a place to flush his growling diarrhea. As the first dewdrop dripped down his thigh slowly, like a run in a nylon stocking, he caught and held his breath and tiptoed through the inconsiderate traffic across the six-lane avenue to enter the Canton Cafeteria. He waddled past the lunch counter to the steam table in the rear. A jaundiced Okinawan cook grinned a mouthful of rotten teeth and crooked a blistered finger to indicate which door it was behind.

31

TOMAS CANALES slouched behind the wheel and talked about how all the churches were nothing but bingo parlors nowadays and how his wife was again as pregnant as pregnant can get and how he caught his mother-in-law sucking on his youngest, "so he knows he's a boy, she said."

"Shoulda busted her for sodomy. Let her in on the secret you're a cop," Sid Struve said, watching a huddle of winos in front of an abandoned store nip at pints of strong port combined with sweet sherry in a mixture known as "pluck."

"What secret?" Canales said.

"There," Struve said. "He's one."

"Who's where?" Canales said.

"Here. Hey. Hey, you!" Struve barked.

Poley Grymes slowed up, turned, and squinted his eyes in the darkness, trying to make out the face peering through the open window on the passenger side of a tannish, black-walled Chevrolet parked in a no-parking zone.

He wondered what the indistinct face in the plainly unmarked sedan could want with him. He gestured with his folded final edition of the New York *Post* to indicate, Who, me?

"Yeah, YOU. Come on. Come here," Struve said.

"Awright, a'ready. I'm here," Poley said, leaning over to the car. "Halloo! Ain't you? Sure, just been reading here in the paper 'bout the two you. Even gotta picture in here from the time youse made that Nazi fruit confess to those murders in the Greenwich Village there. Jeez, never thought——"

"Don't think," Struve said, "just get in the car."

"Why?" Poley said. "I ain't done nothing."

"You'll be doing less, you don't climb in the fucking back. Pronto!" Canales shouted.

"OK . . . OK. I'm in," Poley said, sitting uneasily in the rear and slamming the door that automatically locked with a dull click. "Why'd you do that for?"

"For your own protection," Struve said.

"Protection?" Poley said.

"So you won't fall out on your ass and damage your brains," Canales said roughly, as he had a thousand times before.

"This is Detective Canales, my partner. I'm Mr. Struve. Your name's?"

"Poley. Poley Grymes. You didn't have to bother telling me who you are though. Knew youse was Mutt and Jeff off-the-bat. From the papers."

"Again. This is Detective Canales. I'm Mr. Struve."

"Yeah, I know," Poley said. "Just said that. . . ."

"The newspapers print comic strips," Struve said. "It's their business. Ours is police business. You read newspapers, is fine. You read me, is better. Detective Canales?"

"You better believe it. Cartoons we are not," Canales said, and swung the car southward on Flatbush Avenue.

"Look, I didn't mean," Poley said. "I mean, I didn't know that's the way it was, is all. The newspapers, you know. Alls they ever do is mix things up anyways.

"Still, cheaper than the movies," Poley said. "You know. Go in a bar, read a paper, have a whiskey, drink a couple of beers. Gives you something to talk about. Shoot the crap with some guys. Beats sitting in the dark watching these new Hollywood movies where they don't even speak fucking English. *Godfather Two*. Half the picture's in Sicilian. Gotta look at titles on the screen to know what the hell the guy's talking about. But that music was great. Slept through it three times, the same day, listening to that music. Like being at the Pope's funeral, it was so good."

"Is that what you were doing," Struve said, "going

to have a few drinks, read your newspaper, bullshit with some guys?"

"Matta fact, I was," Poley said. "Yeah."

"Where, Grymes?" Struve said. "Where were you going to spend your cocktail hour?"

"Poley, please," Poley said. "Call me Poley."

Sid Struve turned, draped his left elbow over the back of the front seat, and smiled a tired smile. With the toe of his right shoe, he turned the volume up slightly on the squawk box. The voice on the police band crackled in numerical codes between periods of continued static. A quietly harsh reminder that the vehicle was not a taxi, the detectives not cab drivers.

"Where, Poley?" Struve said. "Where you go to drink?"

"Where I always go," Poley said. "My bar."

"You own a bar?" Struve said.

"No, 'course not," Poley said. "Just I'm a regular, makes it my bar."

"What bar's that, Poley?" Struve said.

"At the saloon," Poley said. "Joe Cobez's place. The Sure Enuf."

"Down the avenue a ways?" Struve said.

"That's it," Poley said. "Been a steady there for years."

"Nowhere else?" Struve said.

"Not anymore," Poley said. "Used to. Now it's like, I like to be someplace I'm known. More relaxed, knowing the crowd around me. Too old for surprises. Don't need the kinda aggravation comes from drinking with strangers."

"Don't strangers come in off the street, sometimes, for a couple cold ones?" Struve said. "The Sure Enuf a private club, or something?"

"Nah," Poley said. "Sure, people come and go there alla time. All I'm saying is, I don't. It's my bar. Where I stay, is all."

"You work there?" Struve said. "Do jobs for this Cobez?"

"Work's a habit I quit long ago," Poley said. "Don't do nothing in that bar, but like I said."

"Morning, noon, and night, huh?" Struve said.

"Weather permitting," Poley said, "most the time."

"You on the welfare rolls?" Struve said. "That where you get your expense account?"

"Helps," Poley said. "My compensation, union benefits is what carries me, though."

"You were in a union, gives you compensation?" Struve said. "For what?"

"A seaman," Poley said. "After the second war, I got my papers. Shipped out a good few years. Real peaceful, the oceans. Sorta like having my own yacht, was the way I felt. Not just part of a crew, you know.

"Anyways, comes the fifties," Poley said, "I'm aboard this freighter in the Pacific on return from Japan, when we heard the general, MacArthur, say what was happening in Korea was really World War Three. Everybody enlist, or get drafted to beat hell outta all the Commies, once for all. Gonna fight half the world. That's when I got my double hernia."

Canales guffawed, saying, "How'd *you* ever manage to get yourself a double hernia?"

"With lotsa money," Poley slipped.

"And you've been collecting compensation ever since," Struve said.

"Well, sure," Poley said. "It happened on the job. I'm entitled."

"See this," Struve said, offering a quick look at his gold shield. "My identification, Poley. Show me yours."

Tomas Canales escaped the late evening rush-hour traffic on Flatbush Avenue by turning into leafless, tree-lined Prospect Park West. Digging a battered, walletlike envelope out of his timeworn surplus parka, Poley Grymes unbuttoned the snap and handed a deck of papers and cards over the front seat. Sid Struve paid no attention to the questioning pleas from the rear, while shuffling through the deck for a specific ID. He separated a plate from the pack and radioed in name, birth date, and other particulars to the Communications and Records Division, asking for a routine computer check to be run on the man.

"A lotta money can get a man entitled to a lotta things, Poley," Struve said. "A few bills, here and

there, to a few right people. A doctor with clear hand-
writing files a medical report, says you got yourself
hurt so bad doing your job, you can't do it no more.
Don't matter, you're standing or sitting, your life's labor's over. Means you're permanently disabled. En-
titles you to collect insurance, rest your livelong days.
Must've cost you a bundle, huh, Poley?"

"A bundle?" Poley said. " 'S not what I said. Cost
me lotsa money, yeah. Getting hurt like I got, not able
to put in a day's work in over twenty years. Sure,
cost me dough. About maybe three, four hundred a
week. Every week, every one those years I couldn't
lift a finger on a job. That's a bundle, right? Bundle
a nothing is what it is. You're twisting it around, making it sound like I bought my way into the union, just
to buy my way right back out again."

"Easy, Poley," Struve said. "It's all right. Figured
you were one of the smart ones, that's all. There's
nothing wrong with being smart. Specially in these
times. Being able to take care of yourself. Looking out
for numero uno is more important now than ever. Why,
I bet if I was to ask Detective Canales here to drive us
over to Kings County Hospital, a good friend of ours
who's a doctor there would be glad to give you a physical. Examine you, make sure you're taking proper
care and all. Can never be too careful, know what I
mean? And you know something else? I bet the
doctor'd diagnose you a perfect case of a man knows
how to take care of himself. So good, he'd probably
write you up a clean bill of health. Xerox some copies,
too. Show others how good you do it.

"Whadda you think, Poley? That a bet I should
make?"

"I don't know from bets," Poley said. "Lookit,
why're you bothering around with me for anyways? I
ain't done nothing to nobody. Never done nothing nobody. Whadda you want from me? Jeez, I thought
youse two were supposed to be chasing the fucking nut
case that's shooting people. Not picking up regular guys
from the neighborhood."

A female voice on the radio called their car number
and Sid Struve responded, raising the volume so the

man sitting in the rear could listen to who he was to the Police Department of the City of New York.

"Grymes, Napoleon, aka Poley. Male, Caucasian. Born Brooklyn, New York, 8-30-20. . . ." What followed was a series of numbers and dates about which Poley Grymes had only a vague notion. His prior acquaintance with the law was largely, but not entirely, misdemeanor. He waited for the detectives to joke about his given name. They didn't. He thought that was strange.

Sid Struve reported their general location in Brooklyn's Eleventh Homicide Zone and spoke further numbers into the transmitter. The female voice responded, signing off with more numbers which he echoed back, summing up the communication. He lowered the volume on the radio and returned the batch of identification to the man whose name he didn't find funny.

"Would've won that bet, Poley," Struve said. "By a long shot. You're even smarter than I thought. That two-eleven in forty-one took some mighty chutzpah. Beautiful, real smart move. To think we've been driving around with a guy's a genius and we didn't know."

"Law of averages," Canales said. "Bound to happen, sooner or later, we get to meet a genius."

"Whadda you mean, that two-eleven, forty-one?" Poley said, trying to stuff his set of papers into the plastic envelope.

"Let's say," Struve said, "it means in the winter of Pearl Harbor, 1941, you're twenty, twenty-one years old, and you walked into the station house of the old sixty-eighth precinct where you told the desk sergeant to tell the detectives upstairs that the perpetrator wanted in connection with the stickup of a certain premises was you, and that you came to surrender for violating the two hundred eleventh statute of the penal code for which you were subsequently booked by the obliging detectives and taken across the avenue to be formally charged with armed robbery and arraigned for the commission of said crime in the Ninth District's Magistrate's Court where you surprised hell outta everyone by asking for and being granted a Legal Aid counsel through whom you pled *not guilty*.

"As a first offender," Struve said, "the judge set nominal bail and your mother, or someone, was right there to put up the bond. You left the courtroom, telling your defense counsel all sorts of third-degree horrors about how the then-not-so-much-obliged detectives coerced you into saying you committed the crime of which you were completely innocent.

"Then," Struve said, "at the preliminary hearing, this last-defense-of-the-oppressed counselor of yours refused to accept a dismissal. Gotten crazed behind your story, he not only wanted a trial by jury and a verdict of acquittal, he's out to make a federal case and a name for himself. Calls for motions, gets continuances, files, briefs. Got more continuances to prepare and file more briefs.

"Meanwhile," Struve said, "the real perpetrator's apprehended during another holdup and you're cleared. But the case's not resolved, 'cause your meshuge counsel's trying to make history first time at bat, putting you on permanent hold in the interest of justice, so you could stand to testify. Which you'd no intention of doing, since it'd been perjury. But it's all keeping you from getting inducted, making the draft board wait on a decision. When the schmuck from Legal Aid finally told you it was almost time, the Second World War was over, and you knew you had to get away from your neighborhood fast, before those unkind detectives in the old sixty-eighth put a frame on you so tight a Rockefeller couldn't a bailed you out. So you hit the high seas those next years, got yourself a double hernia and entitled to a lifetime's disability benefits.

"A man knows how to make it work for him like that's a real genius," Struve said. "Should give lectures at the universities, show the schlemiels how smart smart can be. Am I right, Detective Canales, or am I right?"

"Right as clockwise is right, you are," Canales said.

" 'S that what she was saying onna radio?" Poley said. "That how you know all that? From some meter maid reads you a sheet of numbers?"

"That's part of it," Struve said. "The other part's what the city pays us an exorbitant salary to figure out. The rest's what you told us yourself."

"Alls I told you . . ." Poley said, "I don't like wars, is all. What's wrong with not liking wars? You don't like something, you stay away from it. I don't like wars. What's bad about that? Who in hell likes wars, anyways?"

"Admirable," Struve said. "With you, I agree. But Detective Canales here's a shtarker. Joined the airborne, thinking what that police action needed most was a member of New York's finest. Tried to swim the Yalu River by himself, place all North Korea under arrest for . . . what was the charge?"

"Conspiracy!" Canales said, resounding the word like a thud.

"Of course . . . conspiracy," Struve said. "The one law everyone's born to break. You know, Poley, most people think it takes two to conspire. It don't. Just takes a man and his own brain. Man uses his brain to think of unlawful means to accomplish something lawful, he commits a crime. He just thinks about it, it's hard put to prove. But if he's a man smart enough to do what his brain thinks up, like a bogus way to get himself entitled to some perfectly legal benefit of society . . . he's in trouble. Make a case against a smart man like that, using malice aforethought."

"Malice?" Poley said. "What, whose malice? Why, huh? Why're you doing this for, Mr. Struve? Whadda you gotta do a thing like this? This ain't the kinda thing I read about. Didn't read nowheres where you went around picking on old bums like me. Scaring them they might lose what little livelihood they got comin'. All they got left. 'S that what it's about, Mr. Struve? You gonna take away everything from a nobody's got nothing?"

"Yesterday, Sid, didn't you say about how we maybe should get lucky?" Canales said, curbing the car on Parkside.

"Never figured we'd luck out, though, Tomas," Struve said. "You're a right guy, Poley, a right enough guy. Glad to make your acquaintance."

"Ah, Jeezus Crist, a'ready," Poley said. "Whadda you talking about, now? A right guy? Come on, Mr. Struve, tell me. Willya, please, just tell me what's this all about, huh?"

"We need help with this Godspeed thing, Poley," Struve said. "We're just looking for some help, that's all."

"Help?" Poley said. "What kinda help, you mean?"

"Your help," Struve said. "We'd like for you to give us some help."

"My help?" Poley said. "You want my help? You gotta make me sick to my guts, 'cause you want some help? This's crazy. What's an old bum like me gonna help you?"

"Look at it our way, Poley," Struve said. "We meet regular guys on the job, all the time. Some more regular than others. You, we knew, were a regular guy. Gets what enjoyment he wants from reading the newspaper, drinking with people he knows know him at the bar in the Sure Enuf. That's why we asked you into the car.

"You surprised us," Struve said. "From what you said, on top of what we got over the radio. The way you just came back at that malice aforethought business, we learned you weren't just another regular guy. You're more. A right guy is who you are. Not no old bum. Eight, nine years older than me don't make you old. Figuring out a scheme to get paid for not working the rest of your life don't make you no bum. Makes you a smart man knows how to look after number one.

"We knew you were no straight down-and-out bum," Struve said. "Figured you for a regular guy just had something small and quiet going for him on the side. Didn't get to know you were also a right guy till we had our talk together. We didn't know something else, too, Poley. Something about you makes you important."

"Important?" Poley said. "I'm important now, too? Come on, willya please, Mr. Struve . . . quit jerking my chain. Get to what you're getting at makes a nobody like me all of a sudden somebody important."

"You care about people nobody cares about," Struve said. "People who probably don't even care much about themselves. You care about whether they live, whether they die. Makes you important."

"Who said I care anybody lives, anybody dies?" Poley said. "Who's that supposed to make me important to, anyhow?"

"That newspaper on your lap," Struve said, "the others you talked about reading all the time. Somebody like you buys newspapers, means they care about some things. People don't care about nothing don't buy newspapers. Bums don't buy newspapers. They find them. Gotta have a reason to spend half a buck a day on newspapers. That's the reason makes you important to us. Makes us want your help, Poley."

"What help, Mr. Struve?" Poley said. "What help you need so bad you gotta put me through the mill to find out it's me you want it from? What kinda help's that?"

"The kind of help we always need, Poley," Struve said. "Information. Seems certain members of the criminal element, namely those eminent booth-dwellers at the Sure Enuf Saloon, decided to form themselves a committee. Show the neighborhood what good citizens they are by using their influence to turn up the Godspeed shooter. Word's all over the streets, the honorable CoCo Robicheaux's offering an ounce of cocaine for information leading to the killer's identity. All sorts of rewards, we hear. P.B. Stewart says he'll tear up any markers he's holding on anybody finds out who's the shooter. Leila Russell's gonna contribute her best mother and daughter to play house for a weekend as a prize. Stalebread Charley Stein's gonna make believe the tipster hit the day's number. Ray Ray's gonna let him win at cards. The Squeaker even promises he won't snitch for a month of Sundays. And that gorilla, Typewriter, is going around the avenue slapping guys just to tell them he'll never do it again to the one who turns up the psycho."

"Wonderful," Struve said. "Leaves us nowhere. Who's gonna tell us something for nothing, when they can cash in at the Sure Enuf? Make us look like assholes."

"This keeps on, the way it's going," Canales said,

"we'll get guys coming down from Harlem, bussing over from Jersey, to turn in their mothers. A real fucking circus it'll be. Everybody fingering everybody else."

"And we can't step one foot inside that saloon," Struve said. "Put a quick stop to the bullshit. Find out a few things. We can't even get a ladder, peek in through the window. That's why we need you to help us, Poley. Tell us what we don't know, before it gets crazier than crazy around here and our lunatic shooter murders some more of your kind of people."

"Hey," Poley said, "I can't go mess with them in the booths. You know what'll happen. Everything bad anybody can think of to do to me is what'll happen. Ain't no compensation in that. No, sir."

"That's not what we're asking, Poley," Struve said. "We don't need you poking your nose. All we want is what you hear they heard. Any leads, any talk floating around the bar that's useful. That's all. Not who said what to who. Just information we can't get close enough to to get ourselves. It's simple. What you do every day, anyway. Now you got a chance to save some lives by doing it, is the only difference."

"I dunno," Poley said. "I dunno. Somebody might not like me listening to what I hear. Me being, like you said, a right guy and all. Might catch an attitude about me. Then where would I go to have a few drinks, enjoy a little company? Where would I go, then, Mr. Struve, if I could still walk afterwards? Huh?"

Tomas Canales shifted into gear and pulled the car away from the curb, driving it east on Parkside Avenue. Sid Struve carefully lifted a page from a folder and handed the paper over his shoulder to the rear. The two detectives looked through the windshield, watching the red, white and yellow lights of the moving traffic, ticking off violations to themselves in silence.

In the darkness of the backseat, Poley Grymes batted his eyes at the sheet of paper, moving his lips to read the list of victims' names. Soon he was reminiscing about his old friend Ulric Svensen, always doing things that were funny and making him laugh by refusing to remove the various gloves he constantly wore, gloves strangely missing from his hands on the morning he was found slumped in a doorway. And poor Myrtle Wilson, who had been at the scene and told him of the absent gloves while they were drinking together in the bar on the very night she too was murdered from the shadows by the same nut case who, days later, lodged a bullet in Keel Maroney's numb-skull.

"Motherfucking maniac, you gotta stop him some-ways!" Poley said, looking up from the typed list to see Sid Struve finish jotting in a notebook and Tomas Canales roll through a driveway to park in front of a sign on a building that read KINGS COUNTY MORGUE, where the detectives were going to let this man, Napoleon "Poley" Grymes, fully realize his own importance to them by giving him a memorable look at the waxen faces of his friends' remains, before they were nailed into pine boxes and buried in New York City's potters field on an island in the East River called Hart.

32

WRAPPED IN a gray cotton sweat suit, Leo Warren stood on his hands in the middle of the floor, doing push-ups with his legs stiffened straight in the air. He did this set of exercises as he had almost daily in Folsom over the past five years: with a graceful slowness coordinating balance and power in a hypnotic concentration that made the routine seem effortless. At twoscore and one, he lowered his bare feet and raised his blushed head, letting his arms dangle by his sides while he loosely paced the loft and lessened the depth of his breathing.

Terry emerged from the kitchenette sipping a mug

of reheated black coffee. He sat hunched over on the foam rubber edge of the hidden-away bed. His shoe lazily toed a full shopping bag of bread and peanut-butter protein, canned fruit, and assorted nonperishable nutrients.

He looked down at the .22 Magnum nestled on the cushion beside him and shifted his eyes to Leo, who was no longer pacing, but toweling his sweat. Draping the cloth over his head and folding it into the crew neck of his sweater, he resembled a classy club fighter returning from roadwork. A man capable of taking punishment while performing in a durable, high style.

"Don't have much time, Leo," Terry said. "Gotta get back over to our man there."

"You just got here," Leo said. "You don't have much time. Tell it, then. What went wrong?"

"Me," Terry said. "I went wrong. Went over there wrong."

"Uh-huh," Leo said. "Went over there wrong. That's why this paranoid invited you inside his room? Gave you the keys so you could let yourself back in? 'Cause you went over wrong?"

"No, that's not why," Terry said. "Not what I mean. Those moves I worked fine. Just like we figured. That's not what I'm talking about. What I'm saying, is we misread the man's case. Made him wrong. That crap written in his diary is why I went over wrong."

"You mean this Skidmore's supposed to be a nuclear scientist and he's fucking not?" Leo said.

"Physicist," Terry said. "A nuclear physicist is what he's supposed to be, is. Problem's me not understanding, that's all. See, I'm inside nursing him gin, getting him to talk about things, like why envelopes are manila, how Santa Claus was a Russian, convincing him he gave me his papers himself, just because I found him in the gutter. That's when he turned me around. He was too calm. I mean, I thought certain he'd flip about me having his files, knowing his secrets. Was sure it'd be the roughest hurdle. But no. Hardly even tries to back me off. Throws out a line about not meaning to sound cynical. I begin to lay it on about being kind to all the fucking animals, our

fellow men. How we gotta save the ecology, the fucking bald eagles. But playing it strict and soft, so I can
get in close, real close to him. Then, it starts bothering
me cause it's going too fucking easy. I'm not only
next to him, he's right next to me. Finally found himself a friend, you know, real palsy-walsy.

"What I mean I went over there wrong," Terry said,
"is the stuff in his diary. Took it the man was in stone
terror of all those federal agencies he scribbled about.
So I went over thinking there was no way I was ever
gonna be anything but a threat, and I made my approach like we decided. Reason I got all tangled
around was what's not in his diary. Nobody wants
the doctor, dead or alive, more than he wants himself. Me being there made him real again. I showed
up, he was a lush with the DT's. I leave him, he
thinks he's the same doctor of physics he was, drinking a couple cocktails.

"You see what I'm saying, Leo?" Terry said. "I
not only got myself a mark to hustle. I got myself a
fucking epitaph looking to be written."

"I see," Leo said. "I see we could have us a problem, or no problem at all. You get back there and the
man's still got that look you said he had on his face.
Play the look, not the man. You know what I mean.
If the look's gone, play the man. The way we worked it
out. Start from scratch, you have to. You've the edge
you didn't have before. You're hip to his moves.
Should be easier now."

"Yeah," Terry said. "But what happens, I go back
and the man still has that look and I ask him what
I ask him and he not only answers, he gets some in-
spiration, says, 'Wait for me. I wanna come, too.' I
slip him all these, or what?"

Glancing at the vial of barbiturate capsules in Terry's hand, Leo said, "What kind of shape's he in?"

"None," Terry said.

"Then, you give him all those," Leo said, "you
know what'll happen?"

"Probably kill him," Terry said. "That's why I'm
asking."

Leo paused for a moment, then left the room, walking into the workshop. Terry stood up and pocketed the sleeping pills. His hand reappeared holding a jug of cocaine. He listened to Leo's movement in the back and used his pinky finger to snort a quick dab of white flakes into each nostril. He capped the jug and dropped it into the raincoat, which he started to button when he remembered the revolver. He wished he hadn't. He picked up the .22 Magnum and gripped it, staring at the trigger mechanism, recalling some earlier event experienced with a gun in his hand.

Leo returned, walking quietly on his bare feet across the loft, when he saw that what Terry was gazing at was pointed directly at him. He took several long strides sidewise before he soberly said, "At the floor, Terry. Point it down at the floor."

"Huh?" Terry said, lifting his head in surprise, startled by the location of the voice.

"The gun, Terry," Leo said. "You were pointing it right fucking at me. What's the matter with you?"

"Nothing," Terry said. "A little tired's all. Sorry. I was just gonna pack it away and I got to thinking how much I really hate carrying the thing around. After all these years, you know. I'm thirty years old and I still gotta carry, like it was the Roaring Twenties. Like I was still a kid, and didn't know I didn't need a piece to make out."

"After we finish celebrating George Washington's Birthday," Leo said, "you'll be able to go away somewhere, hire somebody to carry one for you. Chauffeur you around in a limo. Seeing you'll be retired at the ripe old age of thirty."

"Fuck you," Terry said. "What's that you got?"

He eased the revolver beneath his belt at the arch of his back and, complaining about the gin-soaked leather of his gloves, handled what he was given.

"They're Japanese," Leo said. "Made from a special alloy. The lock's practically unpickable. That set of keys is the only way to open those handcuffs without being Houdini, or spending a long time with hacksaws, bolt cutters. There's no master key fits them."

Terry used the keys to open and shut each cuff on the bracelets before putting them in the only remaining empty pocket of his raincoat. He pulled out a pack of cigarettes, sticking one between his lips without touching it with his fingers. He inhaled a mouthful of smoke and drained the mug of lukewarm coffee. The smoke expired inside his lungs. He dragged on his cigarette while he talked, puffing the gray smoke rapidly.

"Feel like a booster," Terry said, "with this coat and all. Got enough stuff in my pockets, open a store. . . . I dunno, Leo, I dunno."

"You're standing in front of a box, Terry," Leo said. "You're standing there with everything you need to crack any safe. But you take a good look at it and you start thinking. You go about it one way, you might freeze the locking bars, or jam the tumblers. You use a torch and the fireproofing ain't too good, you gonna burn all the money's inside to a crisp. So you stand there and you look at it and you got doubts about how to go about it. What's it you do, Terry, you got doubts on how to open a box? What'd you do?"

"Peel it," Terry said. "You peel it."

"Well," Leo said, "go on then. Get over there and peel that fucking grape."

Terry snuffed out his cigarette, finished buttoning his raincoat, snatched up the shopping bag, and left Leo standing alone in the dimly lit loft, fingering the edge of the towel, thinking about his partner.

33

WEARING A gently flared blended wool dress with toast-peach stripes beneath an unwrapped Dacron polyester British-tan cloak, DayDream resembled many a young woman absorbing the crowded drudgery of a plodding subway ride away from the steno pool.

Early that morning, she had arrived punctually to work at the Centennial Insurance Building on the Avenue of the Americas. From nine o'clock till noon, she rode the elevators, emerging at each floor a pert young Kelly Girl to temporarily fill a vacancy which she'd discover with a brief, unassuming look around must be on a different floor. And without a word or pout to anyone, she'd continue searching for the non-existent job.

By lunchtime, she'd seen what she wanted on every one of the fifty-one floors and made sure she was on the nineteenth to mingle with the same group she'd been following to various luncheon waterholes once a week over a period of months. With countless wigs, costume changes, facial makeups to lessen her attractiveness, and assorted props, she had jotted down what her memory could retain from the shoptalk she'd inconspicuously managed to overhear.

After lunch, she'd spent the entire afternoon reaffirming what she already knew about the adjoining buildings, underground garages, taverns, and the four to six P.M. changes in security personnel assigned to guard the properties through the night, as well as the janitorial, custodial, and maintenance employees who worked inside the Centennial after dark.

Satisfied all was normally what it always was, she had boarded the stale, stuffy subway car where her hand was now one of a dozen holding onto the stainless steel pole, bracing herself against the discomforting motion of the train.

When the Lexington Avenue Express stopped at Union Square to allow more daily workers to pack themselves aboard, DayDream felt the long, thin fingers begin nibbling their way beneath the open flap of her Dacron polyester cloak, on across the toast-peach stripes of her blended dress, tapping lightly over her well-formed braless breast, dancing after a nipple to excite.

Like many women trapped in a horde of disregardful strangers, she seemed determined to endure the slurring touch, rather than draw attention to her embarrassing predicament. But she was DayDream; a woman whose distracted air was consciously refined and not the slapdash result of some incidental hand trifling with her bosom.

As the train continued its less-than-rapid transit, the unseen hand grew more daring. The fingers slipped inside the modestly cut dress and tipped about her milky cleavage to slide up the moistened satin of her buxom tit in a flustery caress, cuddling the rosy ripe tomato with a giddy-pated palm.

DayDream did nothing more than remain herself to conceal that she knew the manicured, uncallused hand belonged to the gaunt, felt-hatted top coat pressing against her rear right side.

Once the subway slowed to a crawl inside the tunnel, the Prince Charming really speeded up his act. His right hand squeezed at the fullness of her breast in an effort to make her heart skip a beat. The fingers of his left moved beneath her cloak, pawing the contours of her flanks, on down her shapely ass and up her lusty loins.

Even though her heart would not respond with any irregularity, Prince Charming was certain he'd finally made a conquest. Tonguing long strands of her natural, ebony-black hair, he relinquished her breast to lower his right hand and snatch the final prize. But they lurched suddenly from the tunnel. His paw hesitated on the curve of her slender thigh as the train pulled into the Borough Hall station, where more embarked than disembarked.

When the doors closed and they were again in motion, his hands were startled to feel her body turn. Startled because she did not turn away, Prince Charming raised his eyelids and stared nervously at this wondrous creature who showed no look of anger, fear, or loathing. Just a captivating symmetry of face expressing nothing other than, he thought, submission.

As the express halted at the Nevins Street station to give riders thirty seconds in which to trample one another transferring to various other subway lines, Prince Charming broadened his leer in utter anticipation of performing his entire repertoire of ageless lechery on this youthful woman. He excitedly watched as she eased her tame grip from the pole, as she ever-so-gracefully straightened a gentle forefinger and delicately, accurately, stuck it bluntly into his eye.

DayDream turned on her heels and joined the fringe still pushing their way onto the platform. Ganging along with the people in a hurry up the stairs, she stalled briefly at the token-seller's booth to take a tissue from her shoulder bag. She wiped her fingertip and continued through the station, climbing the final flight to the street.

Calmly DayDream moved to get off Flatbush Avenue before some familiar character's curiosity was aroused by her unaccustomed dress. She intended following her usual route through residential side streets to where the BMW was parked on a quiet household block. But when she rounded the corner, a violent wind iced into her layers of polyester, gathering it up like so much cellophane flapping wildly about her waist. After braving a short distance, she decided there was no percentage in contending with such rough weather, since other means were readily available besides her feet.

She headed back toward the corner to flag a cab. As she reached the bend, the gust wailed hard around the avenue, blasting the tissue from her hand. The tissue whisked sky-ward and, like some crack potshot, drew the bead from Billy Jamaic's stalking eyes. He stood watching the tissue wing high into a dead, unstirring calm, then waft slowly down by a tall young woman whose thick dark hair blustered about her upturned face.

The fine-boned, favored face engaged his memory. It was the face of the denim-clad girl he'd seen kneeling over somebody in that dawn in Prospect Park. The girl who'd also seen him clearly in the light of the pathway lamp post.

"It is her!" he thought, and began to shake. Feeling the primed muscle of his third leg become exalted, he squeezed deeper into the shadowy nook—a ragamuffin swathed in want.

DayDream finally hailed a Checker cab and told the driver she didn't know where she wanted to go, but would show him how to get there. The cabbie immediately obliged by getting thoroughly involved in the knotted traffic which he convincingly blamed on the political midget who was the city's mayor. After some minutes at a standstill, DayDream was about to try another hand at walking when the cab started creeping up Flatbush Avenue.

Billy Jamaic stepped cautiously from the doorway and along the pavement to easily trail behind the snail's pace of the taxi. As to the appropriate destiny of its passenger, he'd await providential guidance. For nothing moved faster than the Supreme Being of Nothingness, except perhaps this Checker cab which somehow crossed into a lane thinned of traffic and was humping its acceleration in high gear, gassing full tilt, and soon pouring it on lickety-split with Billy Jamaic skipping, trotting, then bounding across the sidewalks, scampering madly afterward, before it merged with dozens of others at a fork in the avenue, and whatever was her predestination suddenly had to be delayed because the light changed green and she disappeared, just another passenger being carried away inside just another bubble in a sea of sulphur yellow.

Having run that race and lost, Billy Jamaic faltered, only to stumble upon what he was no longer prepared to encounter: Terry Sage idling inside the entrance of a liquor store with a cardboard case on his shoulder, a shopping bag in his hand, and his eyes off in the opposite direction. Stubbing the rubber soles of his sneakers severely against the abrasive concrete, Billy Jamaic recoiled from his primary target and backpedaled on the rebound through the nearest door.

Terry heard the squeak, but took no notice. He was too busy looking through the store's glass front, watching Poley Grymes nod his head repeatedly at the plainclothesmen whose unmarked Chevrolet he sluggishly climbed from and leaned against to keep on nodding. Terry thought it properly strange that Poley Grymes was intimate with the law and wondered what the schmuck was so diligently affirming. He also thought it best to move, before the rum dummy finished his assurances and came walking up the block to Flatbush Avenue and spied him carrying the case of Tanqueray. Which would start him putting a lot of twos together, trying for an answer.

Tensing the muscles in his back, he could feel his general disdain for Poley Grymes begin to grow particular with the first of many strides he'd have to take in avoiding the man, in circumventing the entire block. An extra three harsh streets because of "That stupid fuck!" Terry spewed, and stomped past the orange sheets of plywood planking the abandoned Melodieu Lounge.

Behind the loosely boarded door, Billy Jamaic waited, panting his shortened breath, despairing his unavoidable blind dodge. He was stunned by the evening's ordeal, dumbfounded by the blank outcome, and deeply depressed by the unknown girl's facile getaway. Her glorious face again began to thrill him with a joy he had never known.

"Oh, she is beautiful," he thought, and happily promised, if given half a chance, to convert her to God's Grand Plan and take her for his mistress. A beatific flower to enshrine full bloom in the stillness of his massed green heritage.

Picturing her servile companionship, Billy Jamaic twirled lightheartedly into the hushed depth of the forsaken Melodieu Lounge. He rested his excitement against the torn, damp velour of the back wall with the stench of his toil reeking off him, like the vile spray from a skunk. He stood in the ghostly strangeness of his own vapor and hummed for the sumptuous-looking woman to be his.

Curled up in a far corner, a pair of big round eyes awoke cautiously from a dull heroin doze and watched what he could smell was more than just another blue-eyed devil's stink. There was fatality lurking in the lethal foulness of the odor. Something which the pin-dot pupils instinctively saw would kick a heroin habit permanently clean in response to any foolish move.

The junkie decided against rushing into any such withdrawal process. He became a still photograph of himself. A black kid who was nine years old.

34

PROPPED UP in his bed, Arthur Skidmore swallowed the cold white of a hard-boiled egg and adjusted his tinted bifocals. The glasses enhanced the look of his face. The look that said he was firmly confident he was himself once more. The resurrected self whose wounded psyche was no longer confused with fear, but ready to recover the cause of the concerned nuclear physicist who now wanted to be addressed by the title prefixing his proper name. David Leigh Rabinovitch asked to be called "Doctor."

Terry Sage was pleased. He was also in no way puzzled, as before. He knew it was mainly his own guile and hokum, his candid and unctuous presence, that bridged the twilight between reality and fantasy, the gap which would inevitably widen into a nebulous chasm where nothing could ever again be the same for this man.

Arranging the jumble of cardboard boxes into a line of shelves to support the stock of items he had purchased, coaxing food into the man, and uprighting the makeshift bar to stir a fresh jar of chilled martinis, Terry dug into his reservoir of research. The Doctor presumed the lead, while it was Terry who actually held the reins, pacing and guiding the canter.

"Technology's just a Greek name for a bag of tools. But it's become such a force in modern society, to refuse it is bad business," Terry said, and paused to reopen the window easily and light another cigarette, as the Doctor asked the question that would send them into the stretch.

"How did you come by this, Dennis?" the Doctor said.

"A simple thing, really," Terry said, sitting down on the straight-backed chair. "A few years ago, I was driving around the country, staying in motels, taking a look around. On the road, was all. At the time, I was checked into a room, eating fried chicken, drinking beer, watching the TV, waiting to go to sleep. Someplace in Tennessee.

"Anyway, there was a special on one of the networks and it was good. All music. No corny skits, just singers singing songs. Don't think anybody talked the whole show. Everything was song and dance. Until they broke for a commercial and up popped the Esso tiger. You know, the 'put a tiger in your tank' tiger.

"Well, he's jumping all around the tube, saying how nice it is to be back, brought back from retirement. Then he quiets down and gets politely serious to explain the special reason he came out of retirement. Like I'm supposed to give a shit, right? But I'm curious to see the product's so special, they gotta use the old tiger to sell it. Sounded important, so I listen. Turns out he's not back to push some new high-octane fuel, propel your car like a rocket. Seems Esso decided to change their name and invited this cartoon to come make the official announcement to the public. Explain the reasons behind the name change. Terrific. What the fuck do I care? Except, that's all he says, and back to the music.

"Ninety seconds, all he said was how glad he was to be back on the air to tell everybody what Esso wanted the country to know and he never says. But on the next commercial break, he's back with all sorts of visual aids and on-and-on reasons about why Esso's changing its name to Exxon. The third segment, he mourns the passing of Esso for obvious sentimental reasons, but times are changing and sentiment can't stand in the way of progress, so remember, 'Exxon.' In the final part, the animated tiger wraps it all up with some futuristic nonsense about why it has to be Exxon. To further illustrate this point, the tiger says he's gonna stay around for as long as it takes to drum it into our heads.

"The tiger wasn't kidding. That month, month and a

half, I drove over seven, eight thousand miles of road. Everywhere I went, Esso was being changed to Exxon. Service stations, as part of America as the corner drugstore, changed into abstract symbols. Esso meant gas and oil. Exxon means power.

"Power's what it's all about, Doctor," Terry said. "Money's just loose change now. And fame's just a game fools are forced to play. Second World War's been over a long time."

"Yes . . . yes, it has," the Doctor said. "You said, you first glimpsed power's abstract reality in Tennessee. Were enlightened by this, this tiger, and became aware of power as an entity."

"Here, there, and everywhere," Terry said. "Yes."

"Traveling in Tennessee," the Doctor said, "were you visiting friends?"

"No. No, no," Terry said. "Surveying the enemy camp's more like it."

"Enemy camp?" the Doctor said. "Enemy camp in, in Tennessee?"

"Oak Ridge, Doctor," Terry said. "Oak Ridge, Tennessee."

"Dennis," the Doctor said.

"Yes?"

"Who *are* you?"

"Who I am doesn't really matter, Doctor," Terry said. "It's what I am that does."

"All right then," the Doctor said, "then *what* are you?"

"A nature lover, Doctor," Terry said, "as simple as like I said before. Just one of a vanishing breed. An ordinary human being, lucky enough to be raised to respect humanity. Not afraid to love, put trust in people. Fortunate to be in a position where I can help. Do some good. A nature lover is all what I am, Doctor. It's my profession. It's all I do. Ever did."

"Is that, that what you were doing in Oak Ridge, Tennessee," the Doctor said, "expressing your love for nature?"

"Sort of, yes," Terry said. "But not out loud. You see, Doctor, that was a few years ago. I was still young, naïve, pretty green at how change is brought about. I mean, I didn't even know what power *really* was. For all I knew then, horsepower was all there was to it. Guess not having a formal education is why it took me so long to be able to see, understand power.

"That's what I was doing in Oak Ridge, Doctor. Taking a look at who these people were at the Atomic Energy Commission down there. Trying to get an idea what they were so uptight about, afraid of. Upset with the environmentalists. Like what was the big secret, you know. Thought the Cold War was through. So why the hysteria all of a sudden? Just because some people were beginning to march, protest on behalf of nature. Save the planet earth."

"Did you," the Doctor said, "were you able to find out what it was you couldn't understand?"

"Yes," Terry said. "Took a while, but I did. Found out there was no big secret. Just seemed that way 'cause everything was hidden. Keep people from knowing, interfering with what they were doing. And what they were doing was manufacturing what I was just beginning to learn about. Power. Man-made power to supply a new source of energy. Developing it as fast as they could to replace all the conventional fuels, like coal and oil, and even the sun. Can only make so many bombs, 'cause there're only so many buyers. But the stuff inside those bombs and missiles's a product could corner the consumer market on power. Nuclear industry's most important material source of atomic energy, plutonium-239.

"That was why they were continuing the strict secrecy imposed during World War Two. They were still trying to safely harness this man-made plutonium, make it a salable commodity. A common utility. They didn't wanna hear about all its deadly, strange properties, or how it was, is, the most dangerous element on the face of the earth. That was the only secret, they didn't want to become too well known. That's why all the fuss about Earth Days and protests. The smearing of plain folks who didn't want their kids turned into fucking jello by the radioactive disaster that's bound to happen. Calling these fathers and mothers a silly bunch of good-for-nothing do-gooders. Filthy subversive freaks talking about what they don't know about. Shooting off their mouths, trying to start a revolution behind 'Green Power' slogans. Like the niggers tried with their 'Black Power' flags. Making too much noise, lots of damaging publicity in the media about how nuclear power is not the solution, but the fucking problem. Which was all very bad for business. And you know the rest, Doctor."

"Perhaps not," the Doctor said. "Please."

"Well, the nonsense was stopped is all," Terry said. "Hard and quick. Made the survival of the environment into an unpopular cause with the phony energy crisis routine's going on. Put ecology down, same way any interference always gets put down. With power. This time using the classic reversal technique. Create a lack, a power shortage. Make out the Arabs ran away with the football. The Statue of Liberty play. Raise the price a few hundred percent on the old-fashioned, natural fuel sources. Show us what suckers we are, falling for such an old, conventional trick. Works beautiful. Who's gonna parade in the streets damning the dangers of nuclear energy during an energy crisis? Maybe a few kids is all. But they'll stop too. After they get their heads broke by some guys from the unemployment line, looking to eat. You gotta eat, you gotta eat is all there's to it. What it comes down to. Power ain't gonna go hungry."

"Power feeds itself, yes," the Doctor said. "Its most charming quality. A triumph that defies defeat."

"Doctor," Terry said.

"Yes, Dennis."

"I got power by the balls."

"You *what?*"

"Tennessee was a long few years ago, Doctor," Terry said. "Learned a lot since then. A whole lot. Enough to do what you wrote about in your diary. What we both know's inevitable. But for reasons that are honorable, rather than selfish terrorism. For the sake of humanity. Out of pure love for nature. Its last hope of survival."

"You mean to say," the Doctor said, "what you read in my journal, garnered from these highly sensitive documents inspired your undertaking some desperate, foolhardy, hopeless course of action. . . ."

"Not exactly, Doctor," Terry said. "Everything was planned to a T, way before I happened to find you unconscious outside in the street there. A total coincidence, you being who you are. When I carried you inside here, began massaging life back into you, you told me about yourself. I expressed interest in what you said, then you showed me those papers, told me how important they were, and asked me to hold on to them for safekeeping until your condition improved. Which is why I returned. Why I'm here."

"This all," the Doctor said, "it's become very confusing. From my standpoint, the implications . . . I mean, a man in my position . . . your being here . . . you're not, not crazy, are you?"

" 'Course not, Doctor," Terry said, refilling their glasses with still another watered-down cocktail. "Just a nature lover happy to make the acquaintance of a respected man like yourself."

"Thank you, yes," the Doctor said. "Thank you, Dennis. I'm honored, touched. Yes, thank you. It's not easy, as you must know. . . ."

"Impossible," Terry said. "The odds, I mean, for your publishing your diary, journal, and these documents to prove how dangerous nuclear power really is. To use their publication to bring about change. Your proof is recorded fact, speaks for itself. Automatically follows that change would occur. Except who'd publish, even print, what you got? *The New York Times?* Like the Pentagon Papers. A test of the First Amendment, freedom of the press. The charges brought against Russo, Ellsberg don't apply in your case, Doctor. Way I see it, you'd be charged along the lines of Julius, Ethel Rosenberg. They got burned for possessing a sketch. No question of freedom of the press regarding your papers, Doctor. There is no freedom. It's against the law. Special laws to even think about disseminating your information to the general public, much less try to publish————"

"I know, Dennis," the Doctor said. "I'm perfectly aware of the consequences that would prevent their publication. The special laws you refer to. The various sections of the National Security Act, the Atomic Energy Act, the NASA Act, and those in Title Eighteen of the United States Code. I know. I know the boundaries limiting the freedom of information, Dennis. Of that you can be sure, as I am that there exists no hope. None at all."

"In serving papers, I agree," Terry said. "It's useless. But to serve notice is an entirely different matter."

"Serve notice?" the Doctor said. "What do you mean, 'serve notice'? To whom?"

"Power, Doctor," Terry said. "We're gonna serve notice on power. Substantiate everything they claim's unsubstantiated. Everything you recorded in your journal, the secret information in the classified documents. We're gonna prove it all. Turn it into the type evidence *The New York Times* will be able to headline on its front page. News. Page-one news in every paper in every country in the world. Make the truth known. Your words universal. Sound the general alarm. Warn everyone, time's up. Power's Day of Judgment."

"We?" the Doctor said. "We?"

"Me, Doctor," Terry said. "Me and a talented group of fellow nature lovers. See, that's what they like to call us, so it's the name we call ourselves. But we're professionals. No amateurs, no in-betweeners. Trained for years for this. Qualified, equipped to nonviolently stem the current violence toward nature. Turn off the most destructive juice. Force power to do what you wrote, told me, they should. Shut down the nuclear program. Redirect the technology. Develop natural energy from solar, geothermal sources. Make it clear power's got no nationality. What the Nature Lovers say goes for Russia, China, France, every continent, corner of the globe. No more!"

"How?" the Doctor said. "How are you, your group, going to realize my hypothesis? Capture the world's attention to the plague enveloping the planet? Have you any idea of the magnitude of such an act? The law enforcement apparatus, the countless agencies you'll unleash upon yourselves?"

"We do, Doctor," Terry said. "We most certainly

do. We also know we're a breed that no branch of law enforcement, no security agency or combination of agencies is effectively capable of comprehending, apprehending. They need targets to see. Something to twenty-one-gun down. They can't see what nobody's going to ever see. Something's nonviolent as shoplifting."

"What?" the Doctor said. "What is?"

"This holiday weekend is what," Terry said. "We're going upstate New York to that same place you used to work, wrote about in your diary. The installation on the river in the Hudson Valley. We're gonna walk through their elaborate security system, right inside with a screwdriver, a wrench, to the part of the plant where the plutonium-239 is stored in those hermetically sealed containers, and we're gonna take some. The kind's reduced to solid metal for transport, those plated with aluminum alloy, weight three-quarters of a pound, about three inches in diameter. We're gonna take half-dozen, dozen of those buttons and leave with them, the same way we came in.

"Then," Terry said, "we're gonna split in all different directions. Everyone goes far away from one another. All over the world. Each of us holding about a pound of plutonium. One button maybe is all. Enough so we each got the same to equal twenty million pounds of TNT. And we're gonna keep it. Use it to ransom nature. Use it like a junkie uses a spike, a needle. Spike power with some of its own medicine. Weaken, stall it from making more leaps over nature. Use what we kidnapped to get the media to report the truth about the dangers come from fucking-over nature. Return power where it belongs. So all the fucking money in all the banks ain't ever gonna buy it back again from its rightful owners. The entire, every last member of the human race. Settle it forever, for all, by not giving it back. All stays invested with the Nature Lovers. No swaps. Only deal's to ensure power controls itself, never again tries to overpower what's nature. All there's to it."

"All there is to it," the Doctor said. "YES! Amazing. Absolutely amazing! Do you know that, Dennis? From all you've said, YES, I actually believe you're sincere about this venture. This master stroke to pull power to its very knees. I deliberated over this same loophole in power's monolithic core myself. But, alas, too long. No matter. You, my boy, are here. Prepared to put into practice what most are terrified to even preach. To initiate the undertaking of my lifelong dream. Awaken the lumpen proletariat to the, YES, inevitable failure of nuclear science's synthetic nature. Instill the masses with the courage to defend life. Save the lives of their very children by opposing the deadly manipulative abuse of power in this godforsaken atomic age. YES! Forestall the servile destiny of misinformed death. YES, MAZEL TOV!"

"Doctor," Terry said. "There is——"

"Now," the Doctor said, "you are certain of gaining access, are you not? Every aspect of this shoplifting thoroughly planned? Your cohorts, YES, your fellow Nature Lovers, fully rehearsed in all arrangements? The detailed necessities required in the accomplishment of such a task, YES?"

"Yes," Terry said. "It's done. We're in. We're out. No problem. There's concern, though, about an accident. One could cause disaster."

"Disaster!" the Doctor said. "I thought . . . now, we're brinking disaster, already!"

"Doctor," Terry said. "Your advice, Doctor, is all we need to prevent any accident. We know how to handle it. About proper ventilation, temperatures, disposal by dissolving the plutonium in concentrated hydrochloric acid, and the rest. We know all the precautions, what to guard against. Except for what exactly causes formation of a critical mass.

"You see, Doctor? What I mean is we think, but we don't *know* for sure. Not enough about what forms a critical mass, makes it into an explosion. You do, Doctor. Your advice can tell me how to stop it from happening. Else we'd be taking an awful chance on doing just what we want to keep them from doing."

"Hmm . . . quite," the Doctor said. "The problem is, Dennis, there are many variables to consider. Not simply what constitutes a sufficient amount to fission a chain reaction. The smallest fissionable mass will support a chain reaction self-sustained by several material conditions. Plus, there's the accompanying lethal emission of neutrons and gamma rays. All of which would rapidly generate enough heat to cause violence scaled according to how quickly the mass forms and how closely it's confined. Gamma radiation detection equipment would certainly provide an automatic warning to any such criticality hazard. But the element's alpha-emitting property must also be reckoned with, since the alpha radiation in itself is more than highly toxic. There's actually no single . . . solution . . . guarantee . . . THE CHAIRMAN! Of course, of course! The Chairman, Dennis, the Chairman!"

"The chairman . . ." Terry said. Wondering whether he'd just lost the Doctor in a sudden crack of final madness, he watched him flip through the confused contents of the manila envelope piled on the bed.

"YES, the Chairman," the Doctor said. "YES, Dennis, the Chairman will do rather well by you and your band of Nature Lovers. Set you at rest. YES. Resolve any and all problems that would, YES, definitely result from the formation of a critical mass of solid metallic plutonium. In fact, the Chairman will negate, YES, the possibility of such a violent occurrence. Here."

He handed Terry a glossy page torn from a magazine for the profession of nuclear science and technology. He bobbed his head to indicate the photograph printed on the page. He continued bobbing his head while Terry looked at the photo. The Doctor was thoroughly pleased with himself, satisfied by something that made him very happy. The Doctor was smiling.

Terry stared at the photo, looking for whatever he was supposed to see. What he saw only deepened his concern about the condition of the Doctor's rapidly deteriorating mind. The photo was a boardroom portrait of men in suits and ties seated at a long table with leather-bound pads and pencils and water glasses neatly placed in front of them. Their heads were all turned toward the camera in a way that suggested its presence was a formal inconvenience, an imposition they annually suffered because of their executive importance. Their names and the positions they held on the board were listed beneath the photo. The man who was the chairman was partially hidden by an ornamental piece centering the table. His eyes said he didn't seem to care. Neither did Terry, since he had seen the photo before and saw nothing in it now that he hadn't then.

He looked up at the Doctor sitting amid the clutter on the bed. When he saw the smile, Terry became angry and had to restrain himself from slapping the smile.

"The Chairman, Dennis," the Doctor said.

"I see him, Doctor," Terry said. "I see him."

"See, what is, YES, in front of the Chairman, Dennis," the Doctor said. "The centerpiece. See it, YES."

"Yes," Terry said, "I see that, too."

"Then, understand, Dennis," the Doctor said, "that what you see is what will enable you, YES, to carry on without fear of creating a critical mass. Achieve, yes, your intended hold around power's very scrotum. Or, yes, as you so phrased it, 'get power by the balls.' "

"I see, Doctor," Terry said. "But I don't understand."

"Look again, Dennis," the Doctor said, "and understand that what you are looking at is plutonium oxide incorporated into a silicate glass formulation. Bound, YES, so tightly in the glass matrix that all danger from handling is virtually eliminated. Once evaluated as a potential reactor fuel, it is, YES, now an arrogant centerpiece, decorating one of power's many boardrooms. The fibers of that glass-shaped mound contain more than enough weight-percent plutonium to satisfy your Nature Lovers' needs. Simply chip, YES, the glass into equal chunks and bear each piece to wherever you're destined to, YES, succeed!"

"Doctor," Terry said, slowly, deliberately, "I don't believe you."

"What!" the Doctor said. "You doubt me? I take you into my confidence. Grant you the benefit of my advice. Give freely of my knowledge. Inform you of a means by which you may proceed safely to demonstrate your love of nature. Dennis, my boy . . ."

"I believe you, Doctor," Terry said. "I believe everything you've said's true. Only, what if it's not there? Suppose this plutonium glass isn't in the boardroom anymore? How do we know . . ."

"Dennis," the Doctor said, "it is. YES, it is still there. For the Chairman who presides over that particular board of cretins in the photo is himself still there. His office adjoins the boardroom where that silicate coil of plutonium-bearing glass sits as a monument to his rise to power. IT'S HIS. And I, YES, tell you it is ALWAYS there beside him."

Terry dropped a dozen ice cubes in the Polish-pickle jar and poured Tanqueray over them. He didn't bother with the vermouth. He used a pencil to swirl the ice, before filling the Doctor's clouded glass. The Doctor swallowed the gin, while Terry dipped his glass into the melted ice water that formed a pool at the bottom of the plastic bag. The cold water made him feel better. He took another mouthful and listened to the Doctor ramble about the monofilament technique of drawing glass fibers from a billet, and the successful incorporation of plutonium oxide into silicate glass forms that were fabricated into a variety of shapes which were not only harmless to handle, but were also imperceptibly disguised in every way, so that the Doctor was soon madly raving about how all the ashtrays in Holiday Inns across the country could easily be bearing the brunt of a nuclear prank by containing some of what the Chairman's icon did indeed contain: plutonium oxide which measured three kilograms in percentage weight.

The Doctor then began ranting about nuclear plants being the Venus's-flytraps of a science whose tentacles would devour mankind. Terry only half-listened while carefully preparing to withdraw from this room where his performance had finally unhinged the brain-sick wreckage of this man.

Terry took another look at the photograph of the Chairman sitting with the members of the board at the long table whose large centerpiece he believed was exactly what the Doctor said it was. He'd assure himself, he thought, when he returned to the loft where he would cross-index every available reference on the subject. If true, this seventh step would prove more than well worthwhile. It would make their job all that much easier and, perhaps, alleviate a great deal of unnecessary media-pressured heat. The plant's board members would obviously be reluctant to publicly disclose the theft for fear of the embarrassing scandal that would undoubtedly transpire in the press.

The picture suggested this attitude. Terry liked that idea and creased the page, folding it inside his raincoat on the floor. He reached into a pocket and squeezed the cap off the vial, removing one of the pills. He palmed the barbiturate in the same hand he used to separate the shell from another hard-boiled egg. He impressed the drug into a piece of egg white and easily force-fed it into the Doctor. He ate the yolk.

The single three-grain capsule wasn't enough to kill. It would simply knock him into a deep twelve-hour sleep. That would begin to happen in roughly twenty minutes, when it entered his bloodstream and stopped the hypermania of his addled wits.

Terry used those twenty minutes to jar the Doctor into silence. He showed him a sheet of paper. On it was typed a list of names and addresses. The Doctor's wife was a professor at the University of Chicago. Terry read off her name first and the address of the house she occupied with their two daughters. He read other names and addresses of people related to the Doctor, ending with his mother, who was convalescing her life away in a Florida nursing home.

He held on to the paper while he matter-of-factly explained the reason for its existence. He said it was to help the Doctor understand that he was not to leave his room until the following week. Not for at least eight days. Especially not before or during the coming holiday weekend of George Washington's Birthday. That, he said, would endanger not only himself but his wife and family as well.

He further explained that the purchase of ample

food and drink was to relieve the Doctor of any necessity for venturing outside. Outside where a member Nature Lover was posted; assigned to guard against the Doctor's jeopardizing their radical course of ecological action by wandering drunk, or screaming out, or anything that would directly, or inadvertently, inform the authorities of their intentions.

Pocketing the sheet of paper, Terry then showed the Doctor the set of handcuffs. He explained their function and demonstrated their use without touching the Doctor's wrist. He attached and locked one cuff to a water pipe beside the bed, telling the Doctor to open and close the other with the keys he gave him. The Doctor blankly did what he was told. While he did, Terry fashioned a string to hold the keys around his neck. This, he said, would enable the Doctor to fasten himself down, if he ever got a sudden urge to leave the room before the appropriate eight days' time. He repeated that this was for his own protection and the safety of his family, since the Nature Lovers would always be watching and become severely angry if he should in any way upset their pursuit of environmental justice.

Terry continued explaining the rationale behind the necessary security arrangements until the Doctor's head dropped, then fell back onto the pillows propped against the bedstead. His mouth parted a little, his body sagged, still erect, against the pillows, his hands relaxed. Terry caught the empty glass as it tumbled from his lap between his legs. The Doctor looked as old and worn as one of Aesop's fables.

Once he was fully asleep, Terry became indifferent to the man and quickly set about completing his visit. He positioned the cardboard boxes shelved with food and drink in a line against the edge of the bed where they could be easily reached. He stripped the shells from a handful of hard-boiled eggs and concealed a single capsule in the white of each. He snapped the cuff on the Doctor's left wrist, leaving it attached to the pipe running up the wall. He made sure both cuffs on the bracelet were securely locked, then bent the keys so they would require straightening to reopen the locks. He strung the bent keys around the Doctor's neck like a pendant and picked up his raincoat.

He shoved his arms into the sleeves and shifted the .22 Magnum beneath his belt at the arch of his spine. He took a last look at the row of food cans, gin, melted ice cubes, shelled eggs, can openers, and moved the bottle of vermouth closer to the Polish-pickle jar. He glanced around the bare toilet facilities squatting inside a closet, considered the situation for a moment, and decided it wouldn't be the first time the Doctor had gone without their convenience. The manila envelope, Terry thought, would suffice as a handy bed-pan in an emergency.

He unbolted the door and locked it from outside the room. He left the lights on to benefit the crazed man in his resurrected role of Dr. David Leigh Rabinovitch, to prevent the oblivion of a dark, anonymous night that might awaken any memory of the frightened bum Arthur Skidmore.

Terry pocketed the latchkeys and walked beneath the stairwell in the dusky-black hallway. He used the corner of a matchbook to spoon cocaine to his nose several times, snorting a good amount into each nostril. The relief came soon. His fatigue vanished and he was refreshed by having gleaned more than was sought from this seventh step.

He bounded down the brownstone stoop and turned the corner onto Sixth Avenue. It was nearly four A.M. and the bars were closing on Flatbush Avenue. To avoid bumping into that raucous scene, he decided to circle the area through the quiet winter of the residential section of the neighborhood. He'd cross Flatbush Avenue farther north and double back through a series of alleys to enter the warehouse from the rear.

The rain began to fall and Terry quickened his pace. It was near the middle of the block that he felt the presence in the shadow of a building line. The figure emerged and came up behind him. It was too late for the Magnum. There was only time for him to drop into a crouch as he heard the sound, "Got spare . . .", and hook his whole body into the left he uppercut at the throat, gagging it on the word ". . . change."

The figure stumbled into a chest-high, cast-iron fence. Terry sprang up and crossed his right fist into the face he could see in no way resembled the God-speed freak. He didn't care. It didn't matter. It could have been. Another right spun the guy's head. He started to go down forward, but his arm caught between the fence pickets above the elbow, lurching him backward. Terry was on him with both hands, pumping his right hard, stiff, fast, whipping his left in short, solid hooks, arching the head upward for more pummeling rights.

The sheet of rain both drowned and echoed the pent-up rage of punches he continued to combine in flurries, whaling on who this should have been; almost was. Until there was a pop and the arm jerked loose. Then the body slumped to the wet pavement and pulled the bloody pulp below the crossfire range of his slap-pounding fists clenched inside the unlined leather gloves that no longer smelled of gin, but were ripped along the ridge where the bones of his fingers joined the knuckles.

The predawn rain became hail, exploding onto the street. Terry walked away, an uneasy, hollow anger gnawing at the pit of his stomach. He didn't like the feel of it.

The hail turned into sleet and then to a wall of gray water. He disappeared in the rainstorm. For the first time in his life, Terry Sage was truly afraid of death.

35

BILLY JAMAIC woke up with the water in the bathtub as cool as custard. He didn't move. Not even to open his eyes. Instead, he remembered the vile disorders he had experienced during the nearly twelve hours since his previous bath, everything that happened to him after he spied Sage in the window across the street. Especially the flowering stalk of a woman.

The memory of her lily face brought back the same excitement that had had him reeling about the Melodieu Lounge in wistful ecstasy. But his momentary bliss was again interrupted by the sudden appearance of an image springing up next to him. Someone in the dark, frantically trying to scramble from a corner. Billy Jamaic jumped out of the tub in a fit of spasm, grabbed his gun, and almost fired at this specter of the skinny black kid he'd already shot and killed and properly anointed.

The little black Sambo, as his father used to say, was dead and gone to heaven. Billy Jamaic stood numb and naked, waiting for the memory to recede. He stared at the murky water waving about the bath. He bent over and pulled the plug. There was a sucking sound from the drain as the bath began to empty. He wrapped a towel around his waist and slipped into a worn terrycloth robe. He tied a knot in the frayed belt and stepped into the adjoining room.

He walked over to the window and looked down at Sterling Place. It was not quite dawn and still very dark. A thin haze was all that was left of the rainstorm. The lights were on inside the room across the street, but there was no silhouette on the shade. He thought that was good. It meant somebody was home. Most likely his shifty target gorging himself on the food and liquor he carried back from the avenue.

The red bubble light of a police car flashed soundlessly in the distance. It rotated its bright alarm up Sixth Avenue and made a sharp U-turn across the wet asphalt two blocks away, rolled alongside a row of parked cars, and slid into a space beside a fire hydrant. The front doors swung open and two patrolmen slipped from the interior. Both hurried onto the sidewalk, out of sight against the line of buildings.

Billy Jamaic wasn't curious to know what happened. He didn't care. All that concerned him was behind the shaded window diagonally across the street. He walked backward through the bedroom and rested his .32 automatic on top of the bureau. He fished through the drawers, pulling out fresh clothes, tossing them onto the bed. He placed a small yellow box next to his gun, a box half filled with rounds of ammunition. Two dozen bullets remained.

He dressed quickly in the light shafting from the bathroom, then switched it off. He took a pea coat hanging in a closet and folded it over the bedstead. He pushed the armchair from the front room up against the wall beside the bedroom window. He filled the teakettle and replaced it on the stove. He turned on the gas, but the pilot light was out and nothing happened. He searched around in the dark for matches. He found some in the refrigerator. He struck a match and the kettle of water jumped up from the burner.

When the water whistled, Billy Jamaic made himself a cup of tea. The sun rose and the night became a wintry, overcast day. He sat down in the armchair with his gun nestled on his lap and the box of shells tucked into his pea-coat, and sipped his tea.

36

TERRY SAGE stood on the forty-fifth landing of the emergency stairwell and waited. An hour earlier, he had arrived at the Centennial Insurance Building and entered through the main lobby. Wearing an olive-brown Brooks Brothers suit, a shirt, a tie, a tweed overcoat, and with his hair comb-dyed and quietly styled, he resembled a young salesman who spent all his money on appearance.

He pressed a button on his digital watch. The numbers glowed. It was 5:07:39 P.M. He opened a large attaché case and removed a pair of thick, colorless rubbers. He tugged them on over his low-heeled Italian shoes. His hands hurt and strained inside his new, thin leather gloves. They were badly bruised, and the knuckle above the pinky finger of his left hand was dislocated. He had used ice that morning to prevent excessive swelling, but the pain still bothered him and made his movements more methodical.

He picked out seven highway flares and, attaching a strip of gaffer's tape to each, stuck them in the patch pocket of his overcoat. He uncapped a spray can of brown paint and lifted the case under his arm without latching it. Holding the master key to the control lock on the fire door, he continued to wait. He leaned back against the wall and immediately pushed himself away. There were several cuts at the base of his spine from the chamber of the .22 Magnum. He cursed the revolver he had refused to ever carry again. The open sores began to smart from the salt of his sweat. He felt like taking a good, long piss. He repressed the urge.

The digits read 5:09:20. Terry watched the seconds tick and caught their rhythm by counting one-one hundred, two-one hundred, until it was time. He unlocked the fire door, pocketed the master key, and entered at 5:10. The floor was newly leased and being remodeled for the future tenants. The construction crew quit work in mid-afternoon. There was minimal lighting. He carefully avoided tripping over structural materials. Conscious of the passing seconds, he ran down the corridor dividing the gutted empty space. There was no one.

He set the case in a remote corner of the floor and propped open the lid, picking out a military canister filled with brightly colored smoke. He moved fast to the center of the floor where a pair of closed-circuit television cameras overlooked the area in front of six passenger elevators. Standing on his toes and reaching up, he sprayed the lens of one with brown paint, then rushed across to the other and did the same. He pulled the snap on the bomb and rolled it behind a stack of sheet-rock. It burst with a blunt noise and swirled around the floor, billowing a dense cloud of red and yellow smoke.

Igniting six of the highway flares, Terry taped one over each of the thermal-activated elevator buttons. Their heat would draw the passenger cars to the forty-fifth floor, keeping them there for as long as they burned. From the case, he took a piece of cardboard with letters cut out and taped it to a wall, spraying it with the paint. The stencil read WOBBLIES UNDERGROUND. He peeled it off and, holding it by the strip of tape, ran with the case to the far end of the floor, where he repeated the procedure in the space by the freight elevator.

With the television lenses sprayed and the stencil lettered on a wall and the last flare burning atop the elevator button, Terry tossed the paint can aside and pulled the pins on three more smoke bombs, exploding them in different directions on the floor. He checked his watch. It was 5:13:25. He snatched up a pair of pepper-gas grenades and reclosed the attaché case. Using the high flame of a Cricket lighter, he torched a corner of the cardboard stencil and stuck the fire up into a sprinkler. Within seconds it reacted, gushing water and signaling a barely audible alarm.

Terry dropped the burning cardboard, lifted the case, and ran to the emergency exit. He sat on the panic bar to open the door and jerked the clips from both grenades, lobbing one back to the shipping area and the other in front of the passenger elevators. He heard the pepper gas explode while running down the old building's staircase, away from the artificial blaze he had created with a riotous mixture of burning flares, colorful smoke, and extremely irritant gas.

A menopausal security guard was sitting alone at his station in front of a central alarm module below the main entrance. His shift had just started and he didn't appreciate the signals being received during these first few minutes on duty. The tape-monitoring system reported a fire on the forty-fifth floor. While the message was automatically relayed to the Fire Department, he pushed a button on the closed-circuit visual alarm. There was no indication the television cameras on that level were inoperative, yet there were also no pictures being transmitted onto the screens. He pushed another button on a panel labeled AUDIO. There was a faint hissing sound. He increased the volume of the audio system covering that particular zone of the building. The hiss grew to a loud whoosh. He listened carefully, trying to understand what it was.

He pressed closer to the speaker box. Suddenly, there was a thunderous rumble. He reached for the control knob to lower the volume, thinking the sound was that of elevator doors opening. The shrill chorus of screams that knocked him straight out of his chair confirmed his suspicions.

With his head vibrating, he was on his feet frantically attacking the dial to reduce the sound. It felt like someone was blowing a bugle in his ear. He flipped a switch to kill the uproar, then pushed another button to activate that floor's public address system. He leaned into a microphone, telling the people in the elevator to remain calm because help was on the way. At least, he thought that was what he said. He could feel his lips mouthing words, but he couldn't hear himself speak.

Terry taped a gas grenade and a smoke bomb back-to-back on the railing of the emergency staircase between the thirty-ninth and -eighth floors. He pulled their pins and continued down the steps. Eight seconds later, he heard them explode. Sweating like a stuck pig, he prepared to plant another pair in the same way with gaffer's tape on the railing several flights below.

Leo Warren stared at the digits on his watch. At 5:15, he left the men's washroom and walked calmly toward the north end of the vacant twenty-second floor. He passed the rack of time cards and the clock where all clerical employees punched out for the day at precisely five P.M., in accordance with their department's security regulations.

Solemnly dressed in a well-tailored suit, a dark camel's hair overcoat, and with his hair and eyebrows comb-dyed gray beneath an expensive felt hat, Leo appeared to be a highly successful business executive. Carrying a classic British umbrella, he casually adjusted his tobacco-brown pigskin gloves as he approached the door of a spacious walk-in maintenance closet.

Entering with a control-master key, he switched on the light bulb and stepped inside, closing the door. He gently hung the umbrella on a coat hook, pocketed the master key, slipped a flat-handled screwdriver from his vest, and crouched before a wall duct, unscrewing its metal plate. Returning the screwdriver to his vest and removing a hand mirror from his overcoat pocket, he turned off the light and squatted in front of the uncovered duct.

The Centennial Insurance Building had been constructed prior to World War II, and its interior had been renovated several times to concur with contemporary standards by the installation of such things as a complex security network which looked good but meant less. The various remodelings of the alarm system to provide maximum coverage of the entire building were certainly comprehensive, but necessarily constricted by the original design of the structure. Leo held the mirror inside the duct and looked down at the major flaw in the system.

Running along the wall were coaxial cables and transmission wires connecting all the protective apparatus of the sophisticated security equipment inside a single terminal attached to the main transformer bank in the basement two hundred feet below. He couldn't see the actual boxes, but he knew they were there. Like every other significant aspect of the building, they were cased the way a dentist cases teeth. What he saw at the bottom was quite enough. Light.

Standing, he pocketed the mirror and checked the time. It was 5:17:20. He turned the lights back on and carefully unfurled the umbrella. Affixed to its ribs were six prophylactics which he delicately removed. Each prophylactic contained a sealed glass tube of concentrated hydrochloric acid. He tucked two between the wires coiled inside the duct. Turning off the light again, he dropped the first of the remaining four

down the shaft. He listened, timing its descent. He
sensed it took five or six seconds to smash on top of
the joint terminal-transformer bank in the basement.
He released the last three in quick but orderly suc-
cession. With the sharp point of his umbrella, he then
burst the balloon-covered glass tubes stuffed between
the wires walling the duct. He also jammed the con-
taminated umbrella down into the same space to be
eaten up by the corrosive acid along with the wires
and basement circuitry. Leo could scent the fumes as
he shut the door on the maintenance room to walk
over to the emergency exit.

The dumbfounded guard monitoring the central
module below the main lobby thought the world
was coming to an end. The control board looked like
Times Square on New Year's Eve, its alarm signals
flashing and the television screens showing crowds
being jostled by arriving squads of police and firemen,
and the audible cries for help coming from the choir
of screamers still trapped on the forty-fifth floor.
Nearly in a state of shock, he answered the telephone
linked to the console.

DayDream was on the line, calling from a sidewalk
booth several blocks away from the Avenue of the
Americas. In a dark green pants suit with matching
cape and her ebony hair piled under a blond pageboy
wig, she looked like a receptionist putting the bitch
on her boyfriend to any passersby who happened to
take notice. What she said to the tormented guard
was simply his name.

Then, in a voice raging with a polyglot of foreign
accents, she introduced herself as X ray, the official
spokesperson for the Revolutionary Commando Unit
of the Wobblies Underground, and went on to identify the horrors occurring on floor four-five as the
direct result of a time bomb planted at three that
afternoon to punish running dog imperialists and cap-
italist pig companies who sought to destroy Third
World Freedom through Zionist treachery.

"YOU BALD-HEADED FAT FASCIST FUCK!"
she said, and slammed the receiver against the aluminum booth. DayDream returned to the curbed Toro-

nado and drove to the spot where she'd listen to the police radio frequencies and wait to make her next move.

The shattered guard tore the phone away from his damaged eardrum. He mumbled to himself. "She knew my name . . . MY NAME . . . she knew . . . a terrorist knows my name!" He lunged at the control board and flicked a switch. The switch activated the public address system in every nook and cranny of the entire Centennial Insurance Building. He raised the volume full blast and picked up the microphone. Clutching it in both hands, he shouted one word many times.

"BOMB!" he yelled. "BOMB!"

Leo and Terry were together on the emergency stairwell landing outside the nineteenth floor. Both jumped like everyone else when they heard the discomposed guard begin to shout over the PA system. But they didn't panic like the frightened evacuees who were approaching them from upstairs, somewhere above the final gas-and-smoke package planted on the twenty-fifth floor. Nor like the security patrol who had been caught with their pants down during the shift change and were struggling with the confused office workers trying to climb the clogged stairway up to the forty-fifth floor. With their portable transceivers crackling, it was obvious the patrol was near.

Leo became tense, thinking about the acid concentrate and the precious time it was taking to work. Terry's face was strained whitish, his eyes watering. They couldn't master-key the fire door because their entry would be promptly recorded on the still-functioning tape monitor. Not wanting the alarm system to identify the exact whereabouts of their intrusion, they had to wait. Their watches said it was 5:19:03 P.M. and behind schedule. Their eyes met in a look that acknowledged it was going to get very crowded within the next minute, also that the inducement of all the pandemonium might not have been such a bright idea. At the time, there had seemed to be no other alternative for gaining quick access.

They were about to quit the scene when the lights flickered and the voice on the PA cracked in mid-yell.

Then everything went completely dark and dead silent. As the thousand voices on the emergency stairway joined together in a gigantic terrified roar, Leo master-keyed the fire door with Terry following him inside.

Terry produced a flashlight and they walked along the corridor to the southwest portion of the nineteenth floor. Their thinking ceased. All was reduced to movement and reaction. Leo stopped in front of a laminated steel door. Terry held the attaché case open at his waist, cupping the flashlight beam with his right hand.

The door was secured by a heavy-duty prison-grade lock generally regarded as unpickable. Leo conceded that fact by removing a cordless, high-powered drill and a large eyedropper from the case. The tip of the dropper was taped to prevent its leaking. He unsealed it and squirted water into the keyhole and onto the multialloyed drill bit. He squeezed the handle and the drill whirred alive. He pressed it into the hole and bored out the key mechanism. He could now move the lock's cylinder, which he did with his screwdriver, unlocking and opening the door.

They entered the room and Leo checked his watch. It was 5:21:30 P.M. There were no windows inside. Terry uncupped the flashlight and shone it between desks and file cabinets to the area in the rear that was the vault. It was a room within a room, a fire-resistant chamber constructed to protect and secure important company records and confidential information. The vault door was six inches of solid steel with a built-in pair of three-position combination locks and a wheel for a handle. The hollows of the side walls were filled with an insulating hydrous compound which converted to steam when exposed to heat. Relatively thin steel covered the walls from floor to ceiling, with the edges embedded in the masonry of the building that also contained the back side of the vault.

Leo sat a chair against the right wall and stood on it, taping a piece of paper onto the steel surface beside him. The paper was a page torn from one of the manuals he'd taken from the safe inside the showroom of the company that had constructed the vault. Terry rested the case on another chair and held the light while Leo used a graduated tape to measure and pencil-mark the distances specified by the page. The lines he drew from top to bottom, side to side, and corner to corner intersected at a spot above the middle and near the front edge of the side wall.

He quickly rechecked the numbers calculated on the page to be sure his measurements were correct, while Terry exchanged the reamer on the drill for another, much larger, fluted bit. Satisfied, Leo dropped the paper, pencil, and tape measure into the case and picked up a heavy hammer and pointed chisel. He sat on the chair and punched the steel surface at the spot his markings indicated on the wall. He handed the tools to Terry, pushed away the chair, grabbed the drill, and pressed against it to bore through the insulation. While Terry assembled a gun-cleaning rod, screwing the sections tightly together, Leo enlarged the hole he had cut in the wall. When it felt right, he put the drill back in the case and took the cleaning rod and flashlight. Terry stepped up to the vault door and gripped the wheel, preparing to turn it counterclockwise at the given signal. Leo shone the light through the hole. The beam bounced off the gypsum dust clouding the interior, making it difficult for him to see inside. He scooped up the dropper, squirting what remained of the water around the rim of the hole, and waited.

At 5:24:55, Leo could wait no longer. He nodded at Terry to get set and peered through the hole. He narrowed the light beam with his left hand and slid the cleaning rod beneath it. At a slight angle, he saw the catch coupling the springs on the locking device. He also saw the jamming mechanism that would permanently freeze the locking bars if he missed, or if Terry didn't react instantly on cue, or both.

The round end of the rod was less than half an inch from the brass catch when he gave it a firm poke. He heard the lock trip, then the dull clank of the tumblers falling. Leo uttered a short, sharp grunt. Terry responded to the sounds by pressuring the wheel, waiting for it to give. It finally did, and he turned it as fast as he could, until it blocked home.

Standing side by side, they both pulled on the wheel. The heavy steel door released and swung slowly open from right to left. Shelves of documents lined the interior walls, and a dozen filing cabinets on casters were crowded in the center of the vault. There was also a medium-sized money safe welded to the floor. Terry took a larger flashlight from the case and moved inside, surveying the rows of documents wthh the legend COMPANY CONFIDENTIAL marked in bold letters on their bindings. He knew what he was looking for. Leo began rolling the filing cabinets out of his way.

On shelves centering the rear wall, Terry spotted the specific category he sought. An espionage notation divided these documents from the rest. For security reasons each set of this bound data was sealed and given a short title, using the first letter of each word of the report's subject, without revealing information relative to the contents of the documents themselves. He pulled the first three off the top shelf. They were arranged in alphabetical order, according to the initials of their short titles. He broke their seals, snapped their binding, and dumped their contents on the floor.

He hunted through the section covering the third letter of the alphabet and quickly found what he was after. He ripped open the thick bound file. There were several folders inside. The one on top was stamped PRO-TEX. Terry smiled through his sweat. In his hands were the detailed procedures and techniques being used in the actual security process within the particular system protecting the mark. The score they were going to take off that holiday weekend. The caper that would surprise George Washington's Birthday right off the calendar.

Terry showed Leo the folder marked PRO-TEX. He handed it to him along with the rest of the binder, then rapidly began the systematic rifling of as much classified material as he could in the brief time remaining. He tore away the seals and unbound the documents, scattering restricted data throughout the vault. This way the insurance company would never really know exactly what classified information was obtained by unauthorized persons. And since nearly a hundred separate sets of documents would be directly compromised by the break-in, the company would likely remain mute about the major security loss for fear of unsettling established customer relations, not to mention losing their accounts.

In any event, there would be no way for them to provide added protection for all their priority accounts without calling in the National Guard. That, of course, being entirely out of the question, they would choose the least upsetting course of action, simply alerting each of the insured premises to be on guard for possible clandestine activity of which their investigators had heard only rumors.

Leo scanned through the PRO-TEX folder. He removed several sheets that outlined the basic security system and detailed alternative plans for weekends, holidays, and various contingencies. He placed the six most informative pages into separate duplicating machines that occupied a cubicle inside the file room, closed the covers, and pushed the ON button for each. He waited for the spare diesel generator in the basement to restore minimal electrical power to the building. Only the regular outlets would be activated by the backup electricity. Not the alarm system. That would have to be rewired before it could ever again supply security.

The IBM clock on the wall was stopped at 5:19:15 P.M. The digits on his watch read 5:26:48. Leo thought the maintenance engineers were taking their sweet time in starting up the backup generator. That was all he allowed himself to think. He passed his eyes carefully over the remaining pages in the folder marked PRO-TEX, reading with speed and digesting only what he deemed important. He continued rapidly through the rest of the insurance documents.

The vault floor was covered ankle-deep in paper. Terry shuffled across to the front left side without lifting his feet. He wanted to avoid stepping on the documents and leaving unnecessary imprints. He paused in front of a section of shelves containing reports to restaurant chains, hotels, and entertainment facilities insured by Centennial. He had an idea. After a quick search through a row he got lucky. He gently cracked the seal and leafed through the bound documents detailing the specifics of an insurance policy that covered every conceivable human calamity that might befall one of Manhattan's most famous hotels. He shifted the hotel's PRO-TEX report from the bottom to the top of the pile and eased the bound file back into its place on the shelf. He hoped it would prove a valuable decoy by diverting enough attention away from the jumble of compromised industrial security data. But he wasn't betting on it.

The lights on the duplicating machines blinked on at 5:28:01. Leo listened to their purr and continued reading, waiting for them to warm up. Terry checked to be sure everything was back inside the case and nothing left behind. Leo turned the knobs indicating the number of copies desired to TWO and pressed the start button on each machine. Terry held the open PRO-TEX folder while Leo retrieved the originals and replaced them in their exact order. Terry ran to the vault with the full set of bound documents and dumped them on the floor, covering them with three unbound bundles of paper from the same section that followed consecutively in immediate alphabetical order. Leo folded the dozen copies into the vest pocket of his suit and switched off the machines. Terry shut the vault, picked up the attaché case, and both men walked over to the door with the unpickable lock.

They used the flashlights to examine one another's appearance in the dark, windowless, soundproof room. Besides sweating profusely, each agreed the other looked all right. The flashlights were placed in the case and the case snapped shut. Leo slowly opened the door ajar, and the hallway light shafted inside. They could hear the noise of the crowd still clammering down the emergency stairway. There was no one in the corridor. They walked along to the fire exit and stood on either side, listening for any authoritative sounds to indicate the presence of guards, police, or firemen. All they heard was the excitement of people fleeing.

Leo suddenly noticed the rubbers on Terry's shoes and motioned him to remove them. He did. Leo reopened the attaché case and Terry stuffed them inside, latching the lid again. He went to take back the case, but Leo held on to it, shaking his head and gesturing at the difference in their attire. Since he was dressed as a mature, successful executive and the authorities probably had nothing other than revolutionary terrorism on their minds, Leo sensed it would be safer for him to carry the outsized attaché case of tools.

Age was the deciding factor. Terry might just be routinely stopped for his under-thirty appearance, while cops on the lookout for youthful radicals wouldn't even see Leo. That is, unless they were detectives from the Safe and Loft Squad and recognized him. Which was a chance he had to take, a much better chance than leaving the tools behind to be matched up with his record of modus operandi. That would connect him as sure as if he had signed his name on the vault.

All things considered, Leo felt the odds were definitely in his favor. He handed the duplicated PRO-TEX documents to Terry, who agreed by slipping them beneath his overcoat, inside his bikini briefs, an act he would later regret and remember never to repeat. He checked his watch. The digits read 5:29:58. He tapped his finger on the blackened dial face to inform Leo. With a curt nod of his head Leo assured him he knew damn well what time it was: too-late-to-get-fucking-nervous-now o'clock. They continued listening.

The circus on the emergency stairwell tapered. The only recognizable sounds were coming from the tail end of a group who passed on by and another arriving from above. Leo pushed the door open and walked on to the landing like he was the Dalai Lama. He waved Terry ahead and firmly closed the door, as the descending troop began to close the gap in the evacuation parade.

Terry plunged down the staircase, taking two and three steps at a time, until he was half a flight behind the group. He slowed his pace to look over the people, making sure there wasn't a guard escort. When he felt it was safe, he gradually blended closer, bringing up their rear.

Wanting to stay separated from Terry but unable to clearly identify the composition of the bunch approaching from overhead, Leo avoided being overtaken by maintaining an equal distance between the two groups. He walked the stairs alone, understanding the danger. Any security personnel would immediately notice the lone man with the large attaché case. His appearance and demeanor would probably carry him through such a confrontation, but that didn't mean he'd pass unremembered. Well aware of this, Leo became especially attuned to every sound. The only way left to play it was totally by ear.

Terry had the distinct advantage, and at the sixth-floor landing he began to work it for all it was worth. A middle-aged woman stopped to catch her breath. She didn't have a chance. Terry looped her arm around his shoulders, grabbed her by the waist and, saying, "I'll help you, lady, I'll help you," lifted her off her feet and down the stairs.

Leo heard what Terry said and rightfully assumed it was time to close the gap. He made his move and reached them as they turned the fourth floor, becoming just another person at the end of a line. With the woman holding on for dear life, Terry maneuvered his way to the front. He intended to dump the woman at the ground-floor exit. When he arrived at the main level and saw what was happening, he changed his mind.

Besides the police, firemen, and unnerved security guards, television klieg lights were already positioned in the lobby with a minicam crew providing live coverage for a local news program and other cameramen set to videotape the bizarre event for the late-night network broadcasts. "Air, lady. Air. Fresh air!" Terry said, before burying his face in the woman's armpit and carting her along toward the main entrance.

When Leo realized they had failed to beat the arrival of newsmen as planned, he covered most of his face with his hand and gurgled and coughed so loud an idle fireman jumped at the opportunity to perform his service. He caught Leo's arm from behind and asked him to put down the attaché case. Leo thought it was a pinch and stopped coughing up phlegm. He was in the middle of a grim sigh when the plastic oxygen mask was thrust over his nose and mouth. He popped open his eyes and could hardly believe it. Out of the massive bedlam in the lobby, he thought, a fireman had to practice lifesaving on him.

He stood there in the middle of all the madness with the sweat pouring from him and with enough evidence in the attaché case to guarantee a life sentence, while this fireman gave instructions.

"Breathe. That's it. Nice and easy now. Breathe." Leo tried faking it, but there was no way. The fireman kept prodding him to inhale deeply and the oxygen soon made him feel light-headed.

A newspaper photographer knelt to frame the victim of the supposed disaster with his camera. The fireman turned to expose his own full face. Leo raised his hand to cover his, pretending to hold the plastic mask while straightening his middle index finger to form a deliberate and widely known obscenity. After taking several shots, the photographer rushed away to continue his coverage of the spectacle. When it was processed, Leo's face would be unidentifiable and his blunt middle finger would prevent the picture's publication in the press.

Removing the oxygen mask, he patted the fireman's slickered shoulder, smiled in gratitude, and abruptly turned away. The fireman tried calling him back to get his name, but Leo streamed into the tumultuous crowd pouring from the building. He lugged the attaché case outside to the front steps. The adrenaline surging through his body helped allay the bitter cold, but not the heightened chaos of the streets.

The Centennial Insurance Building was being besieged by emergency squads responding to an assumed disaster and using every zealous means available to increase the general havoc. Arc lamps flooded the entire area. Twenty fire trucks and other rescue vehicles

packed the surrounding curbs. Uniformed police were
leading evacuees from the vicinity and forming a cor-
don against curious bystanders, while their superiors
issued commands over megaphones to clear the sidewalks of people.

Leo saw a group of firemen wearing breathing apparatus race toward the building. That meant the acid
on the twenty-second floor had gone undetected and
not only helped cause the power shortage but quite possibly an electrical fire whose carbon monoxide fumes
were deadly. He could already see the bold headlines
blocked in the newspapers and briefly wondered if the
media coverage would inspire a revival movement
of Wobblies. That would certainly turn his father over
in his grave, Leo thought.

Lost in the turmoil, he finally managed to shake his
head clear of pure oxygen and escape the vast confusion by following some office workers through a cor-
don of helmeted riot police. Walking normally down
the Avenue of the Americas, Leo spotted Terry un-
loading the woman into a taxi stalled in the jammed
traffic. She fainted when Terry told the driver to hurry
to the nearest hospital. "Heart attack," he said, "heart
attack!" The cabbie never saw him. He was too pre-
occupied with the woman slumped on his back seat.
Glowering at her, he demanded she pay the fare in
advance.

Looking neither right nor left, Terry walked like a
man who didn't fancy the neighborhood. He was also
shaking. He blamed this on the winter weather and his
own perspiration. A sudden chill seemed to confirm his
reasoning but did nothing to explain the queasy void
in the pit of his stomach. The virus, he said deep inside himself. He had caught a virus bug, was all. He'd
be lucky he didn't catch pneumonia from being out in
the rain that morning. Walking and talking to himself,
Terry tripped on a curbstone, stumbled, and almost
fell. His impulsive anger killed further thought.
Lengthening his strides, he hurried down a cross street
with Leo tailing not far behind.

The clock on the dashboard read 5:38:09. Day-
Dream watched the sweeping second hand dip toward

the roman numeral VI. Her partners were more than
five minutes off schedule. Monitoring the police radio
frequencies, she had heard nothing to indicate that suspects were apprehended, nor that the situation at Centennial was understood. She decided to quit the wait
and proceed as prearranged.

Her knee brushed against the butt of the gun
bracketed beneath the dash. She pedaled the clutch,
put the Toronado into gear, and drove up Vanderbilt
Avenue. She had no particular feeling about the revolver's presence, but appreciated the reminder of it
just the same. Turning west toward Madison Avenue,
the crosstown traffic became heavy. It thickened to a
crawl between Madison and Fifth. Beyond there, it was
blocked up in a bottleneck and didn't concern her. She
stayed on the left side of the street to swing south at
the corner of Fifth Avenue.

Seeing Terry approach from the opposite direction,
DayDream unlocked the passenger door and rolled
down her window. Acting surprised, Terry did a double
take when she waved. He bounced over and they gig-
gled and kissed and performed a young lovers' routine
for the benefit of the clockers and watchers in all the
other cars. With her left arm, she made a big thing of
inviting him for a ride. He graciously accepted and
she pushed a button, closing the window made of a
tinted glass that sealed the car's interior practically
from view.

Leo could see the Toronado was three car lengths
from the corner and would make the next light change.
He switched the attaché case from his left to right hand
and headed south on the far side of Fifth Avenue. Day-
Dream responded by erratically blinking her left turn
signal. Leo quickened his pace, walking rapidly after
a bus he'd no intention of catching. The light went
green and DayDream flowed with the traffic, wheeling
the car in a wide-angled turn to end in the farthest
right lane.

Since the Avenue of the Americas traveled northbound and Fifth Avenue southbound, there wasn't an
overflow from redirected traffic. Just the normal rush-
hour congestion of a caterwauling, bumper-to-bumper

midtown jam, an army of rumbling vehicles in a battle
for position on roadways designed for horse-drawn car-
riages. Where a scratched fender, a broken taillight,
or any minor accident was easy to come by, and even
more difficult to avoid. And would definitely impede
the progress of a vehicle whose occupants were felons
in possession of a .22 Magnum, burglar tools,
and enough secret documents to violate the National
Security Act many times over.

This was the contest in which DayDream chose to
compete, rather than race around a rosy track. At once
defensive and aggressive, she paced the two-ton machine like a jockey would a horse, preparing to outma-
neuver the six full lanes of traffic to pick up Leo. A
task akin to stopping in the passing lane of a busy
highway in the dead of night. Favorable odds for getting rammed in the exhaust.

She rolled to a stop at a red light. Leo was less than
a hundred yards down Fifth Avenue. DayDream
needed to put something between her and the undisturbed traffic flow. Leo paused at a newsstand, bought
a paper, and stepped away to plant himself farther
along the sidewalk. DayDream watched a bus load its
final passenger and continue driving down the next
block. Leo stood on a curb with the white newspaper
sticking out against his dark overcoat. DayDream
judged the distance to the bus, and to where Leo was
standing a block in front of it.

She put the lever in first gear and revved the engine. The light went green. She let up the clutch with
a bang and flicked on the supercharger, hurtling the
Toronado over the asphalt to get a jump on the line
of other cars. Flicking it off, she shifted into second,
gunned the gas, and then accelerated into third to over-
run the bus. There was a narrow opening between the
bus and an empty taxi. She glanced in the rearview
mirror. The trailing traffic was coming fast. She hit her
right-turn signal, pushed into the brake pedal, and
downshifted into second gear at the same time.

The Toronado slowed heavily. She let it drop back,
sliding its rear end into the small slot in advance of the
bus. Flashing on her high beams, she tapped the gas

pedal. The front-wheel drive sucked the car forward. She oversteered, drifting the rear wheels farther in toward the curbside. The sudden brightness startled the cabbie, motivating him onward. DayDream turned the wheel, correcting the drift at the back and slipping into the tight squeeze.

She dimmed her headlights and flipped off the turn signal as the first swarm of cars roared past. She cruised slowly, applying the brakes just enough to let the taxi pull farther away and reduce the speed of the bus. Terry was kneeling on the front seat, ready to open the rear door. He kept his eyes on the back windshield, looking up at the bus driver.

DayDream waited until the taxi was nearly ten yards ahead and approaching Leo before she punched the gas pedal. The Toronado lunged across the gap. She braked hard, skidding to a stop behind the taxi as it passed Leo. Terry had the door open, still watching the bus. DayDream shifted into first, her eyes fixed on the rearview mirror. Leo tossed the attaché case onto the seat and was fitting himself into the car when Terry grabbed hold of his lapels. The bus was barreling toward them, the driver apparently distracted. DayDream popped the clutch and floored the accelerator, pitching the car over the black top.

The door slammed Leo inside and Terry locked it. DayDream drove straightaway along with the heavy traffic flow on Fifth Avenue. No one spoke. They listened to the radio frequency being used by the police to report on the scene at the Centennial Insurance Building. An electrical fire of suspicious origin was under control and only minor injuries sustained. There was nothing about the vault, or the break-in on the nineteenth floor. They wanted to be back in Brooklyn before there was.

The dashboard clock read 5:46 when DayDream weaved through an intersection, turning from Fifth Avenue onto lower Broadway. After a mile, she headed east to circle southbound on streets with a minimal volume of traffic and many ways to escape, should a police net happen to drop over all outbound roadways connecting the Island of Manhattan to the mainland.

A voice leaped from the squawk box. Its high pitch distinguished it from the others. The voice rattled off a series of numerical codes. There followed a long moment of silence. DayDream swung north onto the Bowery, then turned right onto the upper level of the Manhattan Bridge. The hush was broken by an official at the emergency command post who asked for the information again. The higher-pitched voice repeated the numbers of each code. Another period of silence followed. DayDream rolled across the East River and down the ramp into Brooklyn.

A man with an unamusing Hibernian brogue identified himself over the radio as the Manhattan Midtown Borough Commander and asked that the information be verified and confirmed. It immediately was. DayDream became unavoidably snarled in traffic on Flatbush Avenue. The Hibernian brogue sounded even less funny, ordering the nineteenth floor sealed and the burglary kept under wraps. After using coded numbers to issue those orders, the brogue used plain words to inform any members of the press who were listening to check with their city editors before filing their stories. Then he signed off to telephone the Police Commissioner, who would enforce a news blackout as soon as he heard the nature of the transgression at the Centennial Building.

DayDream was finally able to swerve clear of the congested Flatbush Avenue and drove through unobstructed back streets. The chief of the Traffic Division alerted all members of his department, directing them to spot-check any suspicious vehicles leaving the Borough of Manhattan by bridge or tunnel. DayDream pulled into a series of connecting alleys.

Terry loosened his tie. He wanted a cigarette, but there was none. There was also nothing else in the car that would help identify its occupants, if it had to be abandoned. Terry draped his left arm over the front seat and, looking at Leo, he said, "Whew!"

"What are you WHEWIN' about?" Leo said, spitting something out of his mouth.

When Terry saw what it was, he laughed. So did Leo. In the palm of his gloved hand was an enamel cap. The cap had been nicely covering a tooth until the conscientious fireman dislodged it by jamming the plastic oxygen mask over his mouth.

DayDream stopped the Toronado by the freight elevator in the alley behind the warehouse and they sat for a moment, letting the laughter come straight out of them, glad they were able to tap their eighth step on that cold Wednesday night in February.

"Whew!" Leo whistled through the gap in his teeth. "Whew!"

37

BY MIDNIGHT, Billy Jamaic had drunk enough tea to put a house painter in business. Sitting in his armchair, he drained another cup and placed it on a saucer and the saucer on the floor. A teaspoon slid from the dish and clinked the rim of a plate covered with toast crumbs. The sound rattled inside the silent, dark bedroom. Billy Jamaic stared down at Sterling Place and watched the lighted room across the street and waited for a silhouette to be cast on the window shade. None was.

He used a clean sock to wipe the condensation off the glass pane. The streets were nighttime cold, winter quiet. A strong breeze ruffled the still air. With his eyes glued on the window, he suddenly saw something he hadn't noticed. The shade was being fluttered by the breeze. A wedge of light became clearly visible between the window frame and the sill. He could see the window was cracked open about an inch. The breeze stopped as abruptly as it began. The shade fell calmly back against the window, closing the interior of the room from view.

Fingering his unshaven chin, Billy Jamaic squared

his jaw and stood up. Careful not to disturb the dishes, or anything else hidden in the darkness on the floor, he stepped over to the bedstead and rubbed his hands with another clean sock. It proved unnecessary. They were bone-dry. There was hardly a bead of sweat on his entire body.

He slipped on his pea coat and poured two dozen loose bullets into the left pocket. He tossed the empty ammunition carton on the floor, kicking it under the bed. The .32 automatic was fully loaded; Billy Jamaic cocked it. A round jumped into the chamber. He started to move slowly through the apartment.

The breeze slicing beneath the window, flapping the shade, bothered Dr. David Leigh Rabinovitch. Besides being cold, it was also a harsh reminder the window was left open. A regrettable oversight which had him prying anxiously at the bracelets cuffing his wrist to the water pipe. But the keys were hopelessly bent. Unable to straighten them, he draped the string around his neck and resumed drinking the breakfast he had prepared upon awakening earlier.

Troubled, but not especially alarmed by the circumstances of his situation, he popped a hard-boiled egg into his mouth and swallowed it with a wash of gin. The alcohol allayed the qualms of his confinement and helped him to consider the handcuffs as merely an awkward inconvenience necessitated by his own illustrious personage and not at all a predicament in which he was imprisoned.

Remembering only what he chose of the previous day, he reveled in the encounter with the young man who had befriended him, and delighted in the confidences they had shared. He thought it duly appropriate that his expert advice had been sought, and found great pleasure in knowing his own radical ideas would soon be realized, implemented by the young man whose name he forgot, as he had the bum, Arthur Skidmore, who used to frequent the bar at the Sure Enuf Saloon.

The Doctor sipped his cocktail, allowing a smile to crease his face, while he fondly recalled how the Nature Lovers appreciated who he really was and treated him with the high regard entitled a principled scientist of his respected standing.

With his memory pleasantly dazed and in a quasi-hypnotic state from the barbiturate capsule he had consumed with the egg white, the Doctor set his martini on a cardboard box, adjusted his glasses, and probed the rumpled bedding in search of a soft lead pencil that had rolled beneath his spindly legs. When he found it, he turned over on his left side to finish what the blowing wind had rudely interrupted.

Clutching the pencil stiffly in his right hand, the Doctor printed letters of the English alphabet on the wall beside the bed. The lettering was grouped in a series of words to form a sentence. The language was Yiddish.

GLAYKHER MIT A HEYMISHN GANEV EYDER MIT A FREMDN ROV.

The Doctor began to scrawl his signature. The point on the lead pencil snapped off in the middle of his first name. He sat up against the pillows, scratching his thick gray beard, wondering how to sharpen the implement. He felt a bit drowsy, so he took a long swig of gin to recharge himself.

Billy Jamaic walked out of his building and rounded the corner onto Sterling Place. He stopped and waited against the trunk of a tree and watched a car pass by. His freckled dish-face was set with a terrible blankness. His pale eyes were vacant, staring out from beneath his crop of rusty red hair. Breath clouded from his mouth, lingering in the winter night like an aura about his head.

He crossed the street and stood on the sidewalk in front of the lighted window. A wrought-iron fence separated the pavement from a stairless well to the basement, a small moat with a fifteen-foot drop and a three-foot span to the brownstone wall. The fence railing was a flat strip of iron unadorned by pickets.

The cold metal bit into his bare hands as he hefted himself up and stepped from the top of the fence to the window ledge in a single motion. Balancing on the soles of his sneakers, he reached down and caught hold of the wooden frame with his fingers and lifted

the window wide open. Quickly drawing his gun from
his pocket, he pushed aside the oilcloth shade and
jumped into the room.

The Doctor was sitting forward in the center of the
bed with his left arm stretched straight back to the
water pipe, straining against the handcuffs. His eyelids sprang up in horror behind his black-rimmed
glasses. He tried to gasp, but his tongue was cleaved
to the roof of his tunnel-gaped mouth. He was frozen
agog by what he saw standing at the foot of his bed.

Billy Jamaic was no less surprised, but he didn't
show it. He held the gun with both hands and kept
it pointed at the Doctor. He darted his bleak eyes
around the room. He could see the toilet space inside
the closet was empty. He walked backward to the front
door and checked the bolted locks. He returned and
looked under the bed. When he was satisfied there was
no one else, he stepped over to the window and closed
it, then moved toward the skin and bones wrapped
in the robe on top of the rumpled bed.

He glanced at the supply of food and drink and with
nothing in his voice he said, "Where is he?"

Though petrified by the gun, the Doctor found
comfort in the question. The muddle of his befooled
mind assumed an appropriate response. "You are a
Nature Lover, are you not?" he said.

Billy Jamaic thought nothing odd and said matter-
of-factly, "I like flowers and I like plants."

"Exactly. YES. Good," the Doctor said. "All's well,
then. For I, YES, I sent him on his way."

"Where did you send him?" Billy Jamaic said.

"Upstate New York," the Doctor said, "to the
Hudson Valley Nuclear Plant, of course."

"The plant," Billy Jamaic said, "what does it look
like?"

The Doctor sat back and began rummaging through
the papers strewn about the bedding. Other than
raising his gun, Billy Jamaic did not move. The Doctor
uncovered a brochure from the pile and proffered it
with his free hand. Billy Jamaic looked at the handcuffs and ran his eyes up the water pipe. He took the
brochure and stared at a picture of two enormous,

identical buildings perched on the bank of a river surrounded by a forest, and listened to the Doctor carry on about what was going to happen there that holiday weekend.

Inside the brochure were more pictures with captions and a page of directions on how to get there by car, or bus. A Greyhound timetable was framed in a box listing schedules. A brief notation advised schools to plan their tours through the public relations department and thanked them in advance for their cooperation.

There was also an aerial photograph of the entire installation, showing the twin buildings encircled by numerous vehicles, a cluster of smaller structures, and a giant parking lot. Billy Jamaic studied it for a moment, then held it in front of the Doctor's ashen face and said, "Where?"

The Doctor stopped his excited monologue and gladly pointed out the building which housed the Chairman's office and the boardroom. The Doctor was proud of himself and went on to explain his valuable contribution to the cause of nature by fingering the whereabouts of the plutonium-bearing glass.

Billy Jamaic didn't know what the Doctor was talking about. But he did understand that the man he sought, and perhaps the woman, were the Nature Lovers who were going to be doing something at the Hudson Valley Nuclear Plant in upstate New York. He wanted to know when.

"This weekend, I told you," the Doctor said. "Friday, Saturday, Sunday, Monday, sometime. Why keep asking? You're a Nature Lover. Who should know better?"

"The girl," Billy Jamaic said. "Is she going to be with him?"

"The girl?" the Doctor said. "Should I know about a girl? Ask him about the girl. Who are you, dropping in through the window? Why didn't he give you the keys to the door?"

"Ah, you're not supposed to leave your post," the Doctor said, "is that it? YES, I understand. Freezing outside. The draught from the window was very cold. Be a nice boy, put the gun away. There's no need. Here's a glass of good, YES, good gin to warm your tuchus. And, YES, an egg, some fruit cocktail. You are just hungry. Come. Take, and fix yourself."

The Doctor began spouting praise for the Nature Lovers and their life-preserving task to ransom the environment from the grip of power's greed. But when Billy Jamaic neither moved nor pocketed his gun, the Doctor visibly trembled and his teeth chattered against the words spilling from his mouth. He bit his wildly flapping tongue several times.

Billy Jamaic folded the brochure inside his pea coat and stared at the babbling Doctor. He was stimulated by the fact that his face was the last the drunken old man would see on earth.

"What is your religion?" he said.

"Religion?" the Doctor said. "Religion! Oh my God! No, God, oh God, no, please. . . ."

Billy Jamaic stepped behind the line of cardboard boxes and pushed the Doctor's head against the pillows. He pressed the gun into the pillows with the muzzle touching the nape of the Doctor's neck and said "Godspeed," before squeezing the trigger. The bullet crashed through the base of the skull and exploded inside his mouth. The report died on the pillows with the man.

The shell casing ejected off the wall and dropped to the floor. Kicking it away, Billy Jamaic pulled the Doctor over to anoint him. He shoved the gun in his pocket and took out a tiny bottle of holy oil. He put the oil on his right thumb and made a cross on the Doctor's forehead. He continued to bless the body while he prayed.

"Te absolvo a peccatis tuis. In nomine Patris et Filii et Spiritus Sancti, amen."

When he had finished performing the rite of absolution and chanting his prayers, Billy Jamaic leaned back and quietly regarded this man he had made dead. He felt warm inside himself.

Then he picked up one of the hard-boiled eggs, replaced the vial of oil in his coat, and stepped across the room. He unlocked the door and switched

keys either. Wasn't a person in the place holding back. Not from CoCo. Not yesterday. Like a animal, he was, the way he roamed the saloon."

"Interesting, hey Tomas," Sid Struve said, checking through his case sheets.

"Extremely," Canales said. "Enough to make one wonder."

"According to this report," Sid Struve said, removing a page from the folder, "the kid's body was discovered by the former owner of said premises and a real estate agent at nine forty-five P.M. Tuesday night. The cause of death remained unknown, until an autopsy was performed the following morning and it was determined the victim died from a gunshot wound fired from a .32 caliber automatic. The spent bullet was subsequently found to match those removed from previous victims of the so-called 'Godspeed' killer. But this and all other related details were not released to the press until six P.M. Wednesday evening, thereby making it impossible for the media to broadcast said findings before seven P.M. on radio, ten P.M. on television, and this cheerful Thursday morning in print.

"So, Poley," Sid Struve said, "you say CoCo Robicheaux was acting mean all day yesterday. Trying to shake information from people at the saloon. Looking for a line on the Godspeed shooter. Is that right?"

"Yeah," Poley said. "That's right. Madder'n hell. From the time he came in around noon, one o'clock."

"How, Poley?" Sid Struve said. "How'd he know what only the bureau knew? What was only confirmed at eleven A.M. yesterday? What the press wasn't informed of until six o'clock. How did CoCo know by noon?"

"You kidding?" Poley said. "The same way those guys know everything, is how. He called the police. Someone at the precinct told him what he pays for. No offense meant, huh, Mr. Struve."

"None taken, Poley," Sid Struve said. "But you take care of yourself. And anything you hear means something, you call that number for another meet."

Canales pulled the car over to a curb a few streets away from Flatbush Avenue. Poley began to get out, but changed his mind.

"You know something?" Poley said. "The black kid."

"What about him?" Sid Struve said.

"He was only nine years old," Poley said.

"So?" Sid Struve said.

"The *Daily News* just gave him a couple paragraphs on page six," Poley said. "You'd think, you know, for a little kid they'd do more. 'Stead, they fill the front page with headlines, stories about how the Centennial Building went haywire over in Manhattan last night. Guess a kid getting murdered don't mean much anymore."

"It happens every day, Poley," Sid Struve said.

"No, Mr. Struve," Poley said. "It only happens once."

The two detectives eyed each other for a moment. Then they watched Poley Grymes walk off down the block in the direction of the Sure Enuf Saloon. He was more than a routine informant and they knew it. They also knew it didn't really matter to either of them.

Sid Struve called in to the sergeant in charge of communications for the Special Homicide Task Force set up in the Brooklyn South Homicide Zone to apprehend the psychopathic killer. He informed the sergeant of their exact location and said they were going to take a few minutes for coffee and a personal at a certain diner.

The sergeant suggested they take care of their palates and bladders in the cafeteria at Kings County Hospital. He said a metal trunk surfaced in the river near Execution Light and was fished out by a harbor launch. Inside was a bloated corpse of a woman wearing expensive clothes, but without identification. An autopsy performed by the medical examiner retrieved a slug from the dead woman's chest. The slug was a .32 caliber and Ballistics verified it could only have come from the same weapon used in the killings they were assigned to investigate.

The sergeant said the body of the woman was covered on a slab in the morgue, awaiting their imminent arrival. He added that the medical examiner made sure to spread her legs wide so the famed Mutt and Jeff duo could proceed with their investigation unimpeded.

Tomas Canales grabbed the transmitter and called the sergeant a very dirty name in Spanish before ending the communication and speeding down the street. Sid Struve attached a red blinking signal to the roof of the car and switched it on. The top light began spinning brightly and the low growl of the siren was soon drawing attention.

A traffic cop was standing in the middle of an intersection, halting other cars, waving them through. Sid Struve could see the traffic cop looked extremely uncomfortable in his job. He tried not to think of himself being assigned to a fixed post in the farthest reaches of Brooklyn to direct traffic for the rest of his career in the Police Department of the City of New York.

"Now a body in a trunk, the schmuck put," Sid Struve said. "And in the water, yet. Like I got to know all about baptism. This, we need . . ."

"Like I need two assholes," Tomas Canales said.

39

TERRY TURNED off the shower and stepped out of the makeshift stall, drying his hair with a towel. Leo sat hunched over a cup of coffee, smoking a cigarette, studying the PRO-TEX documents and the notes he had made from what he remembered reading in the vault room the previous evening. DayDream was already gone, driving upstate to survey the roads in the

Hudson Valley and chart the course of several different routes.

Stubbing his cigarette in an ashtray, Leo glanced at Terry and returned to the papers. Then he moved his hard, dark eyes slowly over to Terry again. Staring at his crotch, he said, "What the fuck's that?"

Terry looked down between his legs. There was a large greenish-yellow blotch discoloring his groin. The skin appeared to be rotten with jaundice. He rubbed it with the towel, but none came off. He lifted up his head. There was a lot of worry in his face. "What the hell happened? What is it?" he said.

"You been playing around with any lepers lately?" Leo said.

"Hey, this ain't funny," Terry said. "Just look. Jesus, it's like gangrene."

"Here," Leo said, "take a whiff of this." He handed Terry one of the Xerox copies.

"So it stinks," Terry said.

"They were still wet when you shoved them in your pants," Leo said. "The chemicals, they gave you the stain."

"Then what's the stain gonna do?" Terry said.

"It's gonna go away," Leo said.

"What if it don't?" Terry said.

"Put it to use," Leo said. "Get yourself a gig in some circus. Be the main attraction in a sideshow. The Man with the Yellow Balls."

"Go fuck yourself," Terry said.

"Listen," Leo said, "you wanna make it go away?"

"Sure, whadda you think?" Terry said.

"Get dressed," Leo said, "and it'll go away."

"For fuck's sake," Terry said.

"Come on, willya. Hurry up," Leo said. "We got enough to think about besides your yellow prick. So forget it."

"How the fuck am I gonna forget a thing like this?" Terry said.

"OK, so worry about it," Leo said. "Every half-hour you can pull down your pants, look at it like a little kid. Maybe it'll even light up for you. Like a glowworm. What's the matter with you, anyway? You bothered about something? Huh?"

"Yeah, this," Terry said. "It's spooked me."

"Like the guy you banged up your hands on the other night?" Leo said.

"Something like that," Terry said.

"Anything else?" Leo said.

"No," Terry said, and got dressed in khaki work clothes similar to Leo's. He poured himself a cup of coffee and sat down at the table. He could feel Leo eyeing him, but he didn't look up. There was nothing he could say. No way he knew of explaining what was happening in his gut. There was a strange confusion inside him, and it was either too early or too late to do anything about it. His jumpy stomach would have to wait until after the long weekend. He did know it had nothing to do with the caper. It wasn't a simple case of nerves. It was something else. Something he'd need time to figure out. And there was none now. So he pushed it from his mind and got down to business.

"What the Doctor told me," Terry said, "about plutonium being mixed in glass formulations checked out. I cross-referenced everything I had available on when, where, how it was done, and the ways to extract, separate the plutonium from the glass for reactor fuel, or whatever. It's all true, what he said. Not only that, it's fucking easy. Much easier than messing with those shipping cases of metal rods. Less dangerous, too. Another angle in favor of the glass is the equipment they got, they use to track nuclear materials. Well, it won't work on the glass. Seems they can track down the aluminum-plated plutonium, soon's it's discovered missing. Which would be soon. They wouldn't even bother to see if the glass was gone, until it was for a long time."

"OK," Leo said. "We went over all this. There's still the same things bother me. For openers, suppose the glass ain't in the boardroom, or anywheres else. Two, suppose it's there and it's just a piece of fucking glass. And three, if it is there, and it does contain three kilos of this plutonium-239, how's Czechmate gonna know it ain't just a piece of fucking glass?"

"It's all in here," Terry said, and handed a rectangular-shaped envelope to Leo. "I cut photographs, plus all they need to know to tell the plutonium content of the glass. They just have to run a single test on the sample we leave at the spot. It'll take about a minute for the Geiger counter, or whatever instrument they're gonna use, to verify the radioactive level. I mean, we gotta assume somebody'll be around, knows about these things. If not, we might just as well unload a crate of lead pipes on them. But for two mill, somebody knows all there is to know about what they're buying's gonna be there. What's in the envelope, he'll understand."

"Back to two," Leo said. "Suppose the chunk we chip off and leave at the drop, suppose it don't register no level. It ain't radioactive, just a chunk of glass like a soda bottle. 'Cause we got no way of knowing, until the man runs his test. It turns out a dud, what then?"

"We still got a million from the bank is all," Terry said.

"And they got Dream," Leo said.

"We buy her back with the second million Czechmate puts in the bank," Terry said. "And Czechmate being who he is, he'll go for it. We also swear to do better next time. Meanwhile, we're a million ahead."

"They're gonna go for that, huh?" Leo said. "Forget who Czechmate is, isn't. A bagman for persons with millions of dollars is all we know. I also know these persons'll disembowel Dream, we play funny with their money, don't deliver the goods. That kinda money don't talk, don't listen. It hurts."

"We'll reach some sorta compromise," Terry said. "We did what was asked. Stuff's no good, well it's not our fault. Not entirely. But we accept the blame, anyway. Deduct our expenses, give them back the rest. *After* Dream's released. They're not looking to, not gonna make a big fucking thing outta it. Czechmate said, all's they want is quiet, not to worry."

"A few minutes ago," Leo said, "you're freaking

out 'cause you got a stain on your cock. Now, you're not worried. I'm telling you, it's a tight dangerous bind she's gonna be in, that stuff turns out to be just some fucking glass. Your Doctor friend's idea of a practical joke. And I don't wanna see it happen. Got me?"

"Gotcha," Terry said. "Dream comes back later, we all talk it through. Let her decide how she wants it worked. OK?"

"All right," Leo said. "But anything wrong with the glass, like it not being where it should in the boardroom, we go for the metallic pluto. The alloyed fuel rods, buttons."

"Absolutely," Terry said. "We gonna have enough time, though? It's a fucking big plant. There's lotsa ground between the boardroom building and the place the heavy metal's stored."

"Time?" Leo said. "We'll have time. Enough and then some. What you said about the government, only insuring these utilities against accidents, was right. Seems from these papers the Feds figure nuclear power's gonna be developed by private industry, let them provide their own security themselves. Something blows up, Feds'll cover damages. Far's anything else, they give them this manual. 'Industrial Security for Nuclear Power Plants.' Fucking thing's only got ten pages. Ten pages of basic fucking nonsense. Couldn't protect a candy store. Wouldn'ta believed half this shit, you didn't show me. It's ridiculous. I mean, we could start a war, we wanted to. That's how crazy it is."

"I know," Terry said. "That's the break, the crack made me decide we could take it off. Fact that protecting nuclear plants from sabotage, any intrusion, isn't considered part of national defense. Only thing the Defense Department does is issue those kinda guidelines to regulate security, try to keep it all a secret. Their role, 'sides inspecting the fucking air, comes *after* something's gone down. After their beautiful security's been breached is when they haul ass. By then, I'll be in Rio, getting married to the first Brazilian chick I can make pregnant, and me safe and suntanned forever. Whadda you gonna do?"

"Stay off the streets after dark," Leo said. "Cultivate the habit of minding my own business, keeping my mouth shut. Whadda you care what? Now, assuming step nine's taken by Czechmate at the bank tomorrow afternoon and all goes well, from what I read here, the best time to take out the passive security is midnight Saturday. Right after the swing shift leaves, the graveyard comes on."

"Take out?" Terry said. "Thought we were gonna disenchant it, not knock it out."

"That's before I knew there's two parts to number ten," Leo said. "See, the system's got a backup library. Can automatically reactivate all the detection devices, alarms. All they gotta do is take the information, feed it into another computer. But the duplicate tapes with that info're locked up at a different location. So we can't disenchant, we gotta blow it. All of it, like Humpty Dumpty. Including the dupes. That way's sure to eliminate their interference. The whole operation'll have to be reprogrammed. And they won't know what's being hit, either. Hudson Valley Plant owns the security firm, but rents its services to all sorts of industrial properties. Guess it's cheaper, saves money by providing surveillance to other companies. Looks like they're making a profit 'cause says here all computer time's booked solid. Oversold. Gonna work for us, though. When the service's discontinued, that'll leave only a dozen industrial guards with guns protecting the plant by the time we show. And like you said, there's an awful lotta ground to cover up at number eleven. We'll be in, out with the pluto in minutes."

"The guards," Terry said, "they got shotguns? What?"

"They're lucky they got fucking jobs," Leo said. "Wait a minute. I took down a note, something I read in the folder last night. Where the fuck is it? Here. Centennial insures the security firm that protects, is owned by the Hudson Valley, right? OK, here's what they're really afraid of. 'The armed uniformed guards deployed at the site by your firm are not highly qualified personnel. In fact, considering the age of some and the,' listen to this, 'the *prison records* of others, it is felt their presence around delicate machinery is frankly undesirable. Therefore it is suggested the caliber of their weapons be appropriately standardized to prevent serious damage, if a gun battle should occur. The liabilities of which could far exceed your premium.'

"What Centennial's saying," Leo said, "is these dings start shooting up the place, they ain't gonna pay the claim. Can you believe it? I mean it's hard. Ex-cons they got guarding atom bombs. These scumbags are really fucking crazy."

"Yeah," Terry said, "but what with?"

"Maximum caliber of all firearms, .38," Leo said. "Plus the regular bullshit. Tear gas, nightsticks. Crap. All we gotta watch for is state troopers coming up on us. But I think the holiday crowds on the roads going for their last ski trip for the winter'll keep them busy. The rest is all laid out here. These PRO-TEX are wonderful things. Just follow the directions."

"Yeah," Terry said, and helped Leo spread the papers over the floor where they would spend the rest of the afternoon studying and discussing the exact details of every move they planned to make in their taking of steps ten and eleven.

Leo sat down on the rough-hewn wooden floor and opened a jug of cocaine. He dipped a finger in the bottle and dabbed the area of his uncapped tooth with crystalline flakes. Rubbing it into his gums, he could feel the numbness set in around the gap between his teeth.

"Lucky we had this," Leo said. "Else I'd be dying. Just hope Dream remembers to buy some dental adhesive. Gonna get fucking high, I keep killing the pain with this stuff. My mouth already feels like a goddamn pillow."

"You know," Terry said, "maybe I shoulda went with Dream. Always use a spare onna run like this. We always."

"Yeah," Leo said. "I was thinking the same thing. But we lost our spare driver. Anyways, you've driven over those roads already. Worse comes to worse, anything happens, you'll just take the wheel and drive over them again is all. Just try the Toronado out to-night, tomorrow morning. Someplace where you can get the feel of it. Out by the beach, the Rockaways. You know where to go. It's an easy, a good car. You'll be able to handle it, you have to."

"How come you never drive?" Terry said.

"It's not what I do," Leo said. "This is what I do. My job."

The absence of a spare didn't disturb DayDream. There was no one available who could duplicate her prowess in any event. Knowing that the ultimate success, or failure, of the entire caper was riding on her alone simply sharpened her awareness and intensified her pleasure behind the wheel. She drove the Toronado with her whole being concentrated on its movement, until she was at one with the machine, and the machine with the road.

The roadway between New York City and the Hudson Valley Nuclear Plant was a thirty-mile course offering numerous alternatives. She'd gone over it repeatedly in the daylight and in the dark and knew everything there was to know about it. The terrain surrounding the plant itself was also advantageous, ranging from wide straightaways to narrow winding roads.

As she often had before, DayDream drove through and around the area again and again. Conscious of every detail. The sharp curves, the clear stretches, the dangerous potholes, the eroding hillsides, the spots with turning room for doubling back, the many unmarked cul-de-sacs, the straights partially blocked by debris, the ways in which various sections of the different roads were banked, the amount of time needed to cover various distances, whether the surfaces were fast or slow, and every other factor that had to be taken into account for a successful getaway.

DayDream would wait to choose her primary course. She'd map out each alternative, but her final decision would be based on a single factor. The weather. And snow was forecast.

It was dusk when DayDream circled the Toronado through the countryside for the last time. She drove without lights, until she neared an expressway. Then she put on her headlights and returned to the city. She purchased the evening newspapers and Leo's dental adhesive in Manhattan, before crossing the bridge to Brooklyn.

She avoided Flatbush Avenue to swing by Sterling Place to check out the Doctor and make sure all was peaceful. Having been told the lights were left burning, she was surprised to see the darkened window. She turned along Sixth Avenue to make another pass. Both sides of the street were lined with empty cars. She rolled by them in first gear and came to a slow stop. The only movement on the block was the fumes from her exhaust. She double-parked directly parallel to the Doctor's window and dowsed her headlights, turning on the halogen fog lights and the yellow standing lights in the rear. She waited a moment, then released the interior lock on the front hood. It popped with a dull bang.

Still dopey with sleep from the barbiturate spansule Billy Jamaic was gradually brushing away the toothpaste caked inside his mouth. The blinking yellow lights drew his attention. He lumbered across to his bedroom window to see if there was some sort of emergency that had anything to do with what he could only vaguely recall. He had never in his life felt so utterly tired.

Looking down at the street, he saw a large car with its hood raised. There was a woman bent over the car's engine with a flashlight. The woman was young and her appearance reminded him of something. She had her head turned in the opposite direction, and seemed to be listening to the engine rather than examining it. He lifted his eyes from the woman bending over the car and stared at the window with the drawn shade and started to remember.

Standing in his bathrobe, Billy Jamaic brushed his teeth and kept his eyes on the dark room across the way and let it all come back to him. Just when he was beginning to savor the good part, the story was interrupted. Light was being reflected on the window, brightening the oilcloth shade. The beam was coming from a flashlight. The flashlight was in the hand of the woman still bent over the engine of the car.

Billy Jamaic thought this was strange. If the woman was listening for something, why wasn't the motor running? There wasn't any sound that he could hear. There also wasn't any smoke coming from the exhaust pipe. If she wasn't really listening, he thought, she must be looking. And since the flashlight was again focused on the window, shining its beam along the wooden frame, he could only conclude that the woman was interested in the room hidden by the drawn shade. He stopped brushing his teeth.

DayDream didn't like the Doctor's lights being out when they were supposed to be on. She liked it even less when the Toronado stalled. Shining the flashlight on the fuel-injected overhead cam engine, she decided to spend the night working on the car at the warehouse. Billy Jamaic watched her close the hood. Clad in denim, he thought she bore a striking resemblance to the girl from Prospect Park. But her hair was much too short. DayDream walked to the driver's side lifting her hair from where it was tucked beneath her jacket, letting it fall across her shoulders down her back. Billy Jamaic dropped his mouth open, spitting the plastic toothbrush loudly against the windowpane. DayDream turned at the sound. Billy Jamaic stepped backward. She opened the car door and looked up at his building. He saw her face and his heart thumped alive. DayDream keyed the ignition, kicked over the engine and drove away. Billy Jamaic not only came awake, he was fast becoming beside himself.

He paced the linoleum floor of his tiny apartment. The girl must have known something happened, he thought. He stood by a mound of plastic foliage and gazed into the neatly framed blank sheet of paper that was the poster of Saint Augustine. Then he scurried over to the bureau where his gun and ammunition were resting. He pulled out the bottom drawer, reached inside the space, and removed an envelope taped to the rear wooden panel. The envelope contained his bankbook and the cash his father had made him put aside for a rainy day, as he used to say. There was almost two thousand dollars he had managed to scrimp together during the past decade. His savings account consisted of what he had collected from the insurance policy on the late William Marcus O'Brien's life. The balance of his bank deposits amounted to more than ten thousand dollars.

Together with the cash, Billy Jamaic thought it would be enough to pay the fare and cover any expenses he might incur on his journey into the Hudson Valley. He set the envelope down next to the gin and the bullets and picked up the brochure. He kept it in his hand while he dressed. He intended to memorize every word of it during the night. He wanted to know what he was doing when he withdrew his savings from the bank in the morning.

Billy Jamaic's only other thought was that his orange beard was growing nicely apostolic.

Terry was standing by the freight elevator as Day-Dream rumbled off onto the floor of the warehouse. Leo came in from the loft area in time to catch the tube of dental adhesive. Terry lifted all the editions of the metropolitan newspapers from the front seat. Pre-occupied with the recapping of a tooth and the published news of the day, both men turned to go. DayDream stopped them. There were some things she wanted to call to their immediate attention.

She told them about the Doctor's unlighted room, and they discussed the possibilities. Since there weren't any police posted by the building, they chose to believe either the bulbs had burned out, or a fuse blown. And left it at that. There was very little else they could do. It was too risky for Terry to go over and case the scene. What was done was done. There were no remedies. There also wasn't any more time.

Then DayDream spoke in a continuous monotone, explaining how she had contacted Czechmate and he agreed to meet her with the first million cash install-ment at one o'clock the following afternoon inside the aviary at the Prospect Park Zoo. She went on to de-tail the arrangements she made with a certain Sergio the Magneto for six legally clean cars to be readied in his garage and left at six different safe locations around Brooklyn by ten the next morning. Since Brooklyn is the fourth-largest city in America, and she was familiar with its every niche, DayDream figured she'd be able to lose any tail before the third car change. The others were simply options she wanted available. Terry would be driving a properly registered panel truck, she said, to use as a crash vehicle in the event of any trouble occurring outside the South Brooklyn Bank. Leo would plant himself in one of the phone booths walling the alcove of a corner building from where he could overlook the entire street.

Regarding the circumstances of the final payment on delivery of the nuclear goods, DayDream wasn't especially concerned with the spot she'd be in if something went wrong. That was why she chose to make the drop at that particular basin of the Gowanus Canal, she said. The place guaranteed her ace in the hole. Not her ass in a sling. What that ace was she'd tell them later. After she finished working on the Toronado.

She shoved a hydraulic jack under the car and watched it lift the front end. "Gotta put studded tires on her," DayDream said. "Gonna snow this weekend."

"You sure?" Leo said. "Those forecasts ain't always fucking right."

DayDream's response wasn't in her mildly staring opaque eyes. The answer was in the way she just kept on doing what she was doing.

"That motherfucker!" Terry said. He was holding open a newspaper. The story headlining the front page was an inaccurate report of the fire at the Centennial Insurance Building. That was not what he read aloud. He chose instead a brief account of a little black kid who died from a gunshot wound in the head to become the ninth known victim of the psychopathic Godspeed killer.

Terry slammed the newspapers down on the hood of the BMW. He was shaking, he thought from anger. He began to rage about how they should have located the punk and taken care of him when they had the chance. "Miserable cocksucker's gonna get fucking away with it," he said.

Leo told him to shut up. There was too much work to be done. After he capped his tooth, they would begin combing the loft, putting aside the clothes and equipment they'd need, and wrapping the rest to be burned in the neighboring incinerator.

"We leave here Saturday night," Leo said, "this place's gotta be clean. 'Cause we sure ain't gonna come back. We split. That's it. Be rid a that Godspeed freak, once for all. Come on."

Terry didn't move.

40

"THE OLD man lives in the ground-floor front at 99 Sterling Place," the woman said over the phone to the desk sergeant at the Brooklyn South Precinct at five minutes past eleven on Friday morning.

"That's nice," the sergeant said. "What's the old man up to?"

"He ain't up to nothing," the woman said. "Just lying still in his bed. *Real* still."

"That's nice," the sergeant said. "Sounds like he's having himself a nice nap."

"Sounds more like he ain't breathing to me," the woman said.

"Hmm . . ." the sergeant said. "How did a nice lady like yourself come to this assumption, if you don't mind me asking?"

"Don't mind the least," the woman said. "It was easy."

"Do tell?" the sergeant said.

"Sure," the woman said. "It was his mouth."

"Was it now?" the sergeant said.

"Yep," the woman said. "It's gone."

"Gone, is it?" the sergeant said.

"Left a big hole," the woman said.

"You don't say," the sergeant said.

"Yep," the woman said. "Looks like the Lincoln Tunnel, ask me."

"That *is* big," the sergeant said.

"Not big's the one between your wife's legs, it ain't," the woman said. *"Or* the one you got your thumb stuck in."

"What'd you say your name was, mama?" the sergeant said.

"Madam Nicety Nice Nice, sucker," the woman said. "Now you jes' send someone over quick. Take this dead old man outta here, 'fore he stink up the whole building."

The woman hung up. The sergeant heatedly dispatched a radio car to the address. When two patrolmen arrived at the building, they knocked on the door of the ground-floor room. There was no answer. Flattening themselves against the hallway wall, they turned the knob and flung open the door. Nothing happened.

They looked inside. Across the room there was a thin, gray man lying face up on a disheveled bed. The patrolmen entered and saw there was a blood-splotched cavity in the middle of the man's face. One of the officers pressed his fingers to the man's wrist. It was stiff and cold and without pulse. The man was a corpse. There were definite indications that the body had reached this state through other than natural causes. The patrolmen suspected foul play. They left the scene undisturbed and called their precinct.

Within an hour, the small room was crammed with various Police Department specialists who'd come to do their work. Everything inside the door remained unmoved while a police photographer snapped away at the victim from several angles and took dozens of photos detailing the murder scene.

An assistant medical examiner labored over the body to determine the approximate time and cause of death. His conclusion was that the man had died from a wound made by a bullet fired at close range through the back of his head between the hours of midnight Wednesday and dawn Thursday. He said the caliber of the bullet, the exact time of death, and all other pertinent data would be revealed by the required autopsy and subsequent laboratory tests.

Sid Struve stood in the doorway and listened to the assistant medical examiner's preliminary findings. Then he asked the obvious question, and the answer was more than likely. "Let you know the results, soon's we lay him open," the assistant medical examiner said. "Until then, Sid," he added as he left, "Godspeed."

When a pair of forensic experts finished combing the bed and the row of stocked cardboard carton shelves, they moved over to the window area. Sid Struve crossed the room and stared at the way the victim's left wrist was handcuffed to the waterpipe. He fingered the bent keys for a moment, and then sifted through the documents on the bed. When he saw the TOP SECRET and other coversheets, he read enough of the information to know the dead man was no ordinary bum. He also had an idea. He collected all the papers in the manila envelope.

Another Homicide detective was studying a saucer filled with cigarette butts. He told Sid Struve that in all likelihood the butts belonged to the perpetrator.

"See, the victim didn't smoke," the detective said. "Ain't no nicotine stains on his fingers. No packs a cigarettes around. The person smoked these definitely knew what he was doing, or gonna do, in this room. Look. There's a dozen butts, and not a brand name left on one a them. Lit the same end every time. Name went up in smoke, the first couple puffs. Definitely knew why, what, he came here to do."

"Good. Bag 'em," Sid Struve said. "Be right back."

"Hey, Sid," the detective said. "Where's that partner a yours?"

"Name's Tomas Canales," Sid Struve said. "He'll be here. Bringing someone in to maybe tell us who our friend in the bed is." Then Sid Struve stepped into the hallway and grabbed the building superintendent and told him he wanted to use his phone.

Driving without beacon or siren, Tomas Canales stopped for a red light. He didn't want attention drawn to the man sitting next to him on the front seat. The man was a puzzled and drunk Poley Grymes. A panel truck pulled across the intersection in front of them. Terry Sage was behind the wheel, wearing a gray work jacket with a trucking company's name over the breast pocket.

"Well, whatdda you know?" Poley said.

"What?" Canales said.

"Nothing," Poley said. "Just thought a friend a mine wasn't working no more and . . . you know."

"No, I don't know," Canales said.

"So, I remembered he was, is all," Poley said.

"What's this friend of yours?" Canales said.

"Nasty," Poley said.

"Alluva sudden you're a comedian, huh?" Canales said, and jumped the light, laying rubber down the white line of Flatbush Avenue, scattering the oncoming traffic to tear around a corner onto Sterling Place where he jammed on the brakes, screaming the tires to a stop.

Poley was so shaken by the sudden frightening experience, Canales had to help him from the car. It was after he was on his feet that Poley noticed the fifty people crowded on the sidewalk, looking at him. Then he saw the blue-gray morgue wagon and the jumble of squad cars and uniformed cops all over the place and he wanted Detective Canales to tell him what was happening, but all he was told was to "shaddup!"

When escorted inside the building, Poley immediately began complaining to Sid Struve about the manner in which he was being treated. "I got rights, Mr. Struve," he said. "And one's to keep alive. Your partner here's a crazy man. Way he was driving was like to kill me. Ain't never gonna get inna car alone with him again, for fucking sure. Lucky we made it, you really wanna know. Like a bat outa hell . . ."

Sid Struve already knew. He could see Poley was fairly drunk, enough to agitate his partner with a wisecrack. He asked Detective Canales to have the police photographers start photographing the bystanders outside. A normal routine that would scatter the crowd, and perhaps produce the photo of a murderer. "It's happened," Sid Struve said.

Then he told Poley Grymes why he was there and what he wanted him to do. He led him into the room packed with men with badges pinned to their coats. A big black detective lieutenant was leaning on the bed with his arms spread wide and his neck craned across to the wall. Sid Struve tapped him on the shoulder. The detective lieutenant straightened up and turned around. The body of the victim came into view. When Poley saw the face of the man with the blown-out mouth, he yelped and held his nausea until a uniformed officer rushed him into the small bathroom, where he vomited all over the toilet bowl.

"What's with him?" the detective lieutenant said.

"Man's got a nervous stomach," Sid Struve said. "You find something?"

"Don't know," the detective lieutenant said. "Take a look. Low on the wall near the mattress. Behind the blanket. Figure he wrote it. But can't make the language. You?"

"Yiddish," Sid Struve said, "it's Yiddish."

"Say anything," the detective lieutenant said, "besides he's Jewish?"

"Says: 'Better with a home town thief than an out-of-town rabbi,' " Sid Struve said.

"Shit. Think he's a been nice enough to leave us a message," the detective lieutenant said. " 'Stead, he scribbles a fucking riddle."

"Why a riddle?" Sid Struve said.

" 'Cause the perpetrator wasn't a thief," the detective lieutenant said. "Lucchesi searched the bed. Found twelve hundred in the left-hand pocket of the victim's robe."

"You sure?" Sid Strue said.

"Sure?" the detective lieutenant said. "What the fuck you talking about, sure?"

"You sure it wasn't twenty-two hundred?" Sid Struve said.

" 'S that supposed to be funny?" the detective lieutenant said. "Or what?"

"A prevalent rumor," Sid Struve said.

"My advice's don't spread it around," the detective lieutenant said. "Understand?"

"Like the writing on the wall," Sid Struve said. "Better with a hometown thief. . . ."

There was a brief commotion at the door. Four men wearing conservative suits and similar hairstyles came bustling into the room, flashing identification that said they were agents of the Federal Bureau of Investigation. The senior agent in charge said his office had received an anonymous tip that highly classified government documents were discovered at the scene. He asked if this was true.

"Don't know whether they're classified," Sid Struve said, "but I found this envelope of papers on the bed. Seemed the victim was going through, reading them, before he was shot."

"May I see them, please?" the senior agent said.

"Lieutenant Idi Amin says it's all right," Sid Struve said, "it's OK by me."

The detective lieutenant flexed his jowls and pulled the manila envelope from beneath Sid Struve's arm. When he opened it and spotted the SECRET coversheets, he dropped the scowl from his face and became seriously officious. The FBI agents huddled around him, exchanging somber looks as the exact nature of the classified information was revealed. The senior agent gave the nod to one of his men, who abruptly turned and left to inform the Manhattan office of the gravity of the situation and the need for additional agents to oversee the local law enforcement officers.

"What're they doing here?" Canales said.

"Is what we got here a circus?" Sid Struve said.

"All we need's a tent," Canales said.

"The tent we got, already," Sid Struve said. "Three rings even. Now, we also got what every circus needs. A putz onna white horse to ride around, bask up the spotlight."

"Beautiful," Canales said. "You're beautiful. Who's gonna ride for us?"

"Efrem Zimbalist Junior, over there," Sid Struve said.

"Mr. Struve, please!" Poley said. "You're gonna break my fucking back, you don't get off."

The pair of detectives were crammed inside the closet-sized bathroom. During their buttonhole conversation, Sid Struve found it comfortable to rest his long, lean 180 pounds on Poley Grymes's shoulder blade. This forced Poley's head down inside the toilet where he had just barfed whatever was left in his stomach.

"Just trying to help, Poley," Sid Struve said.

"Help. Protect," Poley said. "That's all you wanna do. What comes next? Hygiene? Gonna make me piss blood? What?"

"It's for you, Poley," Sid Struve said. "For your own good."

"Good, Mr. Struve?" Poley said. "Grief is what——"

"Who's the dead in the bed, Poley?" Sid Struve said.

"Ah, Jesus, Mr. Struve," Poley said. "Should show some respect, you know? Specially what happened to him. His face, for crissake. Fucking awful."

"Did you know the man, Poley?" Sid Struve said. "Was he a friend?"

"A friend?" Poley said. "Who knows from friends? I knew him. Likable guy, made good conversation. Drank martinis alla time. Doubles. Fact, I used to buy him a round, now and again. 'S not a cheap drink, either. Saw him put away a dozen, last time I seen him. We joked about his name, I remember. Told him there wasn't too many Skidmores inna phone book. Good-natured fella like him, you can say those kinda things. Educated, you know. Polite. Not like a lotta others hang at the bar. Guess you could say we was friendly. Yeah."

"Spelled S-K-I-D-M-O-R-E?" Sid Struve said. "That's his first, last name?"

"The spelling I don't know about," Poley said. "Think it was his last name though. Never heard him call himself anything else."

"He drank in the Sure Enuf Saloon," Sid Struve said. "Anywhere else?"

"Nowhere's I know about," Poley said. "Only place I ever seen him was there, at the bar. A regular."

"When was that?" Sid Struve said. "The last time?"

"Must've been a week," Poley said. "Maybe more."

A young detective called Sid Struve aside. He said the paint was chipped around the window frame and fingerprints found. Then he showed him a brass shell casing ejected from a .32 automatic and one hard-boiled egg with a rainbow-colored spansule imbedded in the white. Both agreed it was a strange twist, but neither speculated further. The young detective also remarked that the food and the case of gin must have been delivered, since the victim appeared too weak to carry the burden.

"The gin'll be easy to trace," the young detective said, "if it was bought in the neighborhood. Stores don't sell a full case of Tanqueray every day. Most don't even stock that much around here."

After telling the young detective to include everything in his written report, Sid Struve advised him to canvass the area's liquor stores himself. "Look good on your record," he said, "you come up with something." Then he turned away, knowing that by the time the young detective located any such leads, the Godspeed case would be closed. At least, he hoped it would be.

He was stepping back to where Canales was questioning Poley Grymes when the morgue attendants entered behind members of the Police Emergency Squad carrying a bolt cutter and various equipment. There were eighteen men crowded into the room. The senior federal agent appeared not to like what was happening, because he shouted for everyone to stop what they were doing. Then he suggested a coffee break, which no one thought was a bad idea. Ten men sauntered out of the room immediately.

With a subordinate taking down notes in shorthand, the senior agent approached Sid Struve and asked him what exactly was written on the wall. Struve said it was classic Yiddish, and translated the words into

English. The senior agent indicated the pencil marking below the line of words and asked if that was also Yiddish. Struve leaned over the corpse and stared at the pencil marks. He said it seemed like a signature, or the beginning of one. If so, he added, the letters D A I were either initials, or the first three of a name.

"What do you make of those handcuffs?" the senior agent said.

"Skip Chasers," Sid Struve said. "The clowns bondsmen hire to apprehend bail jumpers, they use this type. With no master, and only a single set a keys, minimizes the leapers' chances to escape, once the cuffs are put on. Plus, they're exotic. Those faggot bounty hunters go for this expensive oriental hardware."

"Always considered that type a strange breed myself," the senior agent said. "But that's another matter, isn't it, Detective . . .?"

"Struve," Sid Struve said. "Mr. Struve. Plain Sid, you prefer."

"Well, Mr. Struve," the senior agent said, "do you think 'John Doe' attached himself to that pipe?"

"Nope," Sid Struve said. "A man's into binding himself up, he's sick. An S 'n M freak. A masochist. Which the victim obviously wasn't. 'Cause if he was, he wouldn't a cuffed himself to that pipe. It's wrong."

"Wrong?" the senior agent said. "How do you mean?"

"It's cold," Sid Struve said. "The cold-water pipe. Person digs pain, he ain't gonna settle for cold when he can get hot. You can see, it's just as handy. Also, he's no longer a 'Doe-Re-Me.' Man by the bathroom over there's his friend. Identified the victim as his drinking buddy, 'Skidmore.' "

The senior agent shifted his look to Poley. "You come here often?" he said. "Drink and talk with your friend a great deal?"

"Never been here before now, mister," Poley said. "Only time I drank with poor Skidmore's at the bar. At the Sure Enuf."

"Sure enough?" the senior agent said.

"Yeah," Poley said. "Regulars. Both of us regulars at the saloon. JESUS, you know he's the fifth to get himself murdered like this? Five outta ten were regulars. 'S fucking half the people killed. Makes you think this Godspeed's got a beef against the Sure Enuf. Whyn't you cover Skidmore up, Mr. Struve?"

Sid Struve nodded to his partner. The cue sent Tomas Canales's hand inside his coat pocket. He produced a color photograph taken with a Polaroid Instamatic. He held it up in front of Poley Grymes. Looking at it, Poley thought it was a gag. A snapshot of the thing that starred in a horror film called *The Blob*. Then Canales asked if he recognized her. And Poley realized the picture was a bloated body of a woman beached on a stainless steel table, and he doubled over into the toilet and retched.

"Is something wrong with that man?" the senior agent said. "What does he mean, sure enough regulars? Five out of ten murdered? Godspeed? What's he talking about, Mr. Struve?"

Sid Struve cleared his throat, and hemmed and hawed in explaining just enough to get the senior agent mounted without implicating himself in the neighborhood's traditional police-community relations. Once in the saddle, the senior agent became rigid with the discipline of a man who knew how to ride on the back of a horse that was white. He toed the stirrups, preparing to command the charge.

"Where is this saloon, Mr. Struve," the senior agent said.

"Believe it's on Flatbush Avenue," Sid Struve said.

"You believe, Mr. Struve?" the senior agent said. "Meaning you've never been there?"

"Had no reason to," Sid Struve said. "Just another gin mill, these bums drink at. . . ."

"The man in the bathroom stated they were regular patrons," the senior agent said. "That *five* regular patrons were murdered by a psychopath. And you saw no reason to investigate the premises, question other regular patrons, when half the victims regularly frequented this Sure Enuf Saloon."

"Well . . ." Sid Struve said.

"Mr. Struve," the senior agent said, "have you any idea what the victim had in his possession? Who he probably is?"

"A male Caucasian, fifty to fifty-five years of age, named Skidmore, whose alcoholism was cured by a gunshot wound of the head between the hours . . ." Sid Struve said.

"Someone shut the goddamn door," the senior agent said. "Get that guy out of the bathroom. Maybe he can tell me about this Sure Enuf Saloon!"

The burly black detective lieutenant had a vision of himself suspended without a pension, spending the rest of his life watching daytime television with his nagging wife. He looked at Sid Struve with his eyes pleading, "Do something! Anything! Stop him."

Sid Struve shrugged his shoulders and threw up his hands in an exaggerated response. What's to do? he said with the language of his body.

Tomas Canales was shaking his head from side to side to keep from laughing with joy. "An Ivanhoe," he said to his partner, "we got us an Ivanhoe."

A dozen special agents arrived from the borough's field office and were given individual instructions. A member of the Police Emergency Squad was permitted to enter with the bolt cutters. He snapped the chain linking the cuffs of the bracelet and exited. A pair of attendants then entered and placed the victim in a heavy dark green plastic bag. Rigor mortis kept his left arm stretched out to his side where it had been handcuffed. It cracked loudly several times when the attendants buckled it into the body bag. Sid Struve removed the keys draped around the neck, before the pair sealed up the corpse and hauled it away to the morgue in the Medical Examiner's section of Kings County Hospital.

Fingering the bent keys, Sid Struve listened to the senior agent declare that due to the presence of the highly classified documents, the FBI was not only entering the case but officially supervising the law enforcement personnel already involved. This, he said, was on direct orders just received from the Justice

Department, whose decision was based on the Atomic Energy and Smith acts of 1954. Without bothering to elaborate further, the senior agent said what seemed a humdrum homicide was actually a grave matter relating to the internal security of the United States of America.

He did not ask whether there were any questions. Instead, he began issuing commands, as if he were planning an invasion. Then he thanked Poley Grymes for his cooperation and instructed an agent to place him in custody for his own protection as a material witness.

"Witness!" Poley said. "Material? Whadda you talking about, MATERIAL? Who the fuck're these guys anyways? Mr. Struve, please, enough with the protection already. Gonna ruin my life, kill me with all this 'for my protection' horseshit. PLEASE!"

"Will someone kindly restrain this man and take him into custody, now," the senior agent said.

Several agents pounced on Poley and scrambled to finally cuff his hands behind his back. They headed him toward the door, but he struggled loose. When the agents became overly rough, Tomas Canales stepped in, advising them to relax.

With his eyes reddened with rage, Poley looked at the senior agent and let the words explode from his gut. "Who the fuck're you to come in here, say a man's murdered by a fucking lunatic is petty bullshit? But a bag fulla toilet paper alluva sudden makes it all a big fucking deal. A plain killing's too small. Don't make enough difference. 'Cause you don't care, give a flying fuck, about PEOPLE. All you care about's your goddamn game; play Three Steps to Germany. Mr. Struve, Gonzales here. Between them and you's a human fucking mile. You talk, call me 'material witness' like it means I matter. Well, I know the difference. Gotta like people, be able to use people. Wanna use me's some kinda material witness? Show me, you ain't, you got some love inside. All you do's KISS MY ASS!"

After a brief scuffle, three agents managed to tussle Poley Grymes outside into a white sedan. But not be-

fore he spouted his last words at the senior agent.
"Should go wipe your feet onna dead-end street," he
said. "Wipe his feet onna dead-end street!" He was
still shouting when the car sped away.

The senior agent remained aloof, transcending the
verbal slosh of a man whom he referred to as
"Grimey," then continued his command without further ado. Tomas Canales returned from the hallway
confused by Poley Grymes's farewell. He asked his
partner what he thought it meant.

"What? The 'Wipe his feet onna dead-end street'
bit?" Sid Struve said. "Means he's a poet. Who the
fuck knows? Just glad Ivanhoe's still on horseback."

"Think he's riding Western or English?" Canales
said.

"Sidesaddle," Sid Struve said. "Whadda you think
about these keys, Detective Gonzales?"

"Yeah, where'd that come from?" Canales said. "Almost hit him myself, he called me that. OK, OK . . .
the keys. It is my humble opinion that . . . I think
they're bent."

"They're bent, he thinks," Sid Struve said. "No shit,
Sherlock. Take another look, see how they come to
be bent."

"I dunno," Canales said. "Don't see no scratches
. . . rubber pliers! Kind electricians use."

"Rubber's onna pliers' grips, not onna pincers, Detective," Sid Struve said. "No. No tool was used. Just
fingers onna strong pair a hands. Strong's their
owner's smart."

41

TERRY SAGE parked the panel truck at a prearranged location. He doubled back two streets on foot,
then drove off in the BMW. Lowering his window, he
pulled over to the curb at Parkside corner. The newsvendor stepped across the sidewalk. Terry dropped a
quarter into his palm. The newsvendor slapped a
folded New York *Post* up into his hand and walked
away. Terry froze from the pain that shot through his
left arm into his brain and down through his body.

The vendor had slammed the newspaper right
against the pinky of his left hand, bending it sharply
back. The bone of the finger and the dislocated
knuckle were broken.

Sitting motionless, Terry waited for the hurt to settle
inside him. Tears of sweat beaded his blanched face.
He clenched his jaws and held on to the cry. Slowly,
he drew his arm inside the car, dropping the *Post* on
his lap and raising the window. His leather-gloved finger was tipped to the side of his hand. He hoped it
looked worse than it really was. He wondered whether
he should immediately remove the glove, or wait.

The horn blasts from the line of cars backed up behind him suggested he choose to wait. Propping his
left arm upright against the window, his body suddenly feeble, Terry shifted into gear and maneuvered
sluggishly into traffic. There were hot and cold flashes.
Then his eyes welled with tears. He shook the chills
and blinked clear his vision. A dizzy nausea reeled
round the hollow pit of his stomach. He missed third,
grinding the gears. He thought he was going to faint.
He crossed Flatbush Avenue and turned into the al-

leyway behind the warehouse. A frightening confusion swelled inside him. He thought he was going to die.

Terry left the BMW sitting in the freight elevator with its motor running and walked into the loft. Leo looked up from the sofa at the exhaust fumes clouding the elevator. "What happened?" he said.

"My finger's broke," Terry said, and dropped onto the sofa.

"Your finger's broke," Leo said. "So we all gotta suffocate on account . . ." He went over to the elevator and swung the BMW into a space alongside the Toronado, killing the engine. He tucked the folded newspaper under his arm, took a straight razor from the workbench, and returned to the loft. He sliced the glove off Terry's hand. The pinky finger fell limp, dangling helplessly to the palm. It was worse than it looked.

"Gotta get you to a doctor," Leo said. "Dream'll be back soon. She just rang. Must've taken Czechmate for a ride to Jersey's been so long. You see him go in, come outta the bank?"

"Sure, I seen him," Terry said. "Whadda you think?"

Leo thought there was a queer dullness to the sound of his voice. "Little old man," Leo said. "You'd think he'd be taller, bigger, look more like Dream, you know. The way he walked, carried the briefcases, thought he wasn't gonna make it to the front door. Twenty thousand fifty-dollar bills is heavy. Heavy load a paper. Ever see him before today?"

"Czechmate?" Terry said. "No, man. Just heard about him from Dream. What she told me, he fit the description. You make anyone hanging around?"

"Nope. Nobody," Leo said. "But they'll be there, the bank opens Tuesday morning. Be able to see them with your eyes closed. A lotta paper . . ."

"How much?" Terry said. "How much weight's twenty thousand fifties?"

"Bound in stacks," Leo said, "my guess'd be about sixty, seventy pounds. See, air's the difference. Take this *Post*. Folded is one thing, open it, and you . . ." His eyes picked out the subheadline printed across the bottom of the front page. He turned to page three and read the first paragraph of the story. Dumping the newspaper on the sofa, he stood quietly and stared at the wall. Only his eyes said he was thinking.

The headline announced a woman's body was found in the river. Terry switched on a lamp and read the article, while Leo remained on his feet in the darkening loft. Terry wanted to become angry, but he couldn't. He began nursing the fractured bones of his hand, finding comfort in the pain. Relief from his inner turmoil.

Everybody dies, he said deep inside himself. Some fucking consolation prize.

DayDream came up the back stairs. Neither man seemed to notice. She turned on the small spots lighting the loft. Terry greeted her with a silent stare. Leo did nothing. She was about to speak, but Terry waved her over to the sofa, where she sat and read the article about the recovery of an unidentified woman's body in a trunk that surfaced in the harbor. Then Terry showed her his left hand. DayDream regarded the twisted finger without expression. She saw enough to know it could be fixed. It posed no problem. She shifted her look to Leo, waiting for him to make a move.

The movement that finally came wasn't from Leo. It was from outside. An uproar of growling tires, flashing lights, and pounding feet crowding Flatbush Avenue, converging on the Sure Enuf Saloon. Federal agents darted through the front entrance, holding their .357 Magnums barrel-down against their coats. The senior agent was standing alongside a precinct captain who stuttered through a megaphone, declaring everyone inside the premises to be under arrest for suspicion of disorderly, immoral, and criminal conduct. A rookie patrolman began posting bold signs reading THIS IS A RAIDED PREMISES.

From their loft window, the scene below looked like a battle was being staged for television. A Keystone comedy devoid of humor. At least, they saw nothing funny about the production. Especially Leo, who was drawing some fast conclusions. "The guy, the owner," he said, "what's his name, can you reach him? Any chance?"

"Maybe," Terry said, and dialed the private number of a phone set on a stairwell beneath a trapdoor behind the bar. The wall phone didn't ring. It blinked a white light. Joe Cobez grabbed the receiver and in a hushed voice he quickly said, "Dunno what all. Godspeed burned Skidmore is part. These're federal heat. Bust out my place. Me too. Salud!" He hung up just as the floor trap was lifted and an agent pointing the second-largest handgun in the world told him to freeze.

The agent then motioned Cobez carefully upstairs to join the center ring of the circus. In one corner, Stalebread Charley Stein was force-feeding policy slips into a pair of his numbers runners. He was using his own mouth to strongly object to his guests' having been rudely interrupted during the main course of their meal. Since there weren't any plates on the table, the agents found this difficult to believe and insisted he come along immediately. Which is when Stalebread Charley Stein feigned a very convincing coronary thrombosis.

CoCo Robicheaux had two slim jugs of cocaine in his hand. He was about to drop them through a knothole in the seat of his booth when Tomas Canales caught his wrist. Sid Struve advised CoCo to unclench his fist and hand over the drugs before the federal agents intervened. After he did, Canales pocketed the jugs and Sid Struve said no one would ever know about the coke besides the three of them. In return for the favor of not arresting him for possession of narcotics, CoCo was asked what, if anything, he had learned about the Godspeed killings. He swore he knew of nothing that hadn't already appeared in print. They escorted him outside.

In another booth, Ray Ray was calmly playing solitaire. An agent watched him flip over the last card. It was the jack of hearts. He set it beneath a matching queen and lined the rest of the cards in their proper order, completing the game. For some reason, the result did not please Ray Ray. The agent had never

seen anyone win at solitaire and couldn't understand why the well-tailored man was unhappy. When
he asked, Ray Ray said it was because he'd won without having to cheat. The agent wasn't amused and
moved him toward the front door.

One of Leila Russell's daughterly prostitutes managed to turn up the volume on the jukebox. The hearty
voice on the folk record singing "La Chanson de
Cinquante Sous" became a battle cry. The Cajun lyrics
of the song blasted the stable of hookers into a defiant
dance, lifting their skirts, kicking their legs.

> They damned me with a blow and threw me
>   out the window,
> They damned me with a kick and threw me
>   in the street.

An old rusty-gun of a cop went berserk from years
of too much whiskey and emptied his revolver into the
Wurlitzer, killing the record. The tune died on the
phrase "allez jamais dans un restaurant avec cinquant'
sous . . ." The old cop was tackled by a squad of
younger officers as the bums snatched drinks from the
bar and joined the working girls in a mad rush to the
sidewalk. Crouched behind a potted palm, Squeaker
peeked through the fronds to watch the crowd pass by
and to see if it was safe for him to emerge.

Just when the party seemed over, Pinckney Benton Steward exploded from the men's room, holding
up his pants with one hand, and waving several yards
of red-stained toilet paper with the other. He was also
screaming. After he tripped and fell forward, everyone could see why he was upset. There was blood
streaming from his left buttock. The wound was caused
by a bullet fired at the jukebox, splintering on through
the washroom wall. Pinckney Benton Stewart was
shot in the ass and it hurt and he cried all the way
to the ambulance. But he wasn't shedding tears. He
was crying for morphine.

Bumping into Tomas Canales, Squeaker reeled for a
moment, then scooted around the thickset detective
and out the front door into the waiting crotch of a
federal agent. Another agent lifted Squeaker into a

white sedan, saying he was under arrest for assaulting a federal officer with a blunt instrument, his head. Canales thought that was very funny and laughed, until he saw what he really wanted.

In the booth area of the saloon, Typewriter sprang free from a huddle of agents and began racing across the floor toward the shaky old cop. He was obviously full of some very bad intentions with which to avenge his boss, P.B. Stewart. Canales admired loyalty in a man. He also enjoyed practical jokes. And since he didn't consider Typewriter a dues-paying member of the human race, he chose to play the one he liked best on him.

There was nothing particularly fancy about his little prank. Just a touch of sleight-of-hand. Canales simply stepped forward, swung out his arm, and slapped the onrushing Typewriter across the forehead. What caused Typewriter to leave his intentions unfulfilled, flopping straight down in one heap, was an eight-ounce bar of lead tightly bound in burnished leather and cradled in the broad palm of Canales's hand.

He returned the slapper to his coat before anyone saw it. Like most magicians, Tomas Canales was reluctant to reveal the secret of his tricks. That would only spoil the pleasure he reaped from watching the agents marvel at Typewriter's sudden discovery that happiness was a barroom floor. It was also a necessary precaution to avoid a malpractice suit. Performing major brain surgery without a license is a serious offense. Especially if the patient died from the operation. And the blood spurting from Typewriter's brow suggested it was a successful lobotomy.

Sid Struve motioned his partner outside and asked what happened.

"Man wiped his feet onna dead-end street," Tomas Canales said without the slightest hint of a smile.

42

WITH ALL the lights off and the shade pulled down over the window, Terry knelt against the sill watching the activity through the Tasco binoculars. Leo sat in the Toronado, monitoring the special radio frequency being used by the Homicide Task Force and the FBI ever since the agents officially entered the Godspeed case. DayDream stood between the loft and the workshop relaying what one saw to what the other heard, and vice versa.

"Taking them in separate cars," she said. "The bums inna wagon. A federal bus. Three into ambulances. A cop, Typewriter, his boss. First car's pulling downtown. Lotta lights inside the saloon, searching the place.

"Hundred people're on the avenue. Big crowd," she said. "Wait. Head Fed's over by white sedan. He's . . . picked up a mike. Talking. You hear him onna radio?

"Yeah," she said. "Agent at morgue says no positive ID on victim known as 'Skidmore.' Took his prints. Gonna proceed forthwith to Manhattan. Match set against those on file, run a copy to Washington. Says ME autopsy disclosed caliber of bullet, .32. Analysis of oil found on body revealed to be same as that on other victims. Report by ME concludes the perpetrator's MO to be that of Godspeed.

"Material witness," she said, "Napoleon 'Poley' Grymes, to be retained in custody but allowed no contact with others. Repeat. Isolate aforementioned material witness to be interrogated separately. Understood. Ten-four. End of communication.

"Fed's replaced the mike, yeah," she said. "They're

all driving away. Except him, police captain, agents, and detectives cleaning out the joint. That's it."

Terry turned from the window and walked back to DayDream. They both moved into the workshop, looking at Leo sitting with his legs outside the car and his eyes fixed on the dashboard clock.

"Whadda we gonna do now?" Terry said.

"We're gonna score," Leo said. "Gonna fucking score is what we're gonna do. Tonight. It's eight o'clock. Take two, maybe three hours for them to identify Skidmore's the doctor. Gives us plenty of time."

"But when they do find out who he is," Terry said, "they're gonna make a connection between him, the Centennial Building, and——"

"With what?" Leo said. "Their brains? Forget it. They won't know what's happening until it's happened. Question is, we gonna sit here and debate about it, or we gonna go take it down? Split a hundred thou, or two mill? What's it gonna be?"

"Might as well," Terry said. "We gotta get outta here anyway. What with Joanie's body . . . you sure we can take it off, sameway? PRO-TEX lay it all out?"

"I'm sure," Leo said. "Dream?"

DayDream nodded her head. It wasn't enough for Leo. He wanted to hear her voice. He also wanted an answer to another question, formed while he stood outside the South Brooklyn Bank earlier that day.

"Something struck me funny this afternoon," Leo said. "Czechmate. He was different, you know. Expected him to look more like you, like your father."

"Nobody," DayDream said, "could ever look like *my* father."

"But he is. And the money's in the deposit box, like it should be, and you're with us?" Leo said.

"Right. Neck and neck," DayDream said, "all the way."

"Sometimes I think," Leo said, "I think you should be in the movies."

"I am," DayDream said.

"Enough," Leo said. "Let's get busy."

DayDream slipped on a pair of rubber surgical gloves and went into the kitchenette. She took twenty pounds of ground prime beef from the refrigerator and separated the meat into four equal piles. She kneaded half an ounce of pure pharmaceutical cocaine into each mound and bagged them individually in plastic sacks.

Leo was doing something to Terry that tested what has been known to distinguish men from boys: the ability to withstand pain. He splashed alcohol on Terry's left hand, rubbing it clean with cotton. With surgical gloves on his own hands, Leo carefully straightened the fractured pinky, holding it firmly against the ring finger. Using a strip of celluloid as a splint, he taped them tightly together. He then covered his work with three nonlubricated prophylactics, taping them fast to the splint, and eased a rubber surgical glove over Terry's hand, having cut off the last two fingers of the glove below the knuckles for a perfect fit. On top of that he placed a leather mitten, reminding Terry of the fatal damage caused by plutonium penetrating the body through broken skin. Since both his hands were cut and bruised, Terry Sage would have to move extra cautiously to get through the night ahead.

With the drugged beef back in the refrigerator, all foodstuffs, beverages, cigarettes, unnecessary clothing, and equipment were dumped into a pair of burlap bags which already contained other unneeded, traceable items. Training the field glasses on the darkened Sure Enuf Saloon, Leo said there was only a patrolman guarding the door. Everyone else had departed from the scene, leaving the coast clear for Terry and Day-Dream to cart the burlap bags to the adjacent building's incinerator. Before they did, Leo stripped off the business attire he'd worn that day and crammed it all into the bags. They left him standing naked, and walked down the rear staircase to get rid of the garbage, otherwise known as *prima facie* evidence.

Leo didn't stand around long. After he urinated in the nearby kitchen sink, he dressed in navy-blue woolen work clothes and low-cut rubber-soled boots. The wool felt like a hair shirt against his body. But he knew it would soften with his sweat. He was also aware that no matter how much it itched, the wool fabric wouldn't create needless sounds. Which was all he wanted it and the night to be: quiet.

Tossing a dark wool knitted cap on top of the Toronado, Leo folded a charcoal-brown lumber jacket on the roof beside it. Lined with lamb-white cotton, the jacket was also reversible. There were two others like it, but different-sized for his partners. He thought about clothes for a moment, and why Joanie Brown's hadn't been removed before she was placed in the footlocker the newspaper sensationally described as a trunk. He wondered if at least the labels had been torn from what the *Post* said was expensive garb. It didn't make much difference anymore, he guessed. The Homicide Squad definitely knew who she was by now. Godspeed, he thought, and hoped they crucified the bastard. It was when he began remembering Joanie that Leo caught himself and stopped. There'd be time enough to miss her later.

Stepping over to the workbench, he checked the equipment and placed certain tools into his canvas satchel. He then counted a stack of bills and was amused to find it amounted to exactly thirteen thousand dollars. At a thousand dollars a step, Leo figured they had already earned nine. Enough to pay the price for another four rolls of the dice. Perhaps even buy their way out of a surprise pinch. He split the money down the middle. The driver always held half. He'd carry the rest inside with him and Terry.

Terry, his partner, who seemed to be turning into a weak link. Leo knew there was something wrong. Something deep. Something that first became visible after his visit with the Doctor of Physics. It wasn't drugs. A few snorts of coke never hurt anyone. And Leo would have immediately spotted his using heroin, or any other opiate. Neither drugs nor the lack of drugs was the source of the problem. Of that, Leo was certain. It could have to do with Joanie Brown. The bullet that killed her was meant for Terry. Shook him up, all right. But he also shook it off. No, it wasn't just her. The only thing that could get to a tough cookie like him would have to be something he didn't understand.

Knew about, but couldn't understand. Something that'd freak him out.

The thought hit Leo all at once. What was causing his tough cookie of a partner to crumble was Godspeed. The phantom psycho who not only shot at him twice, but was also seen in Long Island City by DayDream during the plumbing supply score. Must have been tailing Terry, which explained Skidmore, the Doctor. Sure, the psycho probably saw Terry, followed him, laid for him, somehow didn't see him come out, got fed up waiting, and broke in to find a drunk asleep in bed. So he just did his Godspeed routine on another bum, and went back into the streets still after Terry.

Now that he sensed what was making Terry Sage fall apart, Leo figured out a possible solution to his partner's problem. As well as his own. For Leo Warren believed in right and wrong. He believed the words meant smart and stupid. And since he did not want anything to go wrong on the caper because of Terry's acting stupid, Leo hoped to set things right again by playing it smart.

He listened briefly, then lowered the volume on the police radio. He was closing the flap on the glove compartment when Terry and DayDream returned up the back stairs. They said it was beginning to snow. Leo raised his hand to stop their talking and looked at both of them with a smile on his face.

"They got him!" Leo said. "Godspeed maniac stopped a bullet by the lake in Prospect Park. Just came over the radio before you come in. Seems he walked into a stakeout team. Shot by a couple cops."

"Dead," Terry said. "They kill him?"

"Don't know," Leo said. "They're taking him to Kings County is all I heard."

"What about his name?" Terry asked. "Who is he?"

"Didn't find no ID on him," Leo said. "But he matches your description of him: short, red hair, overcoat. Also got some oil from his pocket and a .32 automatic. Then the Feds ordered a lid put on all further transmissions about the suspect. Wanna keep it quiet till they're sure, I guess. But it's him. And he's over. Godspeed ran into his dead end."

"Good," Terry said. "Good." Then he stepped into the loft and sat on the toilet bowl in the bathroom, feeling relieved. The knot in his stomach unwound. As it did, Terry realized that death itself didn't scare him. It was to die a meaningless death that frightened him. Everybody dies, but not everybody lives. And Terry Sage long ago decided that when he died it was going to be as he lived. When he died, he was going to die for himself. Not to please someone else. NEVER to satisfy the psychotic whim of a maniac. With Godspeed over and done, Terry once again became his quick, hard, alert, cold self; as nervous as a brick wall.

Leo saw the change begin the moment he announced the news, the lie that proved him right about what was bothering his partner. He was glad it worked, and also sure Terry would be no cause for further worry on the job. He turned to give DayDream the $6,500 and found her unclipping the revolver from the Toronado.

Without a word, Leo hastily replaced the .22 Magnum in the brackets under the dashboard. They exchanged looks. His eyes were sharp, questioning. Hers were calm, shadowy. She nodded her head to say she understood. Though there was nothing in her face to show she fully appreciated the situation, Leo had a definite idea she did.

Due to his bandaged left hand, Terry was having some trouble with his clothes. Leo went in to help him dress in the same dark-type woolen garments he wore himself. DayDream put on a trim brown ski outfit and a pair of lightweight fawn suede boots with crepe soles. Bundling her long hair beneath a fur hat, she resembled the well honed blade of a stiletto. The discarded clothing was bunched together on the floor.

When Terry said he was already holding a thousand dollars, Leo pocketed the rest of the money in his pants. He then handed forged driver's licenses to his partners and stashed the remaining pack of identification along with a kit to falsify others in the compartment concealed inside the trunk of the BMW. Terry went through the car, making sure it was absolutely clean and properly fueled. DayDream attached three different plates to the Toronado. At the bottom of the layer was Minnesota; in the middle, Canada; on top, Washington, D.C. She clipped a wire from the interior of the last plate and checked the set of registrations against the various serial numbers before placing the papers inside the Naugahyde-bound sun visor. She used a warm bar of chocolate to muddy certain details on the official plate from the nation's capital.

Leo organized the loading of their equipment. The Toronado offered enough trunk space for everything including a full oxygen tank. The reinforced springs and special shocks absorbed the weight without any indication that the vehicle was carrying a load. The heavy assortment of gear also would not interfere with the driving, since the car wasn't powered from the rear, but from the front-wheel drive shaft.

Setting the four large Baggies of doped ground beef inside, DayDream closed the trunk, then backed the Toronado into the freight elevator. She descended to the alley, where she parked and locked the car, and returned to do the same with the BMW. Leo and Terry were busy rigging the warehouse for cremation. Several fiber-glass drums were positioned in different areas on the floor. Each contained ten gallons of kerosene into which Terry separated the various pieces of discarded clothes. Using tinfoil, Leo fashioned contact switches for the door, the freight elevator gate, and the inside of the telephone. To these devices he taped wires which were attached to a high-voltage battery, creating a current continuity circuit.

While Terry and DayDream waited in the freight elevator with the BMW's engine turned off, Leo tied another wire to a relay post on the battery. This wire was hooked up to a firing mechanism atop a kerosene-soaked rag draped across the propped lid on one of the ten-gallon drums. This done, he climbed from the workbench over into the elevator without touching the gate, and carefully pulled the ropes to slowly lower them to street level.

Any separation of the conducting tinfoil contact switches caused by opening the stairwell door, the elevator gate, or ringing the telephone would produce an immediate cessation of current flow and thereby release the relay, triggering the mechanism and torching a fire that would engulf the warehouse in a blaze of explosive fumes. If no one stumbled in first, Leo suggested Terry be accorded the privilege of igniting the flaming ceremony with a phone call from the airport, prior to his flight to retirement on the coming Tuesday.

"Hey, wait a minute," Terry said. "What the fuck we gonna do till Tuesday? Where we gonna stay? All this rush, rush, I clean fucking forgot."

"Well, I didn't," Leo said. "We got a place. A good place. I was gonna use it myself, anyway. In Jersey. Right across the Washington Bridge in Englewood Cliffs. Owned by a friend of mine. You'll like him. You don't, he'll eat you for breakfast."

"I don't like him already," Terry said. "But, what with everything coming up Washington, I ain't gonna spoil the run."

"Englewood it is, then," Leo said. "Let's get outta here."

DayDream drove away in the Toronado with Leo on the front seat beside her. Terry followed in the BMW, feeling a stony calm inside himself. The light snowfall thickened toward the outskirts of the city. Northbound traffic was heavy with cars full of people taking advantage of weather that was good for great skiing. But bad for grand larceny.

43

THE DIGITS on his watch said it was 11:15 when Terry parked the BMW outside the crowded lot of a foreign car dealership in a small college town several miles south of the Hudson Valley Nuclear Plant. He left the key attached to the magnet beneath the dash and walked down a lane. DayDream pulled up to meet him without her lights. He got in the front as Leo crawled over the seat into the rear.

DayDream headed the Toronado north on a vacant road where the snow was sticking but the grading was rough. No one spoke, except Leo. He held the PRO-TEX documents, using them to instruct Terry and DayDream on which radio frequencies the various police agencies in the area would use as events developed. Like the one that was about to occur in the expensive shopping plaza of an upper-class village whose snow-blanketed streets the Toronado rolled over in neutral.

A Camaro tilted in a driveway caught her eye. Terry moved behind the wheel when DayDream stepped out the door, walking before her feet touched ground. The keys were in the ignition, but she wasn't interested just yet. She released the emergency brake and let gravity carry the Camaro a block and a half away, before she turned over the engine and came alongside the Toronado. Leo handed her a black box through the windows and watched her steer directly in front of the suburban branch of a world-renowned jewelry company.

The jewelry store cornered the fashionable crescent-shaped shopping plaza. DayDream flipped a switch inside the black box and leaned out the car door, setting the box on the tiled ground of the store's entrance. She swung the Camaro around to the plaza's rear driveway and left it parked with the motor running and the choke on and the lights off. Terry pulled right alongside, allowing her to climb from the Camaro to the Toronado without tracking the snow-covered pavement.

Again behind the wheel, DayDream doubled back through the peaceful residential streets of the village and onto a gravel road that would carry them a mile north to the security firm. Terry listened to the police and security patrol respond to the silent arm signal being transmitted from the jewelry store. The black box contained a powerful electromagnet which was absorbing enough energy through the store's front to disrupt the balance of an electrostatic field inside.

These electrostatic lines of force were created by a capacitive device to protect the premises. What was in the black box caused the internal circuit of the device to break, sending forth the alarm signal. And since the box was black and the Camaro's engine running, the patrols drawn to the scene would be reluctant to make a quick approach. There might be a bomb, or an armed intruder trapped inside, or any number of reasons for them to stall about. From what Terry heard on the radio, the lure seemed to be quite a distraction.

The Toronado passed by the security firm, a single-level, rectangular building made of red brick, without windows, and with an air-conditioning unit on the roof. Rock salt was spread on the ground, melting the snow. There was no movement in the area. A few hundred yards away was a construction site. Day-Dream saw what was needed, and gave Terry the wheel. She got out and scaled a fence, entering the site. She began cross-wiring a dump truck filled with sand, while Terry drove back to the security firm.

Without headlights, he turned the Toronado into the firm's parking facility. Leo took a bolt cutter from the trunk and severed the shank on a padlock attached to a utility manhole. He lifted the unlocked metal cover and climbed down inside to cut all the telephone lines, coaxial cables, and the transmission wire which the PRO-TEX said were there. He was also going to spark an electrical fire.

Barreling the truck through the plywood fence at the construction site, DayDream double-clutched it into high gear and drove to the security firm. Shifting into reverse, she backed the truck in front of the control door that was the sole designated emergency exit. With the tailgate securely fastened, she tripped the dump lever and walked over to the Toronado.

In response to the brief electrical fire, all other doors in the building automatically locked. Leo emerged from the utility manhole in time to see the dump truck being lifted backward by its sealed load of sand. The truck quickly tipped onto its rear end, standing on its tailgate to block the only available exit, and trapping the security personnel inside the building, with all means of outside communication no longer functioning.

DayDream waited in the driver's seat as Terry helped Leo mark the spot on the building's wall indicated by the PRO-TEX sheets. Using a large square reamer with a sharp point, Leo sank the bit into the masonry with the cordless high-powered drill. There was a six-inch water main between the outer brick wall and the inner Sheetrock wall. It cracked, then burst, flooding water into the computer programming tape library and across the floor to short-circuit the brain of the IBM 360–22 computer. Within minutes the electronic data processing facilities in the security firm would be completely paralyzed. Any thoughts of using a standby computer would also be canceled, since the program tapes would by then be thoroughly damaged and possibly destroyed.

Punching the gas pedal, DayDream drove them a mile inland and another mile north to extend the EDP breakdown of the security firm. At an old building temporarily leased for a secondary storage facility, Terry jumped from the car. There was no one and nothing guarding the premises but the passive alarm system that had just been made inoperative. They wanted to be sure it stayed that way.

Terry picked open the door of an exterior tool shed. Parked inside was a forklift. He started it across the rear loading area behind the building. As he neared the rolled-down steel of an electrically operated overhead door, Terry lowered the heavy forks into the snow and rammed them through the steel. He ripped the corrugated metal, forcing the panels upward and clearing a space wide enough for the Toronado to be backed inside.

The building once contained the main offices of a reputable group of accountants and tax consultants who showed the rich how to avoid payment, and the wage earners how to pay through the proverbial nose. Since this reputable group had been relocated to various penitentiaries, the building was unoccupied and empty. That is, except for the security firm's library of duplicate computer programming tapes. These were stored in the departed accountants' vault at whose side wall Terry was chopping away with a fire ax.

When a large slice was cut from the wall, Leo stood the oxygen tank on the floor and ignited an acetylene welding torch. The vault was installed with an internal sprinkler system and was designed to release steam whenever the water particles locked inside the concrete walls reached the boiling point. Which occurred a few seconds after Leo directed the high flame of the torch on the bared hollow of the wall. He waited for Terry to career the forklift into the vault door with a jolt that permanently froze the locking bars, eliminating normal access to the interior. He then taped the torch firmly in place with its constant flame activating sprays of water and clouds of steam that guaranteed the destruction of the security firm's only set of duplicate programming tapes.

Reversing their lumber jackets so that the white insides were out, they traveled toward the Hudson River over three miles of rough back roads. Day-Dream kept the windshield wipers moving slowly along with the rising heat from the defroster. The snowfall became a minor snowstorm, whipping flat wet flakes across the wooded landscape. They rode in silence, monitoring the different frequencies on the radio.

They heard that there was some as yet undefined abnormal equipment malfunction with the central circuitry at the security firm. That automatic coded transmissions of signal trouble were directly received by all local, state, and federal agencies supervising law enforcement in the valley region. That the Cognizant Security Office servicing all industries under contract by the Defense Department within this same geographical region was also routinely notified. As were the company guardrooms at these various industrial facilities.

Then a voice tuned in on the police band, saying he was the officer in charge of the security firm and using a battery-powered transceiver to report that he and six of his subordinates were in big May Day repeat

MAY DAY trouble trapped inside the computer installation without enough air to breathe and with water ankle-deep because the only exit door was
blocked, but they were in the process of removing the
door's hinges and would soon be the hell out of there
right after this last one's removed. . . . The transmission ended abruptly with the sudden sound of several
tons of sand caving through the unhinged door to
bury the officer in charge of the security firm, and
transform the firm into a miniature beach.

Without any lights, DayDream moved the Toronado normally along a service road bordering the
southern section of the Hudson Valley Nuclear Plant.
She shifted down into second gear, pulling the car up
a slight incline off the road. Changing into first, she
then maneuvered between masses of shrubbery
around to a hidden recess facing the plant. Leaving
it in gear, she lowered both front side windows a
crack and cut the engine, to sit and watch and listen
and wait.

Leo removed a pipe wrench from the trunk and
pocketed a set of lock picks. Terry folded a spray canister inside a green canvas duffle bag and slowly
pressed down the hood until the trunk clicked shut.
They stood together on either side of a tree and took
a hard look at the spacious exterior of the Hudson
Valley Nuclear Plant.

A large yellow light was rotating atop a tall steel
spire. According to the PRO-TEX, it meant all security personnel were on full alert. An armed guard
would be posted at each exclusion area to prevent access until the light changed color. Which was not
about to happen, since every sophisticated detection
device protecting the plant had been deactivated by
the paralysis of the security firm's entire central station alarm system. This left only structural barriers,
easily bypassable audio and visual alarms, the sta-
tionary guard force, a trio of security patrol cars
touring in an established routine over a visible, rock-
salted interior roadway, four guard towers overlooking the area and rendered inadequate by the glare cast
from the reflection of the ultrabright protective light-

ing against the snow, and unleashed sentry dogs to keep everybody in their respective place.

Leo motioned Terry over to the trunk. They retrieved the four sacks of coked prime beef and the pair of field glasses. Leo held on to the glasses and one sack of meat. Terry reshut the trunk and, retaining two sacks, gave the last one to DayDream. Using the binoculars, Leo scouted out the dogs, which were considered by the PRO-TEX to be more of a weakness than a strength since they were all thoroughly accustomed to many different handlers. He saw some paw prints in the snow, but not the animals. He had a feeling he would.

A patrol car came into view. They watched it closely. When it continued on its routine round, they stepped up to a twelve-foot-high chain-link fence of woven wire. The gauge number of the American wire was eleven. Leo thought nothing of it. If it meant luck, he didn't need it. Terry didn't even know it.

They entered beneath the fence line where it was raised several inches to accommodate a railroad spur. The tracks ran across the ground into the enormous identical twin structures on the bank of the Hudson River. They went in the opposite direction, heading toward a small cluster of office buildings in an unguarded restricted area. Since there was an insufficient number of security personnel to afford complete penetration of all areas, only exclusion areas were provided with proper coverage.

They moved quickly. Not taking steps, but sliding their feet through the snow. One following in the other's tracks. When they reached the rock-salted roadway, they began to run. A sentry dog came after them. They froze. Terry let five pounds of ground beef slip out of its bag onto the ground. The animal sniffed it briefly, whined, then gobbled it up. They tossed some more far from the roadway and left him to enjoy himself. By the time the dog finished eating, all his senses would be deadened.

They arrived at the two-story building housing the boardroom. Another patrol car was approaching. Leo huddled inside his three-quarter-length white jacket.

Terry hunched down close to the ground in his and wrapped himself around Leo's legs. They became a solid wall of white, a featureless snowman invisible against the snow-blanketed stretch of pavement.

After the patrol car passed, Terry kept watch while Leo gripped the outside rim of the door's key cylinder with the pipe wrench. He turned the whole cylinder slowly in the door. As he did, the bolt withdrew from the jamb and unlocked. They stepped inside, slipping the tightly folded Baggie between the jamb and the door to keep it firmly shut.

The amount of light flooding the plant was the main reason for their carrying small pencil lights, rather than the usual cumbersome flashlights. When they went upstairs to the second floor, they found a reason for regretting their choice. At the top of the stairwell was a secretary's desk similar to those in the office below, and a stainless steel door with nothing on its surface. Neither a handle nor a lock casement; just an absolutely bare sheet of thick metal that was obviously barred from the inside.

Terry was about to give it a kick when Leo pointed to the ceiling. He understood what he saw. With Leo boosting him up, Terry knocked several ceiling tiles from their frames and out of his way. He could see that the partition separating the Chairman's office from the reception area did not extend all the way to the roof. Which was when he did what is known as a "morning glory": a cautious crawl across the metal frames through the ceiling and over the partition to drop into the Chairman's office and unbar the door from inside.

The adjacent boardroom was wide open. Centering the mahogany table was the half-moon-shaped piece of glass, like the Doctor said. Leo was surprised by its weight. He estimated ninety-odd pounds as he shoved it into the canvas duffle bag. Terry pressed the nozzle on the canister, spraying foam inside the bag. Within seconds, it hardened into a rubbery Styrofoam-like substance, filling enough of the bag to cushion the plutonium-oxide glass from harm.

They waited for the patrol car to make another pass.

After it went by, Leo stepped outside and used the pipe wrench to partially return the lock's bolt back inside the door jamb. He exchanged the wrench for the heavy duffle bag which was too difficult for Terry to manage with his splintered left hand. Crossing over the rock-salted roadway, they were again stopped by a sentry dog. Leo stood rigid, while Terry coaxed the animal. Bridging initial resistance, he was finally able to feed the dog five pounds of phamaceutically pure prime protein.

DayDream continued listening to police say they didn't understand what had happened. When their talk turned to a major traffic accident that had just occurred on an expressway, she lowered the volume on the squawk box and climbed out to brush the windshield. She sensed it immediately. Someone was very near, very interested. With unforced poise, she calmly fiddled with the wipers, cleaning the window. Neither her eyes nor ears could pinpoint what she felt lurking. But the scent was there. And it was strong. And it smelled bad.

She swiveled back into the driver's seat, squeezing the car door closed but leaving it unshut. The storm subsided to a gently falling snow. She reached down and gripped the butt on the .22 Magnum. It didn't move. She scanned the magic transparency of the brilliant snowflakes dropping through the floodlight. She didn't see beauty in the view, only Leo and Terry walking toward her. She tugged on the revolver, trying to release it from under the dash where it was somehow stuck fast inside the bracket.

Leo crawled out beneath the fence line, then pulled the duffle bag through the space between the tracks of the railroad spur. Terry was right behind it. DayDream now knew. The run in her spine said it was going to come soon from somewhere. She slapped the horn. Not a sound. It was disconnected to prevent any accidental blast. Terry was outside the fence and getting to his feet when he slipped on the wet rails and fell.

The first bullet slammed through Leo's jacket, shattering his binoculars, and pierced his chest. A second smashed into his temple and killed him. Terry pushed himself up and was hit in the left shoulder. He spun

around. It was blurred, but he caught sight of Billy
Jamaic stretched in a prone position, with his legs
splayed apart and both his hands clasped on the gun.

Terry shouted a single word in astonished disbelief.
The word was "LIE!" The rounds then began flaring
from the barrel of the automatic pistol, tearing into his
thigh, stomach, chest, and neck. He was thrown into
a stark, painful slide across the snow. His punctured
body became a sleigh, riding a shallow slope in a slow,
downward whirl. He didn't feel the next two rounds
pump into his lower back as he lay with his face upturned.

Billy Jamaic hopped to his feet. There was an in-
tense excitement about him. Holding the .32 automatic at his side, he reached into his pea coat for the
holy oil and stepped from behind a tangle of bushes.
He grinned an uneasy boyish smile at the Toronado
and approached the bodies to exact the familiar ritual
of anointment.

When DayDream saw him appear, she neither bothered nor tried to comprehend his presence. She left off
the headlights, switched on the ignition, kept the
gear in first, revved the engine, popped up the clutch,
and flicked the supercharger to send the Toronado
flying from its slot between the shrubbery across the
service road smack into Billy Jamaic, bouncing him and
his holy oil and his emptied gun against the chain-link
fence. She left him stunned and bleeding to check on
her partners.

Leo Warren died in the manner he lived: without
a wince.

Terry Sage was twisted sidewise in the snow, covered with his hemorrhaging blood. It didn't matter that
he was still alive. That he could still feel the whisper
of a breeze. That he could still see the flutter of the
branches on a tree. That he could still think of a seer-
sucker suit, a straw hat, and a cane. That his last
thought was of Maurice Chevalier, he would have
thought funny. If he'd had another. But Terry Sage
didn't. And his life ended; his death began.

A siren blared from the opposite side of the plant.
The first security patrol car would arrive in less than

a minute. DayDream threw away the sack of meat and quickly lugged the duffle bag with the foam-encased plutonium-oxide glass into the trunk. She jumped into the Toronado. There was a loud moan coming from the bearded red head lying against the chain-link fence.

DayDream shifted into first and set the front tires on top of Billy Jamaic. She secured the emergency hand brake and punched the accelerator, churning Godspeed into ground sweat with the whirring front wheels.

She then backed on to the service road and proceeded forward at less than excessive speed. DayDream wanted the patrol car to get close enough for the guards to see and radio their identification of her license plate. It wasn't long before they came up on her. She turned on the Toronado's lights to make it easier for them. She knew there was only the faintest possibility they'd be able to type the customized vehicle with which she was about to give them a driving lesson they'd never have a chance to forget.

When she reached a straightaway, DayDream switched off the lights, flicked on the supercharger, and roared above a hundred miles per hour. The patrol car took up the chase. The security driver's only concern was not to lose sight of her. DayDream was more concerned about successfully negotiating a sweeping hairpin without headlights. She started the turn well in advance, letting the front-wheel drive suck the car across the banked corner rather than steer around it.

The driver of the patrol car didn't remember the hill road curve, until he wandered into it at ninety miles per hour. This rate of speed was substantially reduced when he crashed into a granite cliff wall. The security firm's patrol car went up like a bomb in a burst of instant flame.

DayDream pulled on the wire that ran from beneath the front seat to the rear bumper. The Washington, D.C., plate dropped off to the shoulder of the road as she turned on her headlights. She drove the Toronado up the entrance ramp to the Thruway. Heading along a southbound lane at normal speed, a remote tenderness came to her face. She began to talk to herself. She thought of the miracle and counted on it to come true.

"Thirteen, twelve, eleven, ten, nine, eight, seven, six, five, four, three, two, one," DayDream said. "Thirteen, twelve, eleven . . ."

These books?
Fiction.
Keep telling
yourself that
as you read.

ERIC AMBLER

"THE GREATEST SPY NOVELIST OF ALL TIME!"
—SAN FRANCISCO CHRONICLE